ORSON

A PARAGON SOCIETY NOVEL

DAVID DELANEY

THE PARAGON SCIETY

Join the Paragon Society Newsletter for updates on new releases and more. See details at the back of the book.

Cover Art Design by, Deranged Doctor
derangeddoctordesign.com

For Stephen, Robert, Dean
And of course Shelly

CHAPTER ONE

I prepared myself for battle. Pulling my sword and raising my shield, I roared a challenge to all around me. I grabbed a strength elixir, alchemy magic giving a slight glow to the bottle, and swallowed its contents. I checked those around me, ensuring they were prepared for the coming fight.

"Remy!" I called. "Once we go through those doors, all hell will break loose. Make sure you're in a safe position. We can't afford to lose you."

"Got it." The little gnome leaped in the air in anticipation.

"Is everyone ready? This is it. Everything that's come before has led us here." I wasn't shouting, but I was speaking louder than normal.

"Calm down, Orson. We got this," said Elyse.

"Okay then, let's do it. Elyse, blow the doors. Everyone attack the second they go down."

Elyse, a busty female Elf with clingy purple robes enhancing that particular asset, waved her hands in the air before her. After a short moment, blue light shot from the tips of her fingers and the large iron doors exploded inward.

I was running even before the spell had finished its work, my giant broadsword and steel shield gleaming in the torchlight.

Three massive Orcs were waiting just inside the door. I started swinging, making sure I grabbed the attention of all three. Elyse stood behind me, unleashing fire that set the Orcs ablaze. Arrows sprouted out of the enemies' bodies, just as Richard's large pet tiger smashed into the closest Orc, drawing it away. That left two for me. *No problem.* All I needed was a little healing help from Remy and these guys were dead.

"Remy? Some heals please!"

Nothing happened. The Orcs were getting the upper hand.

"Remy?"

I risked a look back through the doors. Remy was just standing there like a statue—a little, stupid, gnome statue.

"Remy! What are you doing? We're dying here."

"I'm dead!" Elyse shouted.

I checked my other friends. Richard's tiger was dead, and the Orc had gone to work on Richard himself, who was trying to freeze the big, green, ugly thing with an ice trap. Elyse's body was lying to the left of the door. Alec, who had some healing ability, was trying desperately to keep Richard and me alive, but he didn't have enough power to save us both. Realizing this, he poured everything he had left into me. I gave the Orcs all I had. Every move, every ability, years of experience, and muscle-memory came into play.

It wasn't enough.

I downed one of the remaining Orcs, but his comrade took me out with a crushing blow from his massive spiked mace. I fell, and Richard and Alec went down seconds later. They didn't stand a chance with the armor they were wearing.

"Well, that sucked!" I shouted into my headset. "Remy, where the hell are you?"

Just then, Remy's gnome unfroze and he jumped toward the doors. The Orc turned and smashed him once, twice— and on the third blow, the gnome fell over dead.

"Sorry, guys," Remy said. "My game froze. I think my connection is messed up."

"Dude, I thought you were getting a new provider. That cable modem crap you have blows," said Elyse.

"They're supposed to come out tomorrow," Remy replied. "Can we try again?"

"I'm up for it." Alec chimed in.

"It might be nice and sunny in the land of kangaroos and crocodiles, Alec," I said. "But, it's 2:00 a.m. here. I need to get some sleep. Got class tomorrow."

"Yeah, me too," said Elyse.

"So, we're calling it for now?" Richard asked.

"Yeah. We can try again later this week. After Remy gets his fracking internet fixed," I said.

"I hear you, man," said Remy. "Sorry again, guys."

"No worries, mate," said Alec. "I'm going to switch over to my Pally and level him some more. 'Night, everyone."

"'Night, Alec," Elyse replied.

The rest of us said goodbye and logged out of the game. I grabbed my phone and texted Elyse.

lunch tomorrow?

sure. when, where?

i've got Calc until 12:45. how about Taco John's at 1:15?

i'll see you there - nite

nite

I plugged the phone in and collapsed onto my bed. I replayed the last fight in my head. Even if Remy's internet connection wasn't total crap, we might have been in over our heads. The Orcs shouldn't be a problem, but the boss—a dragon—had a couple of attacks that might give us trouble. I'd have to check YouTube again to make sure I knew exactly what my job was as the Tank.

I rolled over and could see the half-moon just setting. Yeah, it was seriously late. I needed some sleep. I started the breathing exercise Aunt Tina taught me, and the next thing I knew my alarm clock was going off.

Oh, man, I was beat. I had sworn off the late-night dungeon runs more times than I could count, but my resolve never lasted longer than two weeks.

Loser.

I pulled myself out of bed. I went through a couple of yoga hassanas that are supposed to energize the body, but I couldn't counteract the lack of REM sleep I'd afflicted my body with regularly.

I dragged myself into the shower, and the hot water did what the yoga couldn't. I soaked probably longer than I should have—water is a premium resource in Southern California. We never seem to have enough of it, and everyday more people kept moving to the State. I couldn't blame them, as the year-round sunshine is hard to beat. I dressed fast. It's easy when you wear the same thing every day: t-shirt, jeans or shorts, and a pair of beat-up Vans.

I love California.

I suspected that I may have used the wrong temperature the last time I washed a load of darks, because my jeans seemed a bit snug and it was an effort to get the fly buttoned. Good thing denim stretches.

I ran a comb through my hair. I would need a haircut soon, it was getting bushy. I'd inherited what my aunt called the Reid family hair curse—thick curls that were more than a match for any brush designed by us silly humans. But, according to Elyse, there were women who would kill for the honey-blond color I'd taken for granted my entire life. My opinion was hair was hair and so I just let mine do what it did naturally. Lucky for me the "messy look" was an actual hairstyle.

I stared in the mirror. My grey eyes were bloodshot from my late-night video game addiction. I rummaged around under the sink, looking for the eye drops. I knew there was a bottle somewhere in the bathroom. Frustrated, I stood up. My eyes were in serious need of lubrication, and I spotted the small bottle sitting on top of the towel cabinet. Ah-ha. The relief was instant. I was enjoying the soothing moisture so much that my brain didn't even register the fact that I had been able to see the top of the towel cabinet without standing on my toes, something that should be impossible.

I hopped down the stairs, two at a time. The house my Aunt Tina and I live in isn't huge. It's a kind of SoCal mini-Craftsman. The coolness of the Craftsman style with lots of wood trim and leaded windows, but on a much smaller scale than the big houses over in Pasadena. We live in a city I call Pasadena-adjacent, Sierra Madre. The weird thing about Southern California is that it's basically one giant city. You can roll from L.A. to Burbank, to Sierra Madre, to Pasadena and points beyond, and unless you're a local, you wouldn't know where one city limit ends and the next begins. Lots of houses, lots of people, and too many cars, but still an awesome lifestyle. The beach is about thirty minutes away, and when I'm not in class or glued to my computer screen on a dungeon run with my guild, that's where I spend most of my time.

If you can do it in the water, I love it. Surfing, sailing, free-diving, scuba diving—you name it, I've tried it or I'm actively involved in it. My Aunt Tina teases I'm part fish or mermaid—or is that merman? I prefer to think of myself as the Sub-Mariner from Marvel Comics. I know, he was sometimes a bad guy, but come on, he is way cooler than Aquaman.

The house was quiet. Aunt Tina must have already left for work. I found a note on my laptop bag.

Working late tonight. Final push on the Cereal campaign. If you order takeout, please get me some of whatever you pick up. Loves.

I smiled.

Aunt Tina is my mom's sister, and she's more like a second mom. My mom, Nancy Reid-Capricorn, is what passes for a hippie in 2017. I have never doubted her love for me, but she was just never good at the responsible adult things parents need to be good at so their kids don't grow up to be psychopaths. My mom and I lived all over the U.S. for the first eight years of my life. She was responsible enough to homeschool me, or at least find someone to help her homeschool me. For my eighth birthday, she decided she would take me to Disneyland, which meant a trip across country to Aunt Tina's house. We ran out of money around Flagstaff, Arizona, and Aunt Tina drove out to get us. It wasn't so bad. I got to see the Grand Canyon.

After two weeks of crashing at Aunt Tina's, my mom's wanderlust kicked in again. She had heard about this "amazing" commune in Baja, Mexico. Aunt Tina put her foot down, and they had a knockdown, drag-out fight over responsibility and me. In the end, I waved goodbye as my mom left on a Greyhound bus bound for the border. I missed her, but life with Aunt Tina was normal. I could attend a real school and make friends that I wouldn't have to say goodbye to in a month or two.

That had been ten years ago. I was now in college. I had been accepted to UCLA, but I was taking a few General Ed. classes at Pasadena City College to get a jump on freshman year.

And this morning, if I didn't get a move on, I would be late for class. I pulled out my phone and set a reminder to order dinner from Aunt Tina's favorite Indian restaurant. I grabbed my keys and laptop bag, and headed out the door.

I drive an ancient, but very loved, Toyota Corolla. I plopped into the driver's seat and fired up the engine. As I pulled out, I had to readjust my rearview mirror.

Odd.

The only time I need to readjust the mirror is after Elyse has driven the car, but that's an adjustment down, since she's a couple of inches taller than me. She's a volleyball superstar who stands at six-one, while I suffer away at the average height of five-ten. This was an adjustment up, just a fraction, as if someone shorter than me had been in the driver's seat. I must've bumped it and not realized. Oh, well. I plugged my phone in and cranked up my iTunes. Calculus, I am your master.

Pasadena City College is about a twenty-minute drive from my house. I turned it into a thirty-five minute drive, because I stopped for a Red Bull and package of Hostess donuts—the breakfast of college students everywhere. Even with my detour, I still made it to class on time. I'm a computer science major, so calculus is kind of like studying Shakespeare if you're an English Lit major. Calculus is the basis of algorithms, and algorithms are what make the tech world spin. Ever searched for anything on Google, or Amazon? Ever tried to find an old post from your grandma on Facebook? Then you are an algorithm junkie. They are the building blocks behind just about everything we do online. And it was my goal to make algorithms my bitch.

"Did you understand the assignment?" Mark whispered.

Mark Becker: not a bad guy, horrible at math, but he wanted to go pre-med and so needed calculus.

I cocked my head and spoke out of the side of my mouth, trying to avoid annoying Ms. Hale, as she explained how the midterm would work. "Why didn't you call me yesterday, if you were having problems?"

"I spent the day with Christy and by 'I spent the day,' I mean I. Spent. The. Day."

"Dude, please. I do not need or want to hear the details of your gross sex life."

Ms. Hale made eye-contact with us, and we shut up. The rest of the class flew by. I'm a bit of a nerd and had peeked at a few upcoming chapters, so most everything was a review and confirmation I had grasped the new concepts.

Ms. Hale reminded us of an extra credit seminar being held the following day. The guest speakers were two former Google employees. I was so going to be there. I bent over to shove my textbook and notes in my bag, when I caught a flash of movement out of the corner of my eye. Someone was about to knee me in the head. I fell back, arms up to protect my face, but there was nobody near me. Two desks over, Mark was talking to Amber—I think that was her name. She had short blonde hair and long legs, and he had her giggling, but he looked over at my sudden movement.

"Jumpy today?"

"Too much Red Bull, I think," I answered.

I took a couple of deep breaths and stretched my arms out. Maybe it *was* too much Red Bull. I fist-bumped Mark, smiled at maybe-Amber, and headed out for my lunch date with Elyse.

CHAPTER TWO

Taco John's is small hole in the wall in the corner of a strip mall. It's owned and run by the Goncalves family—grandma, mom, dad, and their twin sons. They've been serving up tacos and burritos for longer than I've been alive. It wasn't in the most glamorous location and it didn't have the fanciest décor, but the food was top-notch. The proof of my statement was the constant line at the door. Getting one of the five tables was like winning the lottery, and so Elyse and I always got our food to go and ate in my car.

"How was Calc?" Elyse asked.

"Awesome. Or, to be more precise, I should say my continuing mastery of calculus is awesome."

"Glad to see your humility is still in check."

"What did you have today? Art History?"

"Yeah. Had to turn in a paper on the Renaissance."

I finished the second of my two usual shredded chicken tacos with extra guacamole, and I was still feeling hungry. I eyed Elyse's half-eaten carnitas burrito.

"You going to finish your burrito?" I asked.

She snatched it up and held it close to her chest. "Yes, Mr. Eat too fast."

I looked at the line of people. A fifteen-minute wait at least. I dug into my laptop bag and found a granola bar and some turkey jerky. It would have to do.

I tore open the jerky and dug in.

Elyse took a long pull on her soda, let out a sigh, placed her burrito down, and looked into my eyes.

Uh oh. I stopped mid-chew, my mouth full of jerky. "What?"

I was almost one hundred percent certain what her next words would be. I tried to swallow the jerky too quickly and had to take two large swallows of my soda to get it down.

"Are we going to talk about Saturday? Or are we going to continue to avoid the subject?" she asked.

She was still staring into my eyes and no matter how much I wanted to I couldn't look away.

"Uh, yeah. I guess we should."

I had met Elyse when I was thirteen. She and her family had moved to town from Northern California—like way north, almost to the Oregon border. She had been the new, really tall, girl in an eighth grade class of about three hundred students. I first spotted her at lunch; it was hard not to, as she was a head taller than all the other girls and most of the boys. She had long auburn hair—she had to tell me it was that color later. I would've just gone with reddish-brown. She wore it in a ponytail. She had a great tan, and that's what piqued my interest. A tan like that meant she spent lots of time outdoors, maybe at the beach, and I was always looking for more beach buddies, especially if their parents didn't mind driving. Aunt Tina was great about getting out on the weekends, but it never hurt to have back-up contingencies.

I was pleasantly surprised when I showed up for fifth period Biology and she was there looking for an open seat. I introduced myself, pointed her toward two available seats, and that was that. We became fast friends, and over the awkward teenage years we became best friends.

That's why, sitting here in my Corolla, trying not to burp up jerky and chicken tacos, I had started to sweat—just a bit. Saturday had been one of those perfect SoCal days. Elyse and I had met up with a group of friends at the beach and surfed all day. The waves had been epic. We grabbed lunch off one of those fancy food trucks. In the late afternoon, Elyse and Stacey, one of her volleyball teammates, challenged a couple of guys to a beach volleyball game and completely annihilated them. I cheered myself hoarse.

As the day wound down, we got invited to a house party up in the hills above the coast. The view was amazing. Elyse and I sat on a low stone wall and watched the sun sink into the Pacific. It really was perfect. I'm not sure what it was, maybe just a combination of being in the sun all day, drinking a couple of beers at the party, and the gorgeous sunset, but I leaned over as casually as I could and kissed her, and she kissed me back. We stopped for a second, both of us shocked, and then we just went at it.

We couldn't kiss long enough or hard enough. Our bodies couldn't be pressed into each other enough. Fingers twined through hair, necks were bitten, lips nibbled. It was the single greatest make-out session I had ever had, and it had been with my best friend.

Elyse was still staring at me. Her big, amazing, caramel-colored eyes felt like they were staring directly into my brain. I was sure she could hear my every thought. And all I wanted to do was kiss her again. All I've wanted to do since Saturday night was kiss her. Forget eating or sleeping. I wanted to lose myself in her again, to prove to myself that it wasn't the sun or the beer, or getting caught up in the moment. To show her it had meant something, still meant something, everything, to me.

"Is 'Uh, yeah' all you've got?" she asked.

"No."

"Okay. I'll go first." She took a deep breath and blew it out slowly, before continuing. "I just wanted to say—"

I leaned forward, my hand resting on the side of her face, my thumb stroking her temple, and I kissed her.

Her eyes flew open wide for a split second and then she relaxed, reaching out to tangle her fingers in my hair and pull me closer. It was a spicy-Mexican-food-turkey-jerky flavored kiss, and it was pure bliss. We pulled apart to catch our breaths, our foreheads touching.

She smiled and said, "You're such a dork."

"I couldn't agree more." And I kissed her again.

As much as I would have loved to stay in the parking lot outside Taco John's, smooching all afternoon, it was impossible.

Elyse had to meet her mom and sister at a bridal shop for dress fittings—or something like that. Her sister, Jenny, was getting married in a couple of months and the ladies of the Kelly clan were in full wedding-planning mode.

I also had to get to work, and if I didn't stop kissing Elyse in the next five minutes, I would be late for my shift.

"I've gotta go," Elyse said, a little out of breath.

"Yeah, me too."

Neither one of us wanted to let go, though. It was as if we had saved up years of kisses and wanted to get them all out right then, right there, in the Corolla.

"Seriously," she said.

"Right," I agreed.

She fumbled behind and opened the door, sliding sideways on the seat. I followed her as she stepped backward out of the car, still bent over kissing me ferociously. I held in her in place for one more moment and then let her go.

She stood up and took a deep breath, shaking her arms and head out. "I can tell I'm super-flushed. How's my neck? Is it all red? My mom will know exactly what I've been doing."

"No problem. Tell her it was with me. Your mom loves me." I lunged through the open door to grab hold of her hips and pull her back, but she jumped out of my reach.

"You are a bad boy. I need to leave, and you're going to be late for work."

"I don't care."

"Yes, you do. How close are you to reaching the total for your surf trip?"

She knew me so well. I'd been saving everything I could for the past year, intending to take a month-long surfing safari through the Pacific islands before starting school in the fall. It would be the first thing I could cross off my bucket list. Actually, kiss Elyse was the first thing I could cross off the list, and until Saturday I hadn't even realized it had been on the list.

"Go. Go, before my twelve-year-old boy brain overrules my eighteen-year-old man brain."

I shut the car door, so we'd have a barrier between us, and I crooked my finger at her through the open window.

She leaned down, gave me a quick peck on the lips, and then skipped back. "That's it. Call me as soon as you get off work."

"Absolutely. It'll be around seven."

"Orson."

Crap, she sounded all serious again.

"Yeah?"

"You're a fantastic kisser." She winked at me and spun around, almost skipping to her car.

Oh, man, I was in trouble. Elyse Kelly had me body, mind,

and soul. I watched her get into her car, blow me a kiss, and drive away. I sat in the passenger seat for a few more moments. Eyes closed. I could still feel her lips. Yep, I was in trouble, and then I laughed—a deep, happy, belly laugh. I jumped back in the driver's seat and headed to work.

I work twenty to thirty hours a week at the local Costco. I was lead on one of the stock teams. It wasn't hard work, and the pay was great for a college kid like me. I ran into Tony, one of the other leads, punching in at the time-clock.

"Hey, Reid, that's a huge smile you've got on your face," Tony said.

A couple of other co-workers were in earshot and turned in our direction at his comment. I tried to stop smiling, but I swear that only made me smile bigger.

"Oh no, Reid. There's only one reason a guy ever smiles like that. What's her name, brother?"

Tony was smiling now too. We were always teasing each other, and he smelled blood in the water. I shook my head—this was going to be a long shift.

"I'm just happy to be here, my man," I said.

"Uh, huh."

Luckily for me, we had to get to work. It was delivery day, and several pallets worth of canned goods were waiting on the loading dock. Stocking a warehouse store like Costco was nothing like stocking shelves at a local supermarket. Using forklifts, we moved all of our goods on pallets, and something like the fifty cases of chili Tony was maneuvering onto an overhead shelf weighed in at several hundred pounds easy. I was guiding him in; he was a pro, taking it slow and easy.

I've heard stories about people who lived through life-threatening emergencies describing everything as moving in slow motion. I had tried to imagine what that would be like, but nothing could have prepared me for the real thing. There was no time to react. There was an earsplitting metallic screech, and the forklift tilted sideways. And, I kid you not, it seemed to move in slow motion.

I knew by the angle that the pallet was going to slide off. It was going to be really messy and really loud, but there were no customers nearby, and I was standing back far enough that I would be safe from being crushed. That's when Tony tried to stop the pallet from falling by throwing the forklift into reverse and spinning the steering wheel. It wasn't a bad idea, and it allowed me to see what had caused the original problem—one of the hydraulics on the forklift was trashed. I'm sure at the Forklift Center for Safety, if there is such a place, this would be considered a catastrophic failure. The second thing I noticed was that the forklift was now toppling over along with the pallet. This would have only added to the mess, but because Tony was safety-strapped in to his seat, he was going to have a hard landing and maybe be seriously hurt.

I reacted before I could think whether it was a good idea or not. Since everything was moving in weird emergency slow-mo, my mind calculated distances and vectors. I knew how to stop Tony and myself from being turned into paste by hundreds of pounds of wood and metal. The pallet was going to hit the ground to the front left of the forklift. The forklift would then finish its sideways topple, half on, half off the remains of the pallet. There would be a clear space where I could stand and catch Tony—or at least grab him as he fell—and pull him back and to the side. It could work, and we might both get away without major injury. The laws of physics, however, have a way of ruining even the best-laid plans, so one made in a split second while running toward a man-made avalanche had a very slim chance of working. I watched the falling pallet be deflected when it hit a lower shelf—directly toward the space I was currently occupying, hoping to save Tony.

What would you do if hundreds of pounds of chili were

hurtling toward your head? Probably the same thing I did, which was to instinctively throw my hand out to push it away before it crushed me.

The strange thing is—it worked.

Instead of giant body-squishing storage pallet stacked with fifty cases of Dinty Moore Chili, it was as if a large cardboard box full of those Styrofoam peanuts had been falling towards me. I pushed the pallet to the side, sending it crashing to the floor, caught Tony with my other arm, and jumped. Now, when I say jumped, I mean a standing jump while holding a one-hundred-and-ninety pound man in one arm. I cleared the pallet, the forklift, and gained a few feet of clear space.

I dropped Tony, looked over my shoulder at the disaster area, and fainted.

CHAPTER THREE

I opened my eyes. I was lying in the aisle where I blacked out. Yes, I prefer blacked out to fainted. It seems more accurate. There was a small crowd of people standing around me—Becky, the store manager, Steve, one of the assistant managers, and Tony.

"There is an ambulance on the way, Orson," said Becky.

An ambulance? Oh crap. I sat up.

"The 911 operator said you shouldn't move," said Steve. "You could have internal injuries."

"I don't have internal injuries. I don't have any injuries. I think I blacked out from the adrenalin rush or something."

"You totally saved my butt, man," said Tony.

He looked how I felt. Totally strung out from almost dying. Fight or flight, it's a real thing. I stood up and Becky made a hissing sound, shaking her head.

"Becky, really, I'm okay. Just a little shook up."

"Doesn't that hurt?" Steve asked.

I looked at him, confused, and he pointed at my arm. I looked down and almost blacked out again. My entire left forearm was an angry black bruise. It looked like someone had taken a baseball bat to my arm. I touched it lightly with my fingers. Oh yeah, that was sore. "Um, yeah it's a little tender."

Jill, one of the cashiers, came rushing around the corner with two paramedics in tow.

She pointed at me and said, "Oh. He's up. The blond guy with the banged-up arm."

"I'm okay. Really."

The paramedics insisted on checking Tony and me for any other injuries. Blood pressure, light in the eyes for pupil dilation, a few questions like, "what day is it?" and "how many fingers am I holding up?" Satisfied that nobody was in imminent danger of dying, they strongly suggested that I get my arm x-rayed. I didn't want to go to the hospital, but Becky wouldn't take no for an answer. She insisted on driving me. I objected over the fact I would have to leave my car.

"Orson. We are going to the hospital. Right now. End of story."

I could tell I wouldn't win, so I gave in. Tony kept thanking me for saving his life. Co-workers waved, and a few clapped and shouted encouragements as Becky and Tony walked me out to her car.

"Way to go, Superman!"

"Tony isn't worth it, man."

I laughed. This was unreal.

"All I did was push you out of the way. No offense, but you don't weigh all that much."

"Yeah. Well, how much do you think that pallet weighs?"

I looked down avoiding his eyes.

"All I had time to do was get the seat belt off and pray. I knew I was going to get crushed. I just didn't know how bad it was going to be. And then, *bam*! There you were."

Tony stopped walking, which caused me to slow and look

over at him. His eyes were wide. "You tossed that pallet aside, Reid. Like it was made of nothing."

"I know it looked that way, but the bulk of its weight hit something else, the shelf or something." I held up my arm. "That's why this wasn't pulverized into jello."

"I know what I saw, Reid. You saved my life."

"We need to get Orson to the hospital," said Becky.

Tony held out his hand and when I reached out to shake it, he pulled me into a one-armed bro-hug. I gave him a couple of smacks on the back and he let me go.

Becky and I continued to the car. My mind was racing. I played the accident over and over in my head, and I knew against all logic and reason that Tony was right. I had used my arm to whack aside several hundred pounds and only received a bruise for the effort. And Tony hadn't mentioned it . . . maybe the arm thing had all of his attention . . . but what about that completely impossible jump? What the hell was going on?

CHAPTER FOUR

If you ever want to skip the line at the emergency room, just show up with an arm that looks like it was smashed under a boulder and they will usher you right in. Not only did I get an x-ray, but the doc also ordered an MRI, as she couldn't believe there was no internal damage.

"Mr. Reid, you are very lucky man. You'll be black and blue, probably for a week or two if the bruising is any indication, but I don't foresee any other complications."

"Great. Is there anything I can do to help the bruising along?"

"No, it will fade on its own. There's no way to rush it. I'll order a prescription for some pain medication. Tylenol with codeine, take as needed, not to exceed three a day."

"Got it. Thanks again, Doc."

"You're welcome."

She gave me a firm handshake and left me to get dressed. My arm was already feeling a little better. The pain had subsided to a dull throb, instead of the sharp pain I'd been experiencing earlier.

I checked my phone. I had a text from Tony asking what

the doctor had said about my arm. Nothing from Elyse. I wasn't expecting anything, but I was glad I didn't have to explain why I was at the hospital. It would be hard enough keeping her from freaking when she saw my arm. The same went for my Aunt Tina when she'd get a look later tonight. I decided the best course of action would be to send a text, giving her a heads-up and hopefully defusing as much of her worry as I could.

Hey, had little accident at work. Bruised up my arm good. No serious damage. I'm ordering Indian, see you later.

She replied instantly. I love her, and she's usually a calm person, but any kind of sickness or injury in a loved one spins Aunt Tina out pretty quickly.

What? Are you sure you're okay?

I responded with my signature sunglasses emoji. She would still worry a little until she could see my arm with her own eyes, but at least she wouldn't rush out of work, missing her client meeting. I also texted Tony, letting him know the x-ray was clear.

My last stop before escaping the emergency room was the nurse's station to check out. The nurse brought up my record, checked a few of the boxes, and hit print. I was studying the photos she had taped around her workstation, shots of her on some awesome-looking beaches. I was pretty sure Fiji and maybe even Tonga were represented. The nurse turned to the printer to grab my paperwork, and when she turned back, I registered her face in my peripheral vision. It was a twisted monster face! Her mouth was too big, full of what looked like rows of shark teeth, her eyes black like a doll. I flinched back, a small whimpering sound escaping my mouth. When I focused on her face, it was normal.

Her smile faltered, I'm sure due to my strange reaction. "Are you okay, Mr. Reid?"

"Yeah. Sorry. Arm just twinged on me."

Her smile returned and she handed over my paperwork.

I studied her face and that of the nurse behind her. They both looked normal. No monsters. I rubbed my eyes. Maybe I was just tired from the physical and mental stress of the accident. Some kind of short-term micro-PTSD.

"The Tylenol Dr. O'Donnell prescribed will help with that. Remember to take it easy for the rest of the day. Keeping the arm elevated will also help with the swelling."

"Thank you."

Becky was sitting in the waiting room, concentrating on something on her cell. Probably playing Angry Birds. She looked up as I approached. "All done? What did the doctor say? Is your arm going to be okay?"

"Yes, just a bruise, and yes," I replied with a smile.

"Huh?"

"You asked three questions, and I answered all of them. Yes, just a bruise, and yes."

"Oh. Funny."

"Thanks for making me come to the hospital and thanks for waiting with me," I said, with all sincerity.

"You're very welcome."

She insisted on pulling the car around while I waited. I eased myself into the seat, doing my best not to bump my arm against anything. Becky seemed a little tense on the drive back to the store. Her usual non-stop assessment of the store and her performance, and the staff's performance, was replaced by an unsettled quiet.

She pulled into the Costco lot and parked right next to the Corolla. She sighed and turned in her seat to face me.

"I'm sorry about this, Orson, but Regional says I have to ask sooner than later."

"Ask what?"

He answer came out in such a rush I almost didn't follow her. "Are you planning on holding the store responsible?"

"Um. For what?"

"Your arm."

Then I understood the question. She, and apparently the Regional office, were worried I would sue.

"Absolutely not. No way."

She let out a huge breath, her shoulders visibly relaxed, and she said, "Great. I mean good, thank you. The company will, of course, cover all the medical expenses from today and any others that may accrue."

"I think I'm good, but thanks for the info. I'll let my Aunt Tina know."

"Um. Do you think your aunt will agree with you?"

Wow. Becky was worried. I guess it made sense. A sue-happy person could probably get a million dollar settlement for the kind of accident that went down. I wondered if Tony was thinking about suing. He hadn't received any physical injury, but the right kind of lawyer could work up a whole emotional angle that could shake some cash loose.

"Yeah, Aunt Tina will be cool. No worries. Seriously."

Becky let out another enormous sigh and smiled at me. "Thank you, Orson." She patted my leg. "I will credit your time card for today and tomorrow, but I don't want you to come in."

I started to protest.

"Hush. You're going to take tomorrow off. I think you're not scheduled again until Friday, correct?" I nodded, and she went on, "That will give you two full days of rest. And when you come back, no heavy lifting until your arm is back at one hundred percent. Got it?"

"Got it."

"Okay. Now go home and get some rest."

· "Thanks again, Becky."

Before I pulled out of the Costco parking lot, I called the dinner order in to the restaurant, figuring it would almost be ready by the time it would take me to drive over, and I could save the delivery charge by picking it up. I was standing at the counter waiting to pay when the owner came out to greet me. We'd been eating here for years. His eyes went wide at the sight of my arm.

"It looks worse than it feels," I assured him.

"I give you an extra order of Garlic Naan."

I never say no to free food, especially Garlic Naan. I thanked him, paid for the food, and rushed home. I was starving.

I texted Elyse, asking her to call when she was free. She responded with a row of heart emojis. I ripped into the food. No music, no TV, nothing to distract me, just chewing and swallowing. I finally stopped to let loose a loud belch and sagged back into the couch, exhausted from eating. Was that possible? I'm pretty sure it was. I surveyed the table in front of me. It looked like a takeout food explosion. I needed to get Aunt Tina's food into the fridge, and I leaned forward to see what I could consolidate onto one plate.

Empty . . .

Except for a maybe a forkful of Chicken Vindaloo, all the containers were empty. I had eaten all of it—enough food for two people and leftovers, because the only thing better than Indian food was Indian food leftovers.

I jumped when my cell phone rang. It was Elyse.

"Hey," I said.

"Hey, yourself."

"Are you wedding'd out for the night or just taking a breather?"

"We're still at dinner, sampling the courses that will be served at the reception. I snuck away to the bathroom so I could call."

"Ooh. Sounds tasty."

"Poor baby hasn't had dinner yet."

"Actually," I surveyed the Indian food-pocalypse before me, "this will sound weird, because it is, but I just polished off a full dinner order from Siam Café. And I mean I ate it all. I'm going to have to run back out to get Aunt Tina some food."

"Really? That's a serious amount of curry. You could OD. Try explaining that to 911."

It was time to come clean about my exciting day. "Funny you bring up 911. I had a tiny accident at work today and someone called an ambulance."

"What? An accident that required 911 is not tiny, Orson. What happened? Are you okay? Did you go to the hospital? Why. Didn't. You. Call. Me?"

"Whoa. Calm down. I'm fine. All I did was bruise my arm. Becky made me go to the hospital, just to be safe."

"Why was 911 called, then?"

"Well, I sorta passed out."

"I'm coming over right now."

She sounded like she might cry. Wow. It was kind of cool that someone other than my aunt would react that way.

"Elyse. I'm fine. Stay with your family."

"You passed out, Orson. That's not a thing people do if they're fine."

"It was the adrenaline. Tony had a similar reaction. He was totally wigged out."

"Tony? What happened?"

She made me give her a detailed account of the accident, interrupting me to ask clarifying questions. I left out the fact that I had, except for turning green, basically become The Hulk for the duration of the accident.

"Exactly how big is the bruise?" she asked again.

"It's larger than your normal run-of-the-mill bruise, but the doc' said that's all it is. I swear. You need to get back to your family. They're probably wondering where you are."

"All right, but I'm coming over first thing in the morning. I'm serious."

"Then I have something to look forward to on my day off. Say hi to your mom and sister for me."

"I will. Call me if anything changes. If you start feeling weird or something. Okay?"

If I start feeling weird? If she only knew.

"You got it."

I hung up and kind of just stared into space for a few minutes. I needed to get my head around everything going on with me. I pulled out my laptop, loaded a new word document, and started typing. My list included the weird peripheral vision flashes and hallucinations—I didn't like using that word, but how else could I describe monster faces? I wrote out the accident in detail. I stared at the empty food cartons on the table and included "huge appetite" as an item, and I even added the mirror being out of place and my pants not fitting right. When I finished, I read my list of—what were they, symptoms? The only things that seemed even remotely related were the flashes and hallucinations.

I launched Google and searched visual flashes and hallucinations. The results were not cool—terms like Psychosis and Schizophrenia had a much larger return rate than I liked. I bookmarked a few pages and then ran searches on the list items. An increased appetite could be a tapeworm. Gross.

It was then that my brain decided to address the incident of the eye-drop bottle on the towel cabinet that morning. I wasn't tall enough to see the top of the cabinet. What the hell? A thought occurred to me and I set the laptop aside and walked into the kitchen, pulling open the junk drawer. I don't think I've ever been in a kitchen that doesn't have at least one drawer designated for the odds and ends collected through the course of living your life. These drawers all had a combination of batteries, scissors, rubber bands, paper clips, pens, pencils, loose screws, keys to who-knows-what, and of course the thing I was looking for, a tape measure.

Obtaining your height with complete accuracy using a tape measure isn't easy. Luckily, I didn't need an exact number, just my height within a quarter of an inch. I grabbed a pencil and measured out five feet ten inches against the hallway door frame. I then positioned myself against the doorframe and slid the pencil along the top of my head until it touched the frame behind me, making sure I pressed down hard enough to leave a mark. I checked my results.

Huh.

I was wrong. Measuring yourself is harder than I thought. I checked my initial measurement of five feet ten inches and repositioned myself with my back to the doorframe, took a few deep breaths, and held it on the last inhale. I did my best to still my body, raised my arm being careful not to tilt my head, and I measured myself again. I checked the mark, it was in almost the exact spot. This was nuts. I had to be doing something wrong. I measured a third time, and it was the same. I could keep denying what I was looking at or just accept that my boyhood dream of being six feet tall had somehow come to pass.

I went back to the computer and searched male growth spurts. These results were much more encouraging than my first search. It's rare, but there are documented cases of people in college, between the ages of eighteen and twenty, adding up to an inch in height. If my measurements were correct, I had added two inches. Above the norm, but nothing *too* out of the norm. Maybe that's why I was suddenly so hungry all the time? My body needed fuel for some delayed growing. I checked the time. Crap. I needed to replace Aunt Tina's dinner. I shelved my laptop and called in the order.

The drive to and from the restaurant was uneventful. The owner gave me a curious look when I picked up my second dinner order in the space of two hours.

"Unexpected dinner guests," I told him.

As I pulled into my driveway, I noticed Mrs. Giles, one of our neighbors, walking her dog and I waved. She waved back and smiled. As I turned toward the house, I could still see her out of the corner of my eye, and I froze when she began to glow. I kept my eyes forward but watched with my peripheral as she made her way down the sidewalk. A warm golden light shot through with blue sparky streaks emanated from her. I blinked my eyes several times to see if the image would clear. Nope. She was getting close to her house and would soon turn into her yard, where a large tree would block my view. I turned my head to stare directly at her back as she walked away. The moment I focused my attention on her, the light disappeared and she looked like normal, non-glowy Mrs. Giles.

I closed the front door and leaned back against it. Well, I was definitely seeing things. Now I needed to know why. Should I tell Aunt Tina? She would just stress, and if it turned out to be nothing, she would have worried for no reason. We had great insurance provided by the advertising company she worked for and I could do a walk-in to urgent care tomorrow. I was sure seeing hallucinations would get me right in to see the doctor.

I wasn't sure what to do. I needed a distraction, something that would let my subconscious chew on my problem without my logical brain interfering. It was a trick I had learned in my psych class the previous year. Our brains can be tricky to manage. The intuitive side and the logical side sometimes get into turf wars, affecting our problem-solving abilities. The trick was to distract your conscious self by doing something routine: a chore or an activity that you can perform almost on autopilot. Supposedly, this frees up your subconscious to work on the problem without interruption. It doesn't work all the time, but when it does, it's an awesome tool.

I set Aunt Tina's food in the kitchen, pulled my computer back out, and logged into WoW. I didn't think I could do any serious dungeon raiding, but there's so much more to the game and I knew I could kill an hour or two, no problem.

For the uninitiated, World of Warcraft isn't just time spent in a make-believe world running around fighting goblins or some other creature. While there is a lot of that, there is also a whole commerce side to the game. I know people who spend the bulk of their time buying and selling virtual goods in the game, amassing huge amounts of gold.

Anyway, an hour or two of gaming was exactly what I needed to take my mind off my situation. I logged on and inventoried all the items I would try to sell. I wasn't on for more than ten minutes when Alec logged on. I typed a quick hello and told him I was in the middle of bag maintenance. He responded with a hello and asked me to jump on my headset. He probably wanted help with something.

"Hey, Alec. What's up?"

"Orson, did you have an accident at work, mate?"

Did I have an accident at work? How would he know to ask that? Maybe Elyse had logged on and said something, but I didn't know how that would be possible, with her at dinner.

"That's kind of a specific question. Have you spoken to Elyse?"

"Nah, but I have been on YouTube."

"YouTube? What are you talking about?"

"You didn't almost have a tractor fall on you at work?"

"It wasn't a tractor, it was a forklift."

"I knew it was you. You're famous, mate."

"What are you talking about?"

"You need to check YouTube and search for superhero versus tractor."

"What?"

"Just do it. Trust me."

I minimized my game window, navigated to YouTube, and typed in superhero versus tractor. A video popped up in the search results, and my stomach dropped. I double-clicked the thumbnail, bringing the video full-frame. It was footage from a video camera at Costco. My Costco. And there I was, guiding Tony as he maneuvered the forklift. I knew what was going to happen—I had lived it just a few short hours ago— but I was still shocked when I watched myself knock the pallet aside, catch Tony, and jump six feet to the side.

"Oh wow."

"That is you, right?" Alec asked.

"Um, yeah, but it's not what it looks like."

I checked the view count. No way! How could a video just posted already be up over half a million views?

"How's the arm? Did you break it? And what's with that jump? Seriously, mate, it's the craziest thing I've ever seen."

"My arm's a little bruised is all."

Whoever had downloaded the video from the security system had only grabbed the one angle. I tried to remember if there was another camera that covered that aisle. I didn't think there was, but I couldn't be certain. The footage was from a camera in the ceiling, and it was a very wide angle. I took a quick glance at the comments and in between the "OMGs" and the "that's freaking cools" were many posts of "hoax" and "Please, it's total After Effects." So not everyone was buying it as real. I don't know why, but that made me relax a little bit.

"Alec, I gotta log. I'll talk to you later. Okay?"

"Sure. Don't go lifting any cars now, but if you do, make sure you get it on video."

"Right."

I logged out of the game and watched the video several more times. Aside from the obvious reasons of people just can't do those kinds of things, I could see why some were calling it a hoax. The camera angle was wide enough that a lot was hidden from view. With some rope and enough time, a person could rig the pallet into a controlled fall. And while I was no digital video expert, I've seen cats fighting with light sabers, so I knew the technology existed to make my jump look realistic.

This was going to complicate things. I refreshed the page and the views jumped another couple hundred. It was going viral. Who was I kidding? It *had* gone viral. If it kept going, the news media might pick it up. I definitely did not want to be on the news, not when there was a good chance I was sick.

I looked up at the front door opening. It was Aunt Tina.

She locked the door behind her, dropped her purse on a chair and said. "Well, hello, Mr. YouTube. You want to fill me in on your day?"

Oh crap.

CHAPTER FIVE

"It's not what you think." I said.

"Really? And you can read minds now?"

Yeah, she was really pissed. She was still standing, arms crossed, peering down at me with her angry face. I started to respond, but she cut me off before I could utter a syllable.

Here we go.

"I doubt very much that you've become a mind reader in the last ten hours. But if you had acquired that amazing ability, you would know I'm not angry. Well, maybe a just little. What I mostly am is disappointed."

Not the disappointed speech. I'd been able to avoid this one since I'd turned sixteen, and she had caught me sneaking back in from a party. A party where I sampled various kinds of alcohol for the first time to the point of making myself falling down, stupid drunk. There had been no yelling or threats of punishment. She had taken in my drunken state, made sure I hydrated with a ton of water, given me a double dose of aspirin, and sent me to bed. When I regained consciousness, I found her sitting in my room, curled up in an overstuffed chair I used for studying and naps.

It was obvious she had spent the night in my room watching over me. The look on her face was confusing. She somehow looked relieved and upset at the same time. When she finally spoke, it was in a quiet tone. "How do you feel?"

"Horrible."

My mouth tasted like something had crawled in it and died. My body was one gigantic ache. Seriously, my hair hurt.

"You'll feel a little better after a hot shower. I know your stomach will scream no at even the thought of food, but trust me a nice, mild juice smoothie will help your body recover."

"Okay."

Her calm demeanor freaked me out. She should have been angry, yelling, taking away my X-Box, car privileges, and grounding me for life. I had lied, defied a direct "no" to my request to attend the party, snuck out of the house, and returned with a questionable ability to stand up without falling over.

"I want to say a few things, Orson, and I don't want to be interrupted." She waited for me to nod. "First, I'm glad you didn't hurt yourself last night. You were ridiculously drunk and could have easily injured yourself. Second, I understand that part of growing up is pushing boundaries, learning to be your own person. That parties and experimenting with drinking are a rite of passage. But I need you to remember that, for many people, that rite of passage can turn into a life-long addiction."

She was alluding to her dad, my grandpa Stan, whom I'd never met because he had died from complications from alcoholism.

"The last thing is this: life is one long series of choices. Almost every day, we make choices that could affect the direction we are heading. Some may seem inconsequential at the time, but then, with hindsight, we can see how important every choice is.

"I'm not mad at you. I'm disappointed with the series of choices you made that has led to this." She gestured around the room, to me with a lulu of a hangover, her sitting in a chair lecturing me. "It's disappointing that the relationship of trust we've built over the years has been damaged."

"Aunt Tina, I'm sorry."

She went on as if I had said nothing. "I will not ground you or punish you in any way. You're sixteen, so punishing you won't teach you anything you don't already know or should know. You will, however, have to work to gain back the level of trust we had. That's the unavoidable consequence of your choices. And that's the concept I want you to grasp and understand—choices always have consequences. That is an absolute universal truth."

When she was finished, she stood up, left me lying in bed, and went about her day. It killed me, the disappointment I could feel emanating from her like a wave. I would be lying if I said I was a perfect model of obedience from that day on. I was a teenager, after all, but I never again broke a trust with Aunt Tina, or anyone else. I made a promise to myself to never do anything that would cause her that kind of deep disappointment.

It was a promise I had kept—but couldn't keep any longer. Not about this.

I could see it in how she was standing and I could read it on her face. The disappointment was building, but it was warring with some other emotion—hope, maybe. It was obvious she was struggling with the idea I had been involved in an elaborate hoax to gain some internet fame or infamy. What could I say? The video was real? I became Superman for a short time this afternoon and, oh, hey—I'm also seeing things that could mean a brain tumor or schizophrenia? Do I let her be disappointed or do I stress her out about my health? I opened my mouth, not sure what would come out, and then the doorbell rang.

We both looked up at the clock on the wall. It was just after 9:00 p.m., and somebody was making a late house call. I started to rise, but Aunt Tina waved me down. She crossed to the front door and opened it, revealing Elyse. My eyes went wide, and I stood up.

"Elyse?" Aunt Tina said, confused.

"Hi, Ms. Reid. Sorry for the late hour. I know you've been at work all day. I just needed to pick up some calculus notes from Orson."

Elyse flashed her dazzling smile. I'm convinced that smile could disarm an angry rampaging gorilla. My aunt didn't stand a chance.

"Of course. Come in, sweetie."

I hadn't moved. Elyse wasn't in my calculus class. Elyse wasn't in any calculus class. Elyse hated math, she was an Art major. Something was very wrong. Elyse gave me a micro shake of her head.

Okay. I'll play along.

"Again, I'm so sorry to bother."

"No. No. You're good. I need some food and a long, hot soak in the tub," said Aunt Tina.

"Food's on the stove. Siam's," I said.

Aunt Tina smiled at Elyse, gave me a cool look, and said, "Thank you. We'll pick up our discussion later."

I nodded. Elyse smiled. Aunt Tina poured herself a tall glass of sparkling water, grabbed the plastic take-out bag and a fork, and headed up stairs.

"What—" I started, but Elyse held her hand up.

She waited to hear the bedroom door shut and the water in the tub turn on. Satisfied, she turned and pulled me into a hug.

"Hey." My concern grew. "What's going on?"

She held me tight, not saying a word. I held her back, squeezing reassuringly. She released me with a quick peck on the cheek.

"Hold on. I've got to let my mom in," she said.

"Your mom? What?"

Elyse opened the front door and in walked Katherine Kelly. She was every bit as tall and beautiful as her daughter. Where Elyse had auburn hair, her mom's was raven-black. They looked more like sisters than mother and daughter.

"Hello, Orson." She crossed the room, took my hands in her hers, pulled me a little closer and scrutinized my face. I'm not sure what she was looking for, but her gaze was intense and weird. Then it got *super* weird, when she sniffed the air around me.

All I said was a confused, "Hi?"

Mrs. Kelly let go of my hands and Elyse immediately reached out and held one in a tight grip. I looked at her, to her mom, and back.

"Orson, I understand you've had an interesting day." It was a statement, not a question.

"Yeah, I guess."

Elyse said, "We've seen the video. Stacey texted me the link. How's your arm?"

"Not broken."

"Clearly," said Mrs. Kelly.

"Can you show us?" Elyse asked.

I pulled off my hoodie and was shocked to find that the bruising on my arm looked better. I twisted it around for a better look in the living room light. Elyse made concerned noises.

"Huh?" I said.

"What is it?" Mrs. Kelly asked.

"Nothing. It looks . . . I don't know . . ."

"Better." Again, it was a statement, not a question.

"Yeah. A lot better," I agreed.

"Orson, you know I have a medical background, correct?" Mrs. Kelly asked.

"Yeah, you were like a nurse or something back in the day."

"Or something, yes. I've watched the video—multiple times. Your arm, not to mention most of the bones on the left side of your body, should have been crushed. And yet, it looks at most like you fell off a bicycle."

Oh boy. First Aunt Tina's disappointment, and now Elyse's mom was going to voice her displeasure that her daughter would even consider dating somebody who would pull such a horrible prank, hoax, whatever.

"Mrs. Kelly that video—"

She cut me off, "Is a real problem."

"I know it seems like maybe it was some kind of prank. That the trolls on the internet are calling it a hoax, but—"

She cut me off again. "We should only be so lucky that people will believe it's a hoax."

I started to respond, but then her words sank in. *Be so lucky*. What was that supposed to mean?

Elyse gave my hand a squeeze, and I glanced at her. She looked worried, maybe even scared.

I dropped her hand and put my arm around her shoulder. "Hey, are you all right?"

"Orson, I'm so sorry . . ." she said. A tear rolled down her face and her shoulders trembled.

"What's wrong?" I looked to Mrs. Kelly. "What's happening? Why is she so upset?"

"Elyse tells me you had a rather large dinner?"

What? Dinner? I thought she was going to ream me over a fake video that wasn't a fake video. Now she was asking about my diet? What the hell?

"Mrs. Kelly, I'm really confused right now. Elyse is upset.

You're asking about my arm and the video, and what I had for dinner? Can you please just tell me what's going on?"

"One more weird question, if you please." She locked her eyes on mine. "Have you been seeing things?"

That was it. I was done. I let go of Elyse and sat down hard on the couch, staring up at the both of them. The sense that my world was about to implode was over-whelming.

"Please?" I implored.

"Well, I think we can take that as a yes," said Mrs. Kelly.

Elyse sat down next to me, placing a tentative hand on my shoulder. Mrs. Kelly sat on the coffee table in front of me, our knees touching. She took hold of both my hands once more.

"You know the video is real? Don't you?" I asked Mrs Kelly.

"Yes."

"You're not surprised that I have a crazy big appetite?"

"No."

"And you fully expected that I would be seeing things?"

"Yes."

"Why?"

"Because of what you are."

I closed my eyes and took a deep breath. "And what do you think I am?"

"What you are, generally, is something very special. What you are specifically remains to be seen."

What? I stared at her, dumbfounded. That was like the worst Yoda answer I'd ever heard. Was she serious? Mrs. Kelly held my gaze, and I could see she was being as serious as a heart attack.

"You know that makes absolutely no sense, right?" I asked.

Then, she asked a question that came so far from out of

nowhere it almost gave me whiplash. "I understand that you and Elyse recently kissed for the first time."

"I . . . Uh . . ."

I felt Elyse stiffen next to me.

"I'm not upset." She flicked her eyes toward her daughter and said, "No one is in trouble."

"Mrs. Kelly, I'm kind of freaking out right now. What's happening to me?"

"Orson, when I said you are special, a more accurate description would have been unique. The reason that pallet didn't crush you—the reason you're stronger and faster and seeing odd things—is due to your genetic make-up. The reason I know all this is because Elyse and I are like you."

Mrs. Kelly stood in a fluid motion. She cocked her head to one side, as if listening for something.

"Your aunt is still in the bath. We have time."

How could she possibly hear Aunt Tina in the bath? Mrs. Kelly did a quick survey of the room, her eyes falling on three tall iron candleholders by the fireplace. She moved to them, removed the candle from one, and walked back to stand in front of me. She grasped the candleholder in both hands and bent it in half, like it was made of tin. My jaw became unhinged, dropping open.

She held her hand out toward her daughter. Elyse stood slowly and crossed to her mom. Mrs. Kelly held the iron candleholder out to her. Elyse took it and gave me a weak smile. Her eyes looked so sad. Then, without even a hint of effort, Elyse straightened the candlestick out.

"Holy shit!" I exclaimed. Elyse bit her bottom lip. Mrs. Kelly frowned slightly. "Uh, sorry, Mrs. Kelly."

"That's quite all right, Orson. If ever a situation called for a little profanity, this is it."

"Can you do that again?"

Elyse smiled a little wider. She bent it back and forth one

more time, and after making sure it was straight, she set it back down in its place.

"Okay. So you guys are like X-Men or something?" I had a thought and added, "How about Mr. Kelly and the rest of the family?"

"Yes. They are like us. Richard would've been here also, but is attending to an urgent matter that we will discuss later. I must say, Orson, so far you're handling this quite well," Mrs. Kelly said approvingly.

"Well, my self-diagnosis included brain tumors and insanity. This is . . . better. And I also read a lot of comic books."

Elyse let out a snort.

"I see," said Mrs. Kelly.

"So, how exactly did I, all of sudden, become you know . . ." I gestured at them both.

"That is a very reasonable question. The answer is long, but I'll give you the basics," said Mrs. Kelly.

She began to pace as she spoke.

"As I said, you have a unique genetic signature, a marker in you DNA. How do I know this without studying your blood? Because of what has occurred. When you and Elyse kissed, an enzyme that naturally occurs in her was transferred to you. The genetic marker you carry was dormant, and would have remained so for your entire life, if not brought into contact with the enzyme from Elyse."

I looked at Elyse, who dropped her gaze. Why was she afraid to look at me? Was she ashamed? When she spoke, it was a whisper I could barely discern.

"I'm so sorry. I didn't know. I never would have . . ." She looked up at me, eyes brimming with tears. "I didn't know."

I went to her and pulled her to me. She buried her face in my chest.

"It's all right," I said. "I believe you. Please don't cry."

Mrs. Kelly smiled at me and ran her fingers down her daughter's hair.

"So this is like what . . . some kind of magical STD?" I asked.

Elyse pulled back so she could look at me. "Orson, you have to have *sex* to get an STD." Elyse glanced at her mom.

Right. STD equals *sexually* transmitted disease. We'd only kissed. I could be such an idiot sometimes. I felt my face flush red. "Oh yeah, of course. I mean like a magical mono. Um, you get that from kissing, right?"

"Mono is often called the kissing disease," Mrs. Kelly said, smiling.

I wasn't sure, because I was still freaking a little, but it seemed like Mrs. Kelly was teasing me. "So you're saying I've been *infected* with super-powers?"

"You're such a dork," said Elyse.

At least she wasn't crying anymore.

"No. It doesn't quite work like mono. That's a virus and a very contagious one. You already had these "super powers" coded within your DNA. All the kissing did was provide your body with the catalyst needed to activate the genes that control those powers," Mrs. Kelly explained.

"Can we stop saying, 'super powers'?" said Elyse. "It's kind of lame. And there's a big catch."

"A catch?" Uh oh. That didn't sound good.

Elyse was avoiding my eyes again, but she gave a little nod.

"It's best if you see it with your own eyes," Mrs. Kelly said. "Even then, your mind will try to reject the truth of what is occurring. Orson, I need you to have a seat and stay seated. You need to remain as calm as possible. Can you do that?"

I had just witnessed my girlfriend and her mom bend iron like it was nothing. We had entered the twilight zone ten minutes ago. My brain was fried; I didn't think staying calm would be all that hard. I dropped back down on the couch, placed my hands on my knees, and sat up straight.

Mrs. Kelly nodded to Elyse.

"Don't freak out, okay?" Elyse pleaded.

I don't know what I expected, but Elyse getting undressed was not even on the list of possibilities running through my mind. She had kicked off her shoes and pulled her dress up over her head before I realized what was happening.

"Whoa. Wait a second," I said.

Elyse was standing in her bra and panties, black lace and sexy as hell. I shook my head. *Get it together, Reid.*

"Mrs. Kelly, what—" I started.

Mrs. Kelly cut me off. "Orson, remember our deal. This will all make sense in a moment."

"Elyse?" I tried.

"It's okay," Elyse assured me.

I'd seen Elyse in a bikini more times than I can remember, but this was different. She hadn't been my girlfriend then. Seeing her standing there in such a vulnerable way fired up all my primal caveman instincts. I wanted to protect her. I held in a gasp as she pulled off her bra and skinned off her panties. She was gorgeous. A tanned, toned, golden goddess.

Elyse gave me one more pleading smile. I tried to convey my feelings for her through my eyes, hoping she would understand that she meant everything to me. And then she began to vibrate. Just a slight shimmy, almost like she was shivering. Elyse fell forward and I jumped up to catch her, but before my butt even cleared the couch, a golden aura enveloped her body. In the blink of an eye, Elyse was gone and in her place was what I was sure must be a world-record-sized black panther.

I fell back onto the couch. My girlfriend was a giant black cat, a cat with the claws and teeth of an apex predator. She was easily the size of a Shetland pony. I noticed her coat wasn't entirely black. It had a jigsaw of dark auburn-colored patches that gave it richness and depth. It was beautiful. The yellow eyes drew me in. They weren't normal animal eyes. They were intelligent, knowing eyes. They were Elyse's eyes, maybe a different color, but I recognized her, the girl I'd grown up with, laughed with, and fell in love with.

Elyse, because that was the only way to think of this giant cat in my living room—she wasn't an "it," she was Elyse—sat back on her haunches and curled her long tail around her paws. She blinked her eyes at me, chuffed once, and flicked her ears forward. I couldn't hold it in any longer. I laughed.

It was a deep laugh and maybe just a tad hysterical.

CHAPTER SIX

Mrs. Kelly let out a little laugh of her own. "Well, that's an unexpected reaction." She cocked her head and looked up toward the ceiling. Elyse also flicked her ears toward the stairs.

"I'm afraid we are out of time," Mrs. Kelly said. "Your aunt is finished with her bath." She put up a hand when I tried to speak. "I know you have a thousand questions. We just don't have time to answer them right now. I think it's obvious we would like you to keep this," she gestured at Elyse, "to yourself. Your aunt can't know, at least for right now."

"I understand. Like she would believe me, anyway? She'd probably check me in to rehab," I said.

"Elyse, quickly now, shift back," Mrs. Kelly told her.

I couldn't help myself. I stared, completely fascinated by the process. I mean, I was witnessing something that went against centuries of scientific observation and documentation.

Elyse's cat body started the slight vibration I had noticed before—or I guess *shift* was the correct term. At the last moment, she sprang up onto her back legs so that when the shimmery glow finished its thing and she was back in human form, she was standing on her feet.

I tried to be a gentleman, averting my eyes while she quickly dressed. I looked back as she was pulling her dress over her head. "Does it hurt?" I waved my hands in the air. "The shifting, does it hurt?"

Elyse cocked a hip, shook her head, and asked, "You just watched me turn into an abnormally large panther and your first question is, does it hurt?"

I stood up and crossed to her. "Well, yeah. I just want to make sure you're not in pain." I tucked some hair that had come loose behind her ear. It was a casual move, but I hoped it conveyed the message I didn't consider her a freak, or that I was afraid of her now.

Elyse's eyes brimmed with tears and she threw her arms around me. With her lips close to my ear she whispered, "Thank you." I gave her squeeze. She pulled away, but kept a hold of my hand

"Orson, you have always been my favorite of Elyse's friends, and tonight you proved why that is the case," said Mrs. Kelly, clearing her throat and wiping at the corner of her eye. "We have to leave. Your aunt will be down any second. We need you to come to our house tonight. I know it's asking a lot. We were outside long enough to hear part of your conversation with your aunt. Be as kind as you can with her, but don't even hint at the truth. I'm sorry that I'm asking you to lie, but it is for her protection. Can you do that?"

I nodded. I didn't *want* to lie to Aunt Tina, but I also didn't want to put her in danger.

"There is much you need to know and understand about yourself and the world as it really is. This will be a long night. We will wait down the block. You can follow us in your car. Okay?"

"Okay." Elyse and I looked at one another for a moment. I leaned in and gave her a quick peck on the lips. "Give me fifteen minutes."

They both hustled out the door. I just made it back to the couch when Aunt Tina reached the bottom of the stairs. She had on her big terry-cloth robe and a towel wrapped around her wet hair. She dropped the food containers back on the kitchen counter, leaned back, and let out a tired sigh. "Is there anything you want to tell me about today?"

What could I say? I couldn't tell her the video was real. Even if she believed the pallet had been deflected by a shelf and never came into direct contact with my arm, there was no way to explain the jump. A world-class athlete probably could have made it, but not carrying Tony. I would have to disappoint her and it broke my heart.

"We never thought it would get uploaded to YouTube." It sounded lame, even to me.

"You never thought it would get uploaded? That's it? How about responsibility to your employer? I watched the video, Orson, several times, and you damaged that forklift." She was trying really hard to keep her voice calm.

"It looks worse than it is." I tried to sound reassuring, but all she did was roll her eyes and throw her arms up in exasperation.

"You can't be serious! This isn't like you! A stupid prank that damaged property—which is called vandalism, by the way—and on top of that, you could have been seriously hurt. Let me see your arm."

Damn. I thought I could avoid showing her the damage. Even though my arm was looking better, it was still far from normal. "Aunt Tina, really, I didn't get hurt."

"Arm. Now."

I tried to minimize it by pulling up the sleeve of my hoodie instead of taking it completely off. It didn't matter.

When she saw how black and blue it was, she rushed over and kneeled next to me. "Oh my . . . Oh jeez . . . We need to get you to a doctor." She stood up, grabbing for her purse. She paused, looking down at the robe she was wearing, and reversed course for the stairs.

I jumped up. "Wait. Calm down."

"Calm down?" She pointed at my arm. "It looks like your arm was crushed under a car."

"I already had it checked out. And I'm good." I needed her to calm down, so we could finish our conversation and I could get out of there.

"When and by whom?" She stopped at the base of the stairs and crossed her arms.

"I went to the hospital right after—" I almost said *the accident.* "Right after it happened. They x-rayed it, and a doctor checked me out. It looks worse than it is. I promise."

"Orson, what am I supposed to do? You're not a kid anymore. I can't ground you. You're eighteen years old, but this stunt—it was childish and stupid. And you're not a stupid person."

"I know. I know. I regretted it instantly. I really did. I'm sorry I upset you."

"What about your job? People get fired for things like this." She was calming down. I think my messed-up arm transformed all the angry energy into worried energy, and she was now almost back to normal.

What about my job? Becky had given me two days off, but that was before my girlfriend turned into a giant cat in front of me. How do you go back to a normal routine after something like that? Mrs. Kelly had seemed impressed with my reaction, but to be honest, I was still in some kind of denial or shock state. My girlfriend had turned into a cat, and if she and her mom were right, I was currently in the early stages of changing into something too. Would I be a cat also?

Maybe I should have gotten at least a couple of questions answered?

"I'm not sure about my job." I held up my arm. "Becky told me to take a few days to let this heal up. I don't know if anything has been decided." Lying to her was making my stomach hurt.

"I'm exhausted. I need to go to bed," she said abruptly.

"Okay. Um, I'm going to run over to Tony's house." I blurted out the lie as fast I could, throwing poor Tony under the bus as I did. "He's the other guy in the video. I need to talk to him about, you know, how it ended up on the internet."

"Why don't you just call him?"

"I tried. He's dodging me, I think." I smiled. I was terrible at this. How in the world do people lie on a regular basis?

"Okay," Aunt Tina said. "Don't be too hard on him. Remember you were a willing participant." She pointed her finger at me to emphasize her point.

"I know. I'm just hoping I can get him to take it down."

"It's the internet, Orson. It's forever." She leaned over and gave me a kiss on the cheek. "I'm glad you didn't break anything. You are my favorite nephew." It was an old joke, as I was her only nephew. She had been writing that in birthday and Christmas cards for years.

"I love you, Aunt Tina. I'm sorry I disappointed you."

"I'll get over it. Just make sure you never do anything so stupid again."

"You got it."

I waited until I heard her bedroom door close. I grabbed my keys, checked my breath (ugh), grabbed some gum, and stopped and looked at myself in the mirror by the front door. I gave myself a silent pep talk. "This is really happening. You're two inches taller. You're strong enough to shrug off hundreds of pounds of bone-crushing weight. You can jump like a gold medalist track and field superstar. And last, but not anywhere near the vicinity of least, your hot girlfriend can turn into a giant black panther." I took a deep, cleansing breath. Yeah, I'm one bad hombre.

I locked the front door behind me. As I walked to the Corolla parked at the curb, I was searching up the street for Mrs. Kelly's Range Rover. Elyse had borrowed it a few times to drive us to the beach, and it was a sweet ride, tricked out with every option imaginable. I spotted it parked about six houses up. I waved and then nearly had a heart attack when someone right behind me said my name.

"Orson?"

I gave an unmanly shout as I spun around, my feet tripping over where the sidewalk met the grass. I caught myself before I tumbled over.

A face I couldn't place immediately smiled at me. "Sorry. I didn't mean to startle you." A woman in scrubs was standing in the middle of my lawn.

It took me a second, but then it came to me. The nurse from the hospital today, the one whose face went all shark teeth stretchy nightmare. "Oh, hi?" I said. What was she doing here? How did she even know where I lived?

Duh. Idiot, she has all of your medical records and personal information, including your street address.

"I'm sorry, I tried so hard not to come here tonight. I really did." She took a step closer to me.

"No worries, but why are you here exactly? Do I need to, like, sign a form or something?" *Don't be stupid, Orson.* Nurses from the ER didn't hunt down patients late at night to get them to sign forms. Was this a lame attempt at hitting on me? Because she was kind of *old*. Not grey-haired old, but at least a couple of years older than Aunt Tina.

Wait a second . . .

Hunt down patients.

Hunt down.

Hunt.

Shark teeth stretchy nightmare.

The hair on the back of my neck stood up. She took two more steps toward me. One more and she would be able to reach out and touch me.

"I never do things like this," she said. Was her face elongating? Oh, crap. "But it's just . . . what are you?"

Yeah, her face was getting longer, her mouth filling with way too many teeth. Sharp, rip-your-skin-to-pieces teeth.

"Your life force is so . . . enticing." The word *enticing* came out as deep, creepy whisper. She leapt at me. Mouth of razor teeth wide open, claws—yep she had claws curving off each fingertip—reaching for me.

I jumped back and up with enough of my new-found Olympic superstar ability that I landed on top of the Corolla. Not on top of the hood, on top of the roof. With the space I had been standing in suddenly vacated, the shark-nurse-monster-lady smashed head-first into the side of my car, caving in the driver's side door and shattering the window.

An ear-splitting howl ripped through the night. At first, I thought it was the shark-nurse, pissed off at ramming her skull against my well-made Japanese import. But then I noticed movement to my right, and I was sure shark-nurse had brought a friend to share in Orson Tartare I glanced to my right, convinced I would see another shark-nurse or maybe a shark-chef or shark-banker—something definitely sharky and scary.

It was nothing shark-related. It was Mrs. Kelly.

She was running barefoot down the street, and as I watched, her body shimmied once and then *boom,* all of her clothes exploded off her body. That's not exactly right. It was more like her body exploded in a burst of gold light. Her clothes were just collateral damage. Mrs. Kelly was still running straight at me, but she wasn't Mrs. Kelly anymore, and she was definitely not a cat like Elyse. Or, at least, not *entirely* a cat like Elyse. She had cat parts, her head and ears were all cat, but her body was still running on two feet. She was like a person, a really ginormous person, dressed up like a cat. Then, all my years of comic and sci-fi and fantasy reading gave me the term I was looking for—beast form. Something between a person and a cat. All the best parts of both, basically. If comics were to be believed (and after recent events why should I doubt them?), beast form was like the berserker mode of shape-shifting—a near unstoppable rage machine of death.

Shark-nurse hadn't missed the howl either. The header into my car hadn't seemed to faze her much. She looked at Mrs. Kelly, then turned her black doll eyes back toward me. The hunger and desire radiating from them gave me a shiver. She hissed, and I thought it was just to scare the crap out me, which it did, but then a big glob of sticky goo shot out of her mouth, hitting me in the arms and chest. So gross. And then she ran—and damn was she fast. She moved away from me in a blur, down the block and into the darkness.

Mrs. Kelly started to give chase but skidded to a stop. She turned her panther beast form nose in my direction and sniffed.

That's when the burning started.

My chest and arms were on fire. I fell backward off the Corolla, head-first onto the asphalt. I would have screamed my head off, but I couldn't suck in enough air to even gasp.

My world became a black dreamscape with flashes of reality—or what I assumed was reality. Mrs. Kelly, back in human form, naked and yelling at Elyse to avoid the black goo coating my torso and arms. Being lifted into the back of the Range Rover. Street lights flashing by overhead through the windows. Elyse driving, one hand on the steering wheel, the other stretching back to grasp my leg. A loud voice, amplified through the car's Bluetooth, shouting directions at Elyse. Being pulled out of the back seat. A glimpse of my Corolla, its door smashed in, Mrs. Kelly behind the wheel. White walls. Fluorescent lights. People I didn't recognize, standing over me.

Elyse crying and whispering, "Fight, Orson. Please fight. You can't die because I love you, you big dork."

CHAPTER SEVEN

I woke up, instantly alert. I sat up in a strange bed, in a strange room. The sun was peeking out from behind heavy drapes that covered large windows. I had perfect clarity of the attack and the events that preceded it. I gently touched my chest and winced. The skin was red and tender, but the unreal burning was gone. I noticed my phone on a nightstand and checked the time; it was just after 3:00 p.m. I had been out for most of the day. Unless it was Wednesday a week later. I checked the phone. Nope. Just one day. I considered that a win. So, I was attacked by an acid-spitting shark-nurse, and my girlfriend's mom had gone full beast form and chased the shark-nurse off. No biggie. Of course, I was also turning, evolving, metamorphosing (is that even word?) into something different. A giant cat would seem the most likely outcome of my change. I had been infected, or whatever, by Elyse, who could shape-shift into a cat. I wondered if she could turn into anything else, or if it was a one animal form per person kind of thing?

I'd had a busy night.

Aunt Tina. She was probably freaking out. I checked my

phone more thoroughly for emails, voicemail, and text messages. Huh, nothing. I heard someone outside my door. It was Elyse. Don't ask me how I knew that before she opened the door. I could just sense it was her.

She slowly opened the door, pausing when she saw me sitting up. "You're awake."

"Yeah. I just woke up a minute ago. Where are we?"

"My house. Well, the guest apartment behind my house, you know—above the pool house. Let me get my mom. She'll want to check you out."

"Was I at a hospital at some point?" I asked. "I vaguely remember fluorescent lights and a bunch of people. And my chest seems better than I'd expect. Was that like some kind of acid?"

"Yes. We took you to a . . . it's a private clinic." Elyse wouldn't meet my eyes. She seemed uncomfortable.

"Are you okay?" I asked.

"Yes, I'm fine. Let me just get my mom."

"Wait. Aunt Tina?"

"She's fine. At work." Elyse fidgeted, her eyes everywhere but looking at me.

"But where does she think I am?"

"Oh. We left a note. Or, rather, you left a note. I mean, we left a note as if it was from you. It said you had to leave for an early study session."

Her nervousness was starting to make me anxious. I went over the events of the previous night. Maybe she was embarrassed about taking her clothes off in front me? Or after the acid hit, I had become loopy from pain. Maybe I'd said something rude or mean to her.

"Elyse, I didn't do something stupid, did I? Because having a shark-nurse spit black, gooey acid-poison on me seems like a pretty darn good excuse for bad behavior."

She met my gaze, tears spilling down her cheeks. "You

think you did something to me?" Her lower lip quivered, and she bit it. "I've ruined your life. If you hated me and never wanted to see me again, I would totally understand."

I jumped out of bed. Thankfully, I was wearing a pair of sweats. The USC logo down the leg gave away that they probably belonged to Mr. Kelly, Elyse's dad. I pulled her into a soft hug, doing my best to protect my chest. "We covered this last night," I said. "I have a crap-ton of questions, but I'm not mad at you. You're my best friend." I cupped her chin in my hand so she couldn't look away and gently said, "And I love you."

Her body shuddered as she sucked in air. "I know you said you were . . . okay with everything, but that was before you almost died."

"You and your mom saved me. Your mom, by the way, total badass."

"Watch your language, Orson."

Elyse and I jumped. Mrs. Kelly had come silently down the hall behind us. I guess that made sense, as she was some kind of uber were-cat shape-shifter.

Mrs. Kelly smiled and said, "And thank you for the compliment." She patted her daughter's arm. "Go wash your face, sweetie. We'll meet you up at the main house. I'm sure Orson is hungry."

At the mention of food, I realized I was famished. Like, I-could-eat-half-a-cow famished. "Yes, Ma'am. I could definitely eat."

Elyse pulled away, giving my arm one more quick squeeze before walking away to what I presumed was the bathroom. I watched her with a contentment I had never felt before. Maybe this was what it was like to love somebody? Meaning, romantically love somebody. Because I loved Aunt Tina, and I had a warm feeling when I thought about her and what she meant to me, but the feelings I felt toward Elyse were different, more intense and kind of scary.

Mrs. Kelly gave my chest a professional once-over. She seemed satisfied with what she saw and said, "I think Richard left a shirt and a pair of sandals for you also."

"Right. Let me just grab them."

Mrs. Kelly led me out the door toward the main house. The Kellys have one of those big Pasadena California Craftsman houses—my house was a junior version of. It was nestled at the base of the San Gabriel Mountains. It has a gated circular driveway and a backyard big enough for a pool, a volleyball pit (added for Elyse), and a half-court basketball court. The guesthouse I woke up in is part of the rather large pool house. There was a bathroom and changing room for the pool area. A set of outdoor stairs led to a second story entrance and into the spacious one-bedroom apartment I had spent the night in. It included a full modern kitchen and a bathroom bigger than either of the two bathrooms at my house.

I took in the view from the top of the stairs. They looked out over the pool, and to the left was the fence separating the back of the Kelly property from the Angeles National Forest. It was still stunning to me that in the middle of the urban sprawl that was the Los Angeles basin, there was this massive forest. Maybe forest was kind of a strong word, but it's what the federal government called it and who am I to argue with the Feds? It wasn't a forest in the sense that most people think of with giant trees and green mossy stuff everywhere. It was Southern California's version of a forest, and it was pretty cool, if you ask me. And it was big enough that at least once a year some knucklehead or group of knuckleheads would get lost in it. It was home to mountain lions, bears, and wild pigs. So, yeah, people from states with actual mountains laugh when we proudly point to the San Gabriel Mountains and our very own National Forest, but to heck with those interlopers. We native Californians love our conveniently located wilderness.

The Kellys had a gate built into a corner of their back fence that led to a small hiking trail. It wound all the way up to more serious hiking and backpacking trails and even part of the Pacific Crest Trail that ran for hundreds of miles north and south. Elyse and I had covered just about every trail reachable from her backyard and had even blazed a few of our own. Looking out now at the deep brush behind the Kelly house, I couldn't help but feel a little nostalgic for that time —a time before I shoved a pallet weighing hundreds of pounds to the side and before I watched Elyse turn into a cat. I took a deep breath and coughed. The smells that came with the breath were super-intense. I'm talking brain-bursting intense. Chlorine, grass, wet cement, a woody smell I assumed was the fence, and multitudes of other scents coming from beyond the fence that were dizzying. Earthy, primal smells. Even with the layer of city stink on top, I could smell the wilderness and it called to me.

I swayed on my feet.

Mrs. Kelly reached out a hand to steady me. "Are you all right, Orson?" She could transform into a muscle-popping, clawed and fanged were-beast, but she was still a mom.

"Yeah. It's just all of a sudden I can smell . . ." I wasn't sure how to put it into words. "I can smell everything."

"Oh. Of course." She kept her arm on mine to steady me and turned her attention to the hillside beyond the fence. "What do you smell? Try to be exact." She gave me an encouraging smile.

I took another big breath and started coughing again. "Sorry, it's just so overwhelming."

"That's fine, take your time. Close your eyes and take a few smaller breaths. Let the scents flow in."

I tried what she said, closing my eyes, inhaling and exhaling in a slower rhythm. The controlled breathing did the trick and I stopped coughing. I concentrated on what my nose was telling me was out there.

"Chlorine and grass close by."

"The pool and the yard. Yes. What else?"

"I can smell the city. The exhaust of cars, rubber and steel, I think. But under that is . . ." I struggled for the right words. "Earth, you know, soil. Plants, lots of plants. Some of them smell spicy, others sweet, some . . . I don't know . . . tangy? Does that make sense?"

She chuckled. "Yes. That's the sage. I think *tangy* is the perfect word to describe it. What else?"

"I'm not sure. There's kind of a musty smell. It's very faint, but it's there." With my eyes still shut, I pointed up the hill and to the right.

"Excellent. What you're smelling is a jack rabbit."

My eyes popped open. I stared intently at where I had pointed. All I could see were bushes—brown bushes, green bushes, and brown-green bushes. "Really?"

"Yes."

"How?" I turned toward Mrs. Kelly. "How am I smelling a rabbit under a bush, at what, twenty yards away?"

I was surprised at the frankness of her answer.

"Because your animal is waking up and he will make you over from head to toe. Outside." She gently tapped my sore chest. "And inside."

The door opened and Elyse joined us on the landing. She gave me a quick smile and tentatively slid her hand into mine. Her touch was comfortable and reassuring.

"Richard is waiting, and breakfast is getting cold," said Mrs. Kelly. She led the way down the stairs and along a stone path to the large French doors that opened into the main house dining room.

"Breakfast?" I asked, confused.

"Well, breakfast for lunch . . . And a late lunch at that," said Mrs. Kelly. "Elyse told me that breakfast was your favorite meal."

I nodded. "Yeah, she's right, absolutely."

A large wooden table—I think Elyse had once called it a Monk's table—was loaded with heaping plates of pancakes, eggs, bacon, and toast. The table had room to seat eight people comfortably. Mr. Kelly was sitting on one side and motioned for me to sit across from him. I took my seat. Elyse walked around the table to give her dad a peck on the cheek and then she settled in next to me. Mrs. Kelly sat down next to Mr. Kelly and patted his knee.

"Dig in. Then we'll talk." Mr. Kelly had a deep voice. He was tall, like the rest of his family, and toned, but not overly muscled. He was built like a champion swimmer.

I didn't have to be told twice. I was ravenous. Getting acid spooged onto you apparently makes you hungry. Luckily, there seemed to be enough food for twelve people, let alone four. I piled my plate high. I noticed all the Kellys did the same, even Elyse. I've seen her put away mass quantities of food—it's one of the reasons I'd always thought of her as one the coolest girls I knew—but she usually tucked in only after a volleyball match or a day of surfing or hiking.

Elyse saw me watching her. "It's the change. It takes a lot of fuel to recover from a shift," she said, stuffing her mouth with a forkful of pancake and crossing her eyes at me.

In between bites, Mr. Kelly asked, "How's your aunt?"

"Good. A little mad at the 'prank' I pulled at work," I said, making air quotes with my hands. "And my apparent desire for internet fame."

"So, she is convinced it was a prank then?"

"Dad, I told you that's what she thought," said Elyse, exasperated.

"I know what you told me, but he knows his aunt much better than you do. He will know if she is truly convinced or if there is some lingering doubt." He caught my eye and held my gaze. I had always thought of Mr. Kelly as a fun-loving, kind of casual guy. That's not the guy who was staring back at me right now. This guy was serious. This guy looked . . . well, he looked almost menacing.

"No doubts, Mr. Kelly. Hundred percent." I tried very hard to keep the shake out of my voice. I think I succeeded.

Mr. Kelly nodded.

"However . . ." I ventured.

Everyone froze, Elyse reaching for more eggs, Mrs. Kelly wiping her mouth with a napkin, and Mr. Kelly in mid-chew.

"I'm not sure how I'm supposed to explain growing two inches pretty much overnight. She didn't notice last night because of everything going on, but it's only a matter of time."

I counted ten of my own heart beats—weird that I could hear my heart beating—before Mr. Kelly chuckled.

"Yes," he laughed. "I could see how that would be an awkward conversation. Luckily for you, Orson, my young friend, this isn't as the youngsters say 'my first rodeo'."

"No one says that, dear." Mrs. Kelly said mildly.

Elyse laughed so hard she snorted orange juice out of her nose. That did it for me. I laughed right along with her. Mr. Kelly looked at each of us in turn, a cool look on his face. This only made Elyse laugh harder, and she pointed at her dad and mimicked his expression.

Mr. Kelly couldn't keep the straight face and cracked a smile. "As I was saying, Orson, before being so rudely interrupted . . ." He glanced at Mrs. Kelly, who was trying very hard not to laugh. "An explanation of your growth spurt we can handle, but first I'm sure you would like to address the reasons *behind* your growth spurt."

I set my fork down, my laughter and even my smile subsiding. "Yes, sir."

My serious demeanor ended the light mood. I hated to be a downer, but in less than twenty-four hours, my life had exploded into comic book level crazy.

"It's my understanding," Mr. Kelly continued, "that this past Saturday you and Elyse were . . . together."

Oh boy.

Mr. Kelly struggled to say the words out loud. I couldn't blame him. It must be weird for a dad to think about his daughter kissing a boy. "I mean, you and Elyse kissed for the first time." He said it in a rush, just to get it out and move on.

A simple 'yes' didn't seem adequate. I wanted to convey how I felt about Elyse. To help him and Mrs. Kelly understand that the kissing wasn't just a hook-up or convenient, it meant something more. "Yes, sir. And I need to apologize for being such a stubborn idiot." I felt Elyse stiffen next to me. I turned toward her and made sure she was looking at me when I said, "I should have kissed her years ago."

A slow smile spread across Elyse's face. How could such a simple thing be so incredibly sexy? I had to force myself to look away, locking eyes with Mr. Kelly again. I could see Mrs. Kelly in my peripheral vision. She was beaming.

Mr. Kelly cleared his throat. "Right. Good. So, last night, you received a very improvised introduction to the fact that not only do shape-shifters exist, but we can shift into panther form." He gestured to himself and his family.

"All of you? Including Jen and Sean and Kevin?" Elyse was the third child in a family of four kids. Jen, her older sister, was the one planning a wedding, Sean was attending a private university somewhere up north in the mountains which, in light of current revelations, made a ton of sense. Kevin was the baby, and he was a junior in high school.

"Yes."

I had been wondering at the absence of Jen and Kevin. There was enough food for all of us, and I hoped they weren't staying away because of me, and so I asked, "Where is everybody, anyway?"

"Beach day. We thought it would be best if the four of us had this talk in private," Mrs. Kelly explained.

So, the entire Kelly family was a pack of shape-shifters. Unreal.

"I assume Elyse and the others were born this way," I said. "But you, were you bitten by . . . like . . . a were-wolf or were-panther or whatever?"

Mr. Kelly let out another rumbling chuckle. "No, I was born with the ability, as was Mrs. Kelly. The fact is that most shape-shifters—that's a more accurate term than were-panther—are born, not made or created. Actually, I think, the whole bite mythology arose around people like yourself."

"People like myself?" I tried not to sound too confused.

"Yes. Your abilities have lain dormant, and if the histories are accurate, they would have remained so your whole life, had they not been switched on by the . . . ah . . . by Elyse."

"Histories? I'm guessing I won't find them online or at the public library, so that I can study up?"

"No, I'm sorry. I know it must be very overwhelming. Our children, people like us, are raised with this information. Trying to explain it to a man full-grown is a new experience for me."

"When you say people like you, how many are we talking about? And is everyone a shape-shifter, or are there different types of, er, I don't even know the right word to use?" I never realized how hard it was to talk about something for which you had no frame of reference. I didn't know what I didn't know, so how was I supposed to ask questions?

"The Paragon Society, or just The Society, is one of the most common names we are known by collectively," Mr. Kelly said. "And members of the Society can be found on every continent, in every country, but we number less than five million in total. We are not all shape-shifters. There are others with different abilities, but that's not important at the moment. We exist and have existed from the beginning."

"Five million?" I did some quick mental calculations. "That's less than one percent of the global population."

"Correct. Approximately a half-percent of the population," Mr. Kelly said. "Even though our numbers are small, we wield a vast amount of power, and because of that, we have very strict laws. These laws are ancient and the penalties imposed on those who break these laws can be quite severe. And, unfortunately, Orson, you are in violation of one of our most basic laws."

"Wait? What law? How can I break a law if I don't even know it exists?"

Really? I was in trouble with the Paragon Society? Last week, if someone had asked me, 'Hey, have you heard of the Paragon Society?' I would have guessed they were some lame wanna-be punk-folk band. I'm pretty sure that the strict penalties Mr. Kelly had mentioned were not community service. A hidden society of mythical beings—because, let's face it, that's what shape-shifters and whatever else is roaming the world are—was not just going to slap your hand for violating their law. No, violations of law, at least according to Tolkien, Brooks, Martin, and the like, usually include pain and sometimes death.

"Orson, slow down. The law is one of secrecy. If the world at large ever discovered the existence of The Paragon Society, there would be chaos."

The secret part made sense, of course. If average citizens were made aware that what basically amounted to super-humans were among them, they would lose it. Last night, I'd had thick, nasty acid spit on a large part of my body. This morning, I didn't even have a mark on my skin. Just a little redness, but no swelling or scars. My body had healed itself. People would kill trying to figure out how something like that worked and gain access to it themselves. That thought made me wonder if any research had ever been done to try and duplicate the healing ability. The world could benefit from something like that, for sure. I would have to save that question for later. Right now, I was more concerned with the fact that I was considered some kind of lawbreaker.

"I get the chaos thing and the secrecy, but I did nothing on purpose. When the pallet fell, I fully expected to be crushed."

"That's the exact argument I made last night." Mr. Kelly used a very soothing tone. He could probably sense my growing anxiety over losing my head to an axe or being turned to stone, or whatever horrible thing lawbreakers were sentenced to suffer.

"Last night?" I asked "Who did you meet with last night?"

"When Elyse and Katie showed me the video, I knew I would have to get in front of the problems that would arise."

"Dad called the local shifter council," Elyse said. "Think of them as the Society's version of middle-management. They handle all the shape-shifter stuff when it comes up. He explained your situation to smooth things over."

Mr. Kelly nodded. "I called an emergency meeting, showed them the video, informed them of the circumstances and that I believed you were proof of something I have suspected for a long while now."

I was almost afraid to ask, almost. "And what's that?"

"That some of the Society's older legends are not legends at all. And that you may just be something long thought to be myth—Anghenfil, the Ollphiest."

Mrs. Kelly gasped. I mean, she literally gasped. Elyse's hand tightened around mine. It sounded like Mr. Kelly had sneezed, but from the reaction of Elyse and her mom, I assumed he had said something in a foreign language. I held his gaze. I wasn't going to ask. He knew I didn't speak whatever language he had spoken.

"Orson, even the Paragon Society has its ghost stories. Tales they tell one another after too many drinks. Stories used as warnings or to frighten children."

"Like the boogeyman," I said, in disbelief. It sounded like Mr. Kelly was telling me that he thought I was this Paragon Society's version of the boogeyman, the thing that magical shape-shifting cat-people used to scare the crap out of one another.

Great.

"The boogeyman?" Mr. Kelly considered it. "Yes. That's a good analogy. The Ollphiest is the Society's boogeyman."

"Dad?" The pleading in Elyse's voice was clear. Oh yeah, she knew all about the Ollphiest. I bet it was the thing her older brother and sister probably used to tease her with before bedtime. I was sitting at breakfast with a family that could turn into giant, scary-looking panthers, and apparently I was the thing that frightened them the most.

Yay me.

"So, I'm a monster?"

CHAPTER EIGHT

I stared at the food left on my plate. My appetite was vanishing with the realization I was sitting at a table with three people who the world would consider monsters, but who considered *me* to be the monster.

I was the monster that monsters feared. That wasn't an original thought—I'm pretty sure I had read that in a graphic novel or comic book, but it summed up my situation perfectly.

Mr. Kelly broke the silence with another chuckle. "Orson, being a monster," he said, emphasizing the word with air quotes, "is a relative thing. We, all of us at the table, are monsters by the world's definition."

Was he a mind reader? That would be a bad thing, because once I got over the current suck my life was in, impure thoughts about his daughter were sure to cross my mind.

Mr. Kelly said, "You are a shape-shifter. What shape remains to be seen, but in essence, you are like us. It's the how, not the what, that makes you different. If my suspicions are correct and you are what I think you are, I think it will be reason to celebrate. A species of shape-shifter thought to be extinct, or to have never existed at all, suddenly appears, and the Society will have to re-examine its history."

"I'm not sure I understand," I told him. "If I'm a shape-shifter, what makes me different?"

"Popular books and movies have perpetrated false ideas about our kind. That's not necessarily a bad thing. The less the world knows, the better." He stopped and popped a piece of bacon into his mouth, chewing thoughtfully. "For the sake of not confusing you with too much information, I will stick to our kind, shape-shifters."

He waited for my nod, before going on. "As I said earlier, we are born, we are not made. The whole notion of a bite turning a person into a shape-shifter is so much fiction. The specific genes that control our abilities pass from parent to child. Inter-marriage with non-shape shifters does not produce offspring with the ability to shape-shift, at least not in the past two hundred years or so."

I'm pretty sure I understood what he was saying. I knew for a fact that my mom, Aunt Tina, and their parents were not shape-shifters or different in any way. My father, though, was a big question mark. He was in the military and had died while deployed overseas. He had never even known my mom was pregnant before he left. She hadn't wanted him to be distracted by worry while in the field. I know she had loved him and that it was after his death she started moving around, never settling too long in one place. And, lastly, I knew his name was Orson, because my mom had named me after him.

"You're saying my dad had to be a shape-shifter?"

"If you're positive your mother is not, then yes, it seems logical to assume that he was. And I take it by your expression your mother is not?"

"No. And I don't know much about my dad. Only that he

died on a mission for the military." A thought occurred to me. "Could he have passed the genes on without ever having his abilities activated? Is that the right word, activated?"

"It's as appropriate as any other. And the answer to your question is yes."

Elyse held up her hand. "Um, just so we're all on the same page, Dad, you're saying that the Ollphiest, the scary dude I've heard about all my life, isn't just a made-up story?"

"Yes and no. It's my theory that the Ollphiest is just a title, a name used to describe an individual with a specific set of abilities. The only sure thing is that Ollphiests aren't born, they are created. It's why Orson's situation is so intriguing. It has many of the hallmarks the legend describes."

"But the stories, all the things it's said the Ollphiest could do." Elyse stared at me, a look of awe on her face. "Those things are real?"

I had to swallow a laugh. My girlfriend, the supernatural cat, was freaking out about something I could do.

"The short answer is that we just don't know," Mr. Kelly told her. "There are no eyewitness accounts, only vague references in some of the oldest volumes."

"What exactly do the stories say the Ollphiest can do?" I was both interested and horrified.

My question went unanswered as someone knocked on the front door and Mr. Kelly's cellphone rang simultaneously. I didn't need special powers to feel the spike in tension. Mr. Kelly placed his hand on Mrs. Kelly's arm, shaking his head as she started to rise to check on the front door. Mr. Kelly answered his phone. The person on the other end was agitated and shouting, but I couldn't quite make out the words. Mr. Kelly's face stayed relaxed. He even gave me a wink. He was trying to play it cool, but it was obvious something was wrong.

I noticed both Elyse and Mrs. Kelly had their heads

cocked, and I realized they were listening to both sides of the conversation and I remembered Mrs. Kelly doing the same thing last night when she said Aunt Tina was still in the bath. So, I needed to add super-hearing to the list of growing abilities they had and that I could look forward to in the near future. Cool.

Mr. Kelly ended the call and his relaxed look became strained. He wasn't happy. "Thomas and a few others decided on their own to drop by and meet Orson."

"What about the time they promised us?" Mrs. Kelly asked. She didn't look happy either. The doorbell rang again, followed by loud knocking or, as some would call it, pounding on the door.

"Everyone stay here at the table." Mr. Kelly said. "Orson, the people I met with last night—some of them are concerned about what you may represent. They assured me I would have time to talk with you and help you through your first shift. The people at the door are concerned I may be too close to the situation."

"Because you know me, or because of my relationship with Elyse?" I asked.

"Both. Understand there is nobody alive that has firsthand knowledge of what you may be capable of or how your ability will manifest. The only thing we have to go on is shrouded by time and superstition." Mr. Kelly ran a hand through his hair.

"Superstition? Really? You, the Paragon Society, are superstitious? Aren't you guys the living embodiment of superstition?"

How could shape-shifters, creatures of myth and legend, be superstitious, I wondered? They *are* the things that go bump in the night. Fairy tales come to life in living, breathing solid reality.

Mr. Kelly stood. I watched as he walked to the doorway leading from the dining room to the front of the house. He paused and turned back toward me. "No thinking being can avoid superstition. It's encoded into our brains to wonder what may be hiding in the dark. For us, that thing is the Ollphiest, and the fact that may describe what kind of shifter you are has rattled some nerves. Wait here. If I can't convince them to go away, then when I bring them back, just remain calm and answer any questions they ask, if you can. There is no need to lie or make up what you think they want to hear. Understand?"

I nodded. He walked out of the room.

Mrs. Kelly smiled at me. "It will be okay." I wasn't sure who she was trying to reassure, herself or me.

My mouth was dry. I picked up my glass and took a long swallow of juice. Elyse adjusted my collar and ran her fingers through my hair in an attempt to make my bed head more presentable. Somehow, I didn't think the people at the door cared about what my hair looked like.

The three of us remained quiet. I heard Mr. Kelly open the front door and speak to the uninvited visitors, but my super-hearing not having kicked in yet, I couldn't make out the conversation.

It was frustrating, because I knew Elyse and her mom could hear every word. "What are they saying?" I whispered to Elyse.

Elyse put her finger to her lips. She picked up her cell phone and started typing. Only when my phone buzzed did I realize she had texted me.

If we can hear them, they can hear us,
even if we whisper. Uncle Tommy wants
to meet you. Dad is saying no

.   .   .

Uncle Tommy? One of these guys was related to Elyse? I responded to her text with that question.

He's your uncle?
  No. old friend of family, known
  him forever always called him uncle Tommy

Mrs. Kelly motioned for us to put our phones away, just as I heard the front door close. Mr. Kelly had been unsuccessful in turning them away, because even I could tell there were several people walking back toward us. I set my phone down and took a deep breath. Elyse placed her hand on my leg.

Mr. Kelly walked back into the dining room, followed by a man almost as tall as Mr. Kelly and with skin the color of chestnut, a shaved head, bushy eyebrows and goatee. Uncle Tommy, I presumed. There was also a man who looked like a younger version of Uncle Tommy, with the exception he had a full head of hair. A son, maybe. It was only the three of them. Mr. Kelly must have worked a compromise, allowing only the two of them to come and meet the extinct shifter freak.

Uncle Tommy was all smiles. The only problem was that nobody had informed the rest of his face. And you could see the tension in the way he moved. He leaned down and kissed Mrs. Kelly's cheek, saying "Katie," and as he winked at Elyse, "Sweet pea." When he finished greeting the ladies, his eyes locked on me and didn't waver. The younger guy just stood in the doorway, still as a statue, looking from Elyse to me.

Yeah, I didn't like these guys at all.

"Hello, Tommy," said Mrs. Kelly.

Mr. Kelly introduced us. "Thomas, this is Orson Reid. Orson, this is Thomas French and his son Kyle."

I stood and offered my hand. I might not like the guy, but

my aunt raised me with manners and to respect my elders.
"Mr. French."

Uncle Tommy hesitated, almost as though he thought I
might be contagious or something. But he quickly recovered
and grasped my hand. Firm, but not a dominating crushing
shake like some guys feel is necessary to assert their manli-
ness. No, Thomas French was as confident and cool as they
came. "Orson, nice to make your acquaintance."

Liar, I wanted to shout. Instead, I nodded, pulling my
hand back. I glanced at Kyle, who hadn't moved from his
position. I nodded at him too, and he gave me the barest of
nods back, his hands clenched in fists at his side. Jeez, the guy
looked like he was ready to pop. I wondered what his deal
was. I sat back down, and Elyse took my hand in hers in a
gesture of solidarity. Man, I loved her. Uncle Tommy's eyes
flicked briefly to our hands, and then he turned his attention
back to Mr. Kelly.

"Have a seat, Thomas. Kyle, have something to eat or
drink. There's plenty." Mr. Kelly gestured toward the table.

Uncle Tommy seated himself next to Mrs. Kelly, which
put him across from me. Kyle continued to stand. The guy
was starting to give me the willies. Uncle Tommy got straight
to the point.

"I'm here, Orson, because you present a quandary. I'm
sure Richard has been explaining." He paused and stroked his
goatee. "Explaining how the world you thought you lived in is
much more than it appears."

"Yes, sir."

"Thomas, or Tommy, please." He smiled and I couldn't
help it—images of shark-nurse flashed through my mind. He
didn't have the rows of pointy teeth that shark-nurse had, but
he had the same predatory vibe. "You can understand that
keeping the knowledge of our existence secret is of utmost
importance. Displays like the one you engaged in yesterday

are a no-no, and to be recorded on video . . . well, laws are laws."

Mr. Kelly told him, "Actually, Thomas, we hadn't broached the specifics of the law just yet. We were trying to lay a foundation first, a reference point to help Orson not be so overwhelmed."

"Oh, I see. Well, Orson, public displays of power are strictly forbidden. We can't have the media crying 'super-human smashes up local Wal-Mart' now can we?" Tommy asked, the condescension dripping off every syllable.

"It was Costco," I mumbled.

Elyse tightened her hand around mine a fraction. I could read her warning loud and clear. *Watch it, dork*, she was saying, without even looking in my direction. Kyle shifted his weight.

"Excuse me?" Uncle Tommy's eyes narrowed.

"I said, it was Costco. The place where I work." I would not let this jerk intimidate me. "And I can assure you, *sir*, I'm not one for displays of attention. I reacted to a life-threatening situation. As the video clearly shows, my co-worker and I were in serious danger of being smooshed. As Mr. Kelly said, he was just getting me up to speed on the *laws* governing this sort of thing, but I have to imagine that a 'save your ass' exemption must be part of it?" I gave him my best smile. Actually my *I just pulled a straight to your three of kind, and I'm taking all your money, you stupid noob* kind of smile.

Tommy's eyes bored into mine. He was giving it all he had trying to force me to look away. No way. Not today. I'd had a really stressful night and the morning wasn't starting off great. I wasn't about to let this jackass push me around. Out of the corner of my eye, I saw Kyle shift his weight again. He was barely keeping himself contained.

Mr. Kelly slammed his hand down on the table, not hard but enough to rattle the dishes. It worked. Uncle Tommy and

I dropped our eyes at the same moment, and we both looked at Mr. Kelly.

"Thomas, the decision was made last night." Mr. Kelly held up a hand to stop Uncle Tommy from interrupting. "Katie, Elyse, and I are going to help Orson through the transition. The council agreed to that course of action."

"Not unanimously," snarled Uncle Tommy.

"No, not unanimously, but a unanimous vote isn't necessary and hasn't been since the rules were amended—by you, I might add, decades ago."

So, good old Uncle Tommy had forced through a rule change. From my brief encounter with the man and his less than sunny disposition, I was guessing he changed the rules to push through some nasty piece of business to suit his needs. But now he was on the wrong end of a decision, and he was pissed.

What a tool.

Mrs. Kelly said, "Tommy, you know we would never do anything to endanger Elyse. Let us work with Orson." She smiled at me. "He is smart and a fast learner. There is nothing to worry about."

Uncle Tommy stood up. "I hope not." He once again locked eyes with me. "I will be monitoring the situation closely. No need to show me out."

Uncle Tommy spun on his heel and walked out of the dining room. Kyle hesitated and it looked like he might actually speak, but he reconsidered and followed his father out. A moment later, I heard the front door open and slam shut.

I started to voice my opinion of Uncle Tommy, but Mr. Kelly waved me off. "Wait."

The three Kellys did that head cocked to the side thing again, listening. I strained to hear what they were hearing and faintly heard car doors slam and a vehicle pull away.

Mr. Kelly turned his attention back to me. "Thomas and

Kyle and those with them have hearing every bit as good as ours. It's always best to wait until hostile visitors are in the car and down the driveway before resuming conversation."

"Hostile? It seemed to me that if he could have killed me and buried me behind the back fence, he would have," I said. "And what's up with that creepy kid of his? It was like he was trying to murder me with his eyes."

"Tommy's scared, Orson. They all are, even those who voted to give us time to work with you," said Mrs. Kelly.

"And what was up with you getting into a staring contest with him?" Elyse asked.

"I . . . it was . . . he started it." Oh man, that was lame. What am I, a five-year-old?

"Seriously?" Elyse dropped my hand, turned in her seat, and crossed her arms to give me the full body disapproval.

"I know it's lame. It's just . . . I can't explain it. From the minute he walked in, he just made me angry."

"It's perfectly normal," said Mr. Kelly. I watched Elyse's face go from ticked off to surprised at her father's words. "Isn't it obvious? Orson, your body is transforming from the cellular level up. The anger you felt is a natural reaction to another shifter trying to dominate you."

"Dominate? Like an alpha dog kind of thing?"

"Exactly. I'm assuming you don't normally challenge people you've just met?" Mr. Kelly asked.

"No." I looked to Elyse for support.

Elyse sighed loudly. "No, he's usually totally easygoing." She offered her hand palm up, and I took it in my own.

"Sorry," she said to me.

I shook my head and crossed my eyes at her. "So . . ." I looked at each of them, stopping with Mr. Kelly. "You've been given time to help me transition, get up to speed. When do we start?"

"As soon as you do two things. First, you will need to quit

your job." Mr. Kelly held up a hand. "No, let me finish. Second, we need to leave, this afternoon, for our cabin in Lake Arrowhead. Do you think it will be a problem convincing your aunt?"

"No, it shouldn't be. I'll just tell her you guys have invited me up to the cabin for a long weekend. She'll probably want to talk to you." I inclined my head toward Mrs. Kelly. "Just to make sure it's a real invite. But why do I have to quit my job? I kind of need the money for school."

"All that will be taken care of. The only thing you need to concentrate on for the next few days are the changes occurring in your body. It will get very difficult, both physically and mentally. I need you to prepare yourself for that."

"The store opens in about an hour. I'll head over there and give notice."

"Sorry, no notice. You have to quit straight away." I searched Mr. Kelly's face. I had never seen him this serious.

"If that's what's required, you got it. But I still have to tell them personally. I owe Becky that much."

"Good. We have to get a few things ready here. It's 9:00 a.m. now. Can you be back by noon?"

"Yes."

"I should go with him," said Elyse.

I was pretty sure her parents would say no to that. I was the boogeyman, after all. But Mr. Kelly nodded.

All he said was, "I agree."

CHAPTER NINE

Oh, man. My Corolla was in bad shape. The passenger side door was completely buckled. Someone had brushed out all the shattered glass from the window. I tried to open the door for Elyse, but it was stuck. I pulled with everything I had.

"This would be a good time for my super strength to kick in," I told Elyse. "Is there, like, a special power word or something?"

She giggled. "No. Right now, your abilities are still in flux. If you're in danger or stressed out, they can trigger, but otherwise—not so much." She snuggled up to me. "You want to let me give it a shot?"

I stepped aside. "Please, knock yourself out."

Elyse stepped up to the door. She ran her hands over it, testing the handle. She squatted down to inspect the dent. "I don't know, Orson. This door may be history." She stood back up, slipped the fingers of both hands in between the door panels, and flexed. The dent popped out. She tried the handle and the door opened with a loud metal groan.

"Is it wrong I'm turned on right now?" I arched an eyebrow at her. It was a total Spock move, and I nailed it.

Elyse grabbed a hold of both my ears, pulling my face toward hers. "Dork." She gave me a quick kiss and slid into the passenger seat, pulling the protesting door closed behind her.

The drive to Costco was quick. The store was only ten miles from her house, but in L.A. traffic that could mean anywhere from fifteen minutes to twenty-five minutes, depending on the time of day. We were hitting medium traffic with it being the middle of the week and the late breakfast crowd was out, but I was cool with that because it gave me time for some strategic questioning. I knew her dad had given Elyse strict instructions to avoid answering my questions. He wanted to be there for any question and answer sessions, and I couldn't blame him. He wanted to make sure everything was done properly, so the council wouldn't get all worked up over proper protocol.

Still, I needed to know stuff.

"So, you can turn into a giant cat?" *Smooth opening, Orson. You're such a wordsmith. I don't know how the ladies don't swoon on your every word.*

My ridiculous lack of skill stringing together a more coherent question was not lost on Elyse.

"Really? That's the best you got?"

"I'm still in shock or something from recent and ongoing events. Give me a break." We stopped at a red light and I gave her my best puppy dog look, or at least I thought I did, because she laughed.

"You look like you have gas," she said. So much for the pity play. The light turned green and saved me from further embarrassment.

"There are certain things, a lot of things actually, that you need to wait for my dad to explain. But ask me what you want, and if I can answer, I will. If I can't, I'll tell you so. Deal? She turned in her seat to face me.

I kept my eyes on the road, no need for unsafe driving. "Deal."

Where to start? I had so many questions, but most of them I'm sure she would defer to her dad. I figured sticking to her experience, growing up and living every day with her abilities, was a safe place.

"It's called shifting? When you turn?"

"Yes. It describes it perfectly. 'Are we going to shift?' 'Did you shift?' See? It works well for just about every usage. We also use the term *form*. 'Was she in cat form.' Like that."

"You can shift anytime? It's not, you know, contingent on the full moon?"

"Yep, anytime. The moon thing came about because it's just a lot more fun to go running in the moonlight."

"As a kid, or a baby, how did you control your shifting?"

"That is a great question." She leaned over and kissed me on the cheek. "The answer is in-depth and technical, but what I can tell you is that, until we hit puberty, we don't mingle with the public much. I attended a private school until junior high."

"So, there are control issues?"

"For the young, yes."

"But for adults, there isn't a problem?"

Elyse was smart. She was able to read between the lines of my question and she stiffened slightly. "Are you asking if we're dangerous?"

"Well, yeah. You can turn into a pretty wicked-looking panther, and your mom went full beast form last night. Knowing if control is ever an issue seems like a valid question." I snuck a peek at her to see if she was upset.

"You weren't afraid of us, were you?" Elyse asked, and the worry in her voice drew my attention away from the road for a moment.

I reached over to hold her hand. "No. Absolutely not. You

guys were awesome. But that guy today, Uncle Tommy, he looked like he could do some serious damage and didn't seem as cool and in control as you, and your mom and dad."

Elyse didn't answer right away. I glanced over at her again. The evidence of an internal struggle was written across her face. That was answer enough for me. Uncle Tommy was a jerk of the first order, and I had pissed him off. *Super, Orson, just super.*

When she spoke, it was quietly. "I can't say much. You get that there are rules—laws—that govern our behavior?"

I nodded.

"There are some of those rules that, if violated, carry a . . . heavy penalty." She paused, waiting for me to figure it out.

Okay, I thought, what would be considered a heavy penalty? Maybe there was a shape-shifter jail? Then I realized what she was saying. "You mean, like the death penalty?" I already knew the answer.

"Orson, you have to understand. If the Society were exposed . . . The world just isn't ready. You love the X-Men. How does being a mutant usually work out for them?"

"It's okay," I tried to assure her, but my voice wasn't cooperating. "I get it."

But I didn't get it. I'm a product of growing up in a world where people weren't put to death for telling secrets. Sure, there was the death penalty, but that was reserved for serial killers, and even then, it was super-controversial. In California, convicts could sit on death row for years, decades even.

"My dad can explain it better."

"So, our buddy Uncle Tommy, he's like what? An enforcer or something?" I'm pretty sure I knew the answer to that one too. The guy had stared at me with menace in his eyes.

"He is on the council and they decide things like that, yes. I don't think I should say any more. Dad can explain it so much better."

"All right. But should I be worried that he obviously doesn't like me?"

"No, he was just trying to be intimidating."

"Well, it worked. He's a scary dude. Uh, what does he turn into, a panther also?"

I glanced at her. She was biting her lip again. If Elyse was nervous or anxious, she nibbled that bottom lip. I've always thought it was cute, but in the current circumstances, I didn't think it was a good thing.

"You can't tell me?"

"I'm not supposed to."

"Well, I—"

"A wolf," she blurted out. "You can't tell anyone I told you?" She couldn't keep the pleading out of her voice.

"Of course not." *A wolf. How original.* "Not a peep. Ever."

Elyse took a deep breath. "There may be a more personal reason Uncle Tommy was upset." She was looking straight ahead.

Uh oh.

"And that would be?"

"As you can imagine, it's hard, if not impossible, for a shape-shifter to be in a . . . um . . . a romantic relationship with a regular person."

Oh no, this wasn't happening. I gripped the steering wheel a little tighter.

"Kyle," Elyse said, not looking at me.

I couldn't believe it. It was something so ridiculously cliché.

"Kyle and I grew up together. Went to the same school, when we were younger. We've known each other our whole lives."

I couldn't let her dangle and sputter. I loved her. "He was your boyfriend."

"Kind of."

"How is someone *kind of* your boyfriend?"

"You took Brooke Little to every dance, junior year. Was she your girlfriend?" Elyse asked, crossing her arms.

"Uh."

"Exactly."

"So, does Kyle still think you're dating?"

"He shouldn't. Not after prom."

Elyse and I had gone to prom as a couple. Neither one of us had been dating anyone seriously. At least, I hadn't been. So we decided to go together. We were best friends, and we had a blast.

Like the idiot man I freely admit to sometimes being, I asked, "Why? What changed after prom?"

I had been there, and I knew exactly what had happened at prom. There had been lots of dancing and laughing, and in the middle of a slow dance, toward the end of the night, we had a moment.

I had tossed my tux jacket, my tie and loosened my collar. Elyse ditched her heels. We swayed around the dance floor to a slow song, Elyse resting her head on my shoulder. It was the oddest thing—I started feeling little jolts, not exactly shocks, just a kind of zing in all the places our bodies touched. The zings grew in intensity and had the effect of me wanting to draw her closer. Who wouldn't? The feeling was amazing. She tilted her head back to look at me, and I could see it in her face she was feeling the same thing. We stared at each other, our breathing getting heavier, and then I pulled her close. Our arms wrapped around each other, our cheeks touching, and the world melted away. We clung to one another, the exchange of energy between us escalating. At one point, I had to open my eyes to make sure—and I know this sounds crazy —that we weren't glowing.

The song ended. We stood motionless for a second. Then Elyse excused herself to freshen up. I agreed that was an awesome idea and I spent a few minutes splashing cold water on my face, staring at myself in the mirror, wondering what the heck had just happened. We didn't talk about it. We just spent an awkward few weeks ignoring it, until the party last Saturday.

Elyse pulled me out of my memory. "What. Happened. At. Prom?" I'd like to say she sounded more hurt than angry, but I'd be lying.

Idiot.

I pointed to myself. "Post-traumatic stress. It causes unpredictable behavior. That's science. I'm just saying." I smiled, pleading.

Her eyes narrowed. She reached over and flicked my earlobe, held up a finger, and said, "That's one." She tried, unsuccessfully, to stifle a grin. "As I was saying, after prom, I told Kyle that things had changed. He wasn't happy."

"And I'm assuming his dad wasn't thrilled either."

"No. Even my parents were—I don't know—surprised, I guess. It's not something that's supposed to happen. One of us falling for one of you."

"One of you? Don't you guys have a term like Muggle or something? You know, to describe the rest of the people in the world?"

"We use the word mundane sometimes, but it sounds kind of rude, don't you think?

"So you broke little Kyle's heart, and now his dad is out to get me?

"That's probably a part of it, yes, and unfortunately he has Society law on his side because of the whole forklift thing."

I pulled into the Costco parking lot. "Well, we're about to start damage control on the 'whole forklift thing,' so hopefully Uncle Tommy and his mini-me can get their little girl feelings under control."

"Be nice. Kyle is a good guy."

I thought about the way Kyle had stood motionless at the Kellys'. He didn't seem like a good guy; he seemed more like a crazy guy.

"In my experience, guys with jerk fathers are almost always little jerks themselves."

Elyse frowned a little. She wasn't happy. If I was acting like a jealous idiot, it was because I was a jealous idiot. She'd had a lifelong relationship with some other guy, a guy who had shared in her secret life. They had gone to school together, spent days probably just hanging out and chilling. What can I say? I'm a regular guy—well, except for the part where I may be the legendary monster of monsters—but as far as romantic mushy stuff went, I was just a red-blooded, jealous-of-guys-named-Kyle man.

"Sorry, I'm a dude," I said. "We say stupid things like that when we realize we are totally into our hot best friend." Yeah, when needed to, I can apologize with the best of them. I'm not a total idiot. "Am I forgiven?"

Elyse leaned over and put her arms around my neck. "Always."

I gave her a peck on the lips. "Excellent. Let's go spread some Men in Black style misinformation," I said enthusiastically.

Costco wasn't crowded that early on a Thursday morning. The crew working the customer service desk stopped what they were doing to stare at me as I walked in. I waved, and they immediately went back to looking busy. Weird.

I led Elyse back toward the manager's office, drawing quick glances and some straight-up stares from the cashiers on duty. Elyse stopped walking, pulling me to a stop beside her. Tony was standing in front of us, blocking our path.

"Hey, Tony. What's up?" I asked.

He looked tired and a little dazed.

"They're calling us liars," he hissed. Okay, not dazed. Agitated.

"What?" I didn't have to fake my confusion. I didn't understand what he was talking about.

"Liars. The news people, the people on the internet, they're saying we faked the accident. Like that would be possible? The forklift flipped over." Tony was rocking on his feet, running his hand through his hair. "I'm not a liar, Reid." He looked over at the cashiers and yelled, "I don't lie!"

We resumed our walk toward the manager's office. I said, in a low voice, "Follow us, Tony, and we'll talk about it, but not out here." I did my best to herd him without being overly aggressive. Tony is a good guy, and I hated seeing him so worked up. Elyse still had a hold of my hand and gave it a squeeze in encouragement. "Tony, I don't think you've ever met my friend, uh, girlfriend." I needed to get used to using that new introduction for Elyse. She had been in my life for so long it was weird I had to qualify her to people. "This is Elyse. Elyse, this is Tony."

"Nice to meet you, Tony," said Elyse. She let go of my hand and reached out for a shake, never breaking stride. This helped me get Tony moving in the right direction.

Tony is well-mannered, and so he took the offered hand and gave it a couple of pumps. "Nice to meet you too." His face softened. "So, you're the reason Reid has had that goofy grin on his face lately?"

"Goofy grin? Really?" Elyse gave Tony one of her million dollar smiles.

"Oh yeah, all the time. And I can see why. I'd be grinning too."

Elyse laughed.

I could see the tension in Tony's body relax a little. It wasn't much, just a rounding of the shoulders and a loosening of the jaw. Wow. It must be my new super-powers kicking in, because I don't think I would ever have noticed those things before. They were so slight. What's the term I learned in Psych class? Oh yeah, micro-expressions.

We reached the manager's office. The door was open and Becky was at her desk. I pulled back a couple of steps and turned to Tony, giving him my full attention. "I'm sorry for what's been going down."

Elyse asked him, "What exactly were you talking about, Tony? The lying thing?"

Tony's face tensed again, but his shoulders remained relaxed. "There's a guy on the internet, on YouTube, some science nerd. He shows, step by step, how the video could be faked, and concludes that we are both lying, for attention or something stupid."

I hadn't seen the video Tony was talking about, but if the guy used real science to refute the forklift incident, it made sense that people were jumping on the 'it's a fake' band-wagon. What's easier to believe, an elaborate prank or super-natural shenanigans?

I asked Tony, "Do you know who uploaded the security footage in the first place?"

Tony shook his head, looking back over his shoulder to the retail floor. "Any one of these jerks could have done it." He looked back to Elyse and me. "Some people think that kind of crap is funny."

Elyse said, "So this science nerd had a whole forklift rigged up and everything?" I realized Elyse knew something, or at least was on to something. I paid closer attention to what she was saying and, more importantly, what she wasn't saying.

"Nah. He has a copy of the video, and he freezes it and writes on it with arrows and stuff. Pointing out exactly how he thinks it was done. He also uses some video effects soft-ware to recreate that jump." Tony looked at me and I could see he wanted to ask about the jump again. I looked away before he got the courage to ask.

"And this science nerd's YouTube video is what the news is using to talk about the story?" Elyse asked.

"Yeah, pretty much. Like I said, they're calling us liars. I think we really need to be interviewed or something and tell our side of the story. That it's real and all the . . ." Tony paused and caught my eye again. "All the stuff you did, was like an adrenaline rush or something."

"Um." I wasn't sure how to respond. Speaking to reporters seemed like the last thing I should be doing. I wanted less attention, not more.

Elyse squeezed my hand meaningfully. When I looked at her, I could see that my instinct had been correct. No news. No interview. She didn't speak, but she didn't have to. She was shouting at me with her eyes and I heard her loud and clear.

I had to answer Tony very carefully. "You know, that might be a good idea. Let me talk to Becky for a minute, and I'll see you before I leave."

The radio on Tony's belt squawked and he snatched it up. "What's the problem?" Someone had spilled a carton of eggs in the dairy section and they needed Tony to help with cleanup. "I'll be right there." He slipped the radio back into his belt. "Before you leave?"

"Absolutely," I lied.

Tony nodded once, gave Elyse a smile, and strode off to clean up eggs.

"You know we can't give him any more information, right?" Elyse asked.

"Yeah, I got that." I blew out a big breath.

"The video, the news coverage. It has the Society written all over it."

That thought hadn't occurred to me. I just figured talking

to the press would piss off Tommy and the other council members who sided with him.

"That's them? The YouTube guy? You think?"

"Disinformation is a proven tactic in keeping secrets. Governments have been using it for decades. The Society, for centuries."

"So, I will be made out to be a lying idiot?" This didn't make me happy. I understood why Tony was so angry. To have my integrity called into question—I'm not going to lie, it was going to hurt. Funny how most people—well, honest people —would take physical pain, like a broken arm, over having their integrity questioned.

"You understand why, right?" Elyse was looking at me intently. "They have to make people disbelieve what they are seeing with their own eyes. An eighteen-year-old kid knocking aside hundreds of pounds, catching his friend, and performing a Spiderman-like jump—it's impossible. But their brains can't deny what they're seeing. It's right there on video. They can watch it over and over, in slow-motion if they want. So, the Society gives them something to explain it away. Something their rational minds can wrap around. Special effects. A prank. Internet silliness." She caressed my cheek.

I nodded in agreement and kissed her palm. I knew what I had to do. "I have to lie to Becky, don't I?"

"If she asks if it was a prank gone wrong, and I'm almost sure she will, then yes. I'm sorry." I knew she meant it, but it didn't make it any easier.

"Okay. Let's do this."

Becky's office wasn't overly large. She had just enough space for a medium-size desk, with two chairs positioned in front of it. The manager of Costco can usually be found out on the floor, helping the staff to keep operations running smoothly. Costco was superb about promoting staff from within, so most managers, Becky being one, had worked most of the positions in the store. Her experience in how things should run was vast.

I stopped in the doorway. Becky was typing on her computer. I knocked on the doorjamb. "Becky, do you have a minute?"

She looked up from her typing, surprised. "Orson? I thought you were going to take the day off?"

"I am. I mean, I'm not here for a shift, but I need to talk to you."

She waved me in and her eyes widened when Elyse followed me into the office. I know it's bad form to bring your girlfriend to a meeting with your boss, but due to the current, otherworldly, circumstances, I needed the back-up.

"This is Elyse."

Becky stood and she and Elyse shook hands. She then motioned to the chairs and we all took our seats. "I just want to say I'm sorry for the mess yesterday," I began.

Becky said, "Before you continue, can I say a few things?"

"Of course."

Becky took a moment to gather her thoughts. She glanced at her computer screen, and at Elyse, who gave her a reassuring smile. Becky then focused back on me. "I've been on the phone all day with corporate. I've been dodging reporters' calls for interviews and have had to chase a few bold news crews out of the store." She paused, obviously searching for the right words to ask what I'm sure was the burning question from corporate and the news media.

I let her off the hook. "You want to know if it was really an accident?"

Becky shook her head. "I was there moments after the pallet went down. I saw you and you were out cold, not faking. Tony was shaking, he was so freaked out. There was no way that it was staged. No way."

Elyse tapped my foot with hers. I couldn't tell the truth,

but I also couldn't lie. Becky had been there and she had seen the aftermath.

Becky went on, "I've seen the video. I'm still trying to find out who leaked it, and when I do, they will be looking for a new job. But I've also seen the video of that debunker guy. His explanation makes sense, but I was there, Orson." It was clear she was confused, and a little freaked out herself. The video of the accident clearly showed inhuman or superhuman abilities. A rational person living a normal ordinary life would naturally doubt what they saw and would assure themselves that there had to be a rational explanation.

How do I help her accept what she saw, but still keep the secret I had sworn to keep? There really was no answer. I thought about all the crazy shows I'd watched over the years about UFOs, alien abduction, and my favorite, the Ghost Hunter shows. Where regular people agreed to be inter-viewed about strange, unexplainable things they had seen or encountered. Just about all of them came across the same way, confident about what they had experienced, but with an underlying understanding that they sounded ridiculous and fully expected not to be believed. I could see it in Becky's eyes. She was almost to that point, and I was going to have to shove her over the edge.

I ignored the question I could see burning in her eyes and simply said, "I'm here to give notice. I have to quit immedi-ately, today."

Becky sat back in her chair. Whatever she had expected from me, it hadn't been this. "You're quitting?"

"Yes." I should have just left it at that and walked out, but it just wasn't in my nature. I had to soften the blow, at least a little. "This has been a great place to work. You've been a great boss, but due to a personal situation, I need to leave."

"But the video? Corporate wants to send their own insurance investigator." Becky was trying to process the bomb I had just dropped into her lap.

"I guess they can call me. You have my contact information." I stood up, Elyse following my lead.

Becky came to her feet too. "Orson, what do I tell them?"

"Tell them the truth."

"And what, exactly, is the truth?"

"Whatever it is you saw. Let them make up their own minds," I said. I was leaving her and Tony to dangle in the wind, and I hated myself for it. There was nothing else I could do. The truth would lead to a place they weren't allowed to go and carried a heavy penalty for those who didn't guard its safety.

Elyse slipped her hand into mine.

"I'm sorry, Becky." I turned, and Elyse and I left, leaving Becky standing behind her desk with a dumbfounded look on her face.

I scanned the front of the store, looking for Tony. The coast looked clear. We hustled for the exit. I didn't make eye contact with anyone. When we reached the Corolla, I collapsed into the driver's seat.

Elyse slid in next to me, putting her arm around my shoulder. "I know that was hard. I'm sorry." She stroked my hair.

"Is this the way it's going to be for the rest of my life? Having to lie to everyone?" I couldn't keep the disgust out of my voice.

"No. When this blows over, you'll have a secret that you don't share, but you won't have to overtly lie to anyone." She turned my head so I faced her. "I've never lied to you. I've kept a part of my life private, but I've never told you an outright lie."

"That sounds like total BS. You know that, right? A lie is a lie."

"So, you think that people aren't allowed something

private? Something only they know about themselves? That everything must be out in the open?"

I'm not a naïve person. At least, I don't consider myself as such. I understand the difference between a lie and an omission. While there are many who would argue that's just semantics, I didn't suffer from any such illusions. Some secrets needed keeping, if for no other reason than to protect those you loved or, in the case of governments, citizens they're sworn to protect. Elyse knew I understood this concept from countless conversations we'd had about politics and current events. Now that I thought about it, all of those late-night conversations about whether some secrets, especially those to do with national security, were necessary may have been her way of telling me that *she* had a secret she couldn't share.

"I'm just feeling sorry for myself." If talking to Becky was difficult, I could only imagine what my first conversation with Aunt Tina was going to be like. She could read me like a book. I had no idea how I was going to pull it off. "I know you didn't lie to me. You protected me by withholding information. I get that it's not the same thing. I'm just not sure how well I will do when I have to talk to Aunt Tina."

"We will figure something out." She gave me a peck on the lips. "I promise."

I nodded, trusting in her certainty. "Okay. Where to next?"

"Tina's at work, right?" Elyse asked, pulling her phone out.

"Yes."

"Good. We have to go to your house. You'll need clothes for the weekend." She was texting somebody, her thumbs flying over the keyboard.

"Right. Arrowhead. Is it cold up there this time of year?"

I asked, starting the car and checking my mirrors before pulling out.

"The nights can be cool, but I don't think that's going to be a problem."

I gave her sidelong glance. She smiled at me and went back to texting. Why wouldn't it be a problem? Oh, that's right. Because everyone can turn into giant animals. Elyse was a shape-shifter. She came from a family of shape-shifters. A bunch of the people she knew were shape-shifters. And sometime, probably in the next twenty-four to forty-eight hours, I would be a shape-shifter as well. I guess, technically, I already was. I just hadn't shifted yet. The question was: What would I shift into? A panther was pretty cool. A wolf, even though a little cliché, wouldn't be too bad either, except that I didn't want to shift into the type of animal Tommy shifted into—*shifts* into? Could shift into? I didn't even know the right terminology. Anyway, I didn't want to turn into a wolf like Tommy. A juvenile attitude on my part, you bet, but I didn't care. The guy was a douche-nozzle, and I didn't want to have anything in common with him.

Of course, I may be the Ollphiest everyone seemed so worked up about. Which, by the way, was not confidence-building. How was I supposed to remain calm and cool when all the giant cat-people and wolf-people were flipping out at just the possibility that I could be the dreaded shifter boogeyman?

Elyse finished texting. "Dad wants to be on the road in the next hour. Is that doable?"

"Sure. Hey, I have a few more questions."

"Dad is the best source of answers, really."

"All right. But can you just answer one?"

"Maybe. It depends on what it is," she said carefully.

"The name Ollphiest. Your reaction was interesting."

"Yeah. Your pronunciation is horrible, by the way."

"Excuse me, but ancient Gaelic . . . it is Gaelic, right?" She nodded, and I continued, "Ancient Gaelic is not exactly in my skill set."

She ignored my sarcasm. "It's pronounced 'ul-feist' Take the 'ul' from ultimatum and combine it with 'feist' from feisty."

"Ul-feist." I repeated back.

"Perfect."

"Okay, now that we've got the language lesson out of the way, spill. Is the Ollphiest really like the boogeyman?"

"Kind of. Ollphiest literally translated means monster."

"But what kind of monster?"

"That's the thing. Nobody knows. It's a scary story kids tell each other. If you're bad, the Ollphiest will come in the night and eat you. Things like that."

"Eat people?" I felt nauseous.

"Don't sound so worried. You're not going to suddenly want to eat people. It's a stupid kid's story."

"But you don't know for sure. Even your dad isn't positive I'm the Ollphiest. And if it turns out I am, nobody knows what I could be capable of." I was starting to understand why Tommy was being such an a-hole. A shapeshifter with unknown abilities could be disastrous for the Society.

That reminded me of another question I'd had earlier but had been embarrassed to ask. "Um. Elyse, like, how old is your dad?"

"That is a question you have to ask him."

"But you're only eighteen, right?"

"You've known me since junior high, Orson. Of course I'm only eighteen."

"And you've been eighteen for only, you know, since your last birthday?

"You are such a dork. I have only been *alive* for eighteen

years. Does that answer your question sufficiently?" She glared at me.

"Yes. I just wanted to make sure I wasn't unknowingly making out with a senior citizen or something." I tried to say it with a straight face, but failed. Elyse punched me hard in the arm. "Ow."

"Don't be a baby. I didn't hit you with even a fraction of my strength." I glanced over and she wore a mischievous grin.

"Oh, so that's the way it's going to be, huh? Well, once your dad helps me get all Hulked up, I might just have to teach you a lesson."

"Promises, promises," she taunted.

The trip to my house was quick. I packed a couple of changes of clothes. Elyse insisted on sweat pants.

"Why?" I asked. "I'm no fashionista, but sweat pants are made for one thing only, marathon gaming sessions. I don't want to look like a homeless person in front of your parents."

Elyse insisted and I don't know if I've mentioned this, but I'm a total sucker for a pretty girl. Especially pretty girls who let me kiss them and squeeze their bottoms.

After one such kiss and squeeze, she put her foot down. "Enough," she said, breathing a little heavy. "Grab your bag. I'm driving, so you can call your aunt."

Elyse is an excellent driver. We are talking super-precision. When she gets behind the wheel, it is always impressive. Even in my old Corolla. She drives fast and weaves the car through traffic like a NASCAR driver. It dawned on me that it had to be because of her super spidey-senses or, in this case, cat-like agility. I grinned and shook my head again at the comic book quality my life had taken on.

Elyse noticed and asked, "What?"

I was about to hit 'dial' on Aunt Tina's number. "It just struck me, how surreal this all is. You're like this awesome superhero from a family of awesome superheroes. And you're driving me, the new guy, to my destiny. We are living an origin story moment."

Elyse rolled her eyes.

"I know, I'm a dork," I said.

"Yes, you are. But it's not just that. This life, hiding from the other seven billion people on the planet, isn't exactly easy. You don't know how many times I've almost messed up around you."

I didn't say anything. I just looked at her and let her talk.

She said, "Don't get me wrong. I love my life and the things I can do, but it's not all . . . I don't know."

"It has its pros and cons?"

"Yes. But it's more than that. I know it sounds corny, but it's the whole 'great power, great responsibility' thing."

I tried not to laugh. "So it's not a comic book. It's a movie based on a comic book?"

"Hilarious. You know what I mean."

"Yeah, I get what you're saying." I laid my hand on her thigh. "I really do."

"You need to get Tina called. We're almost to my house."

I dialed Aunt Tina, and she surprised me by picking up. I gave her the agreed-upon story. I was really glad this conversation was over the phone because, in person, she would have sensed the lie instantly. Even over the phone she was suspicious. Luckily for me, we pulled into Elyse's driveway and I could pass the phone off to Mrs. Kelly.

Two minutes later, I was back on the phone with Aunt Tina, and she was telling me to behave myself and to offer to wash the dishes all weekend or something as a thank you. I agreed, told her to have a relaxing nephew-free weekend, and ended the call.

CHAPTER TEN

Lake Arrowhead was not that far from Pasadena. In light traffic, the drive was only about an hour and a half long.

I used my time wisely.

"Mr. Kelly, do you mind if I ask a few questions while you drive?" I asked.

"Not at all." If it was possible, his driving was even more amazing than Elyse's. I could imagine that his heightened senses would allow a level of multi-tasking, including driving, that was significantly above the norm.

I figured that was a good icebreaker question. "The way you drive, is that a heightened senses thing?"

Mr. Kelly said, "Yes. Being a shape-shifter is more than just turning into another form. The ability makes us stronger, faster, and more agile than regular people. An enhanced sense of sight, smell, hearing—all the normal senses—allows us a greater awareness of our surroundings." He glanced at me in the rearview mirror. "And we have a few extra abilities that add an even greater dimension to how we experience the stimuli of the world around us."

"Like what, if that's cool to ask?"

"Orson, everything is 'cool' to ask. We will try to cover every aspect of what it means to be a shape-shifter, and your questions will help us. Remember, all of us were born into this life and for us it's second nature. We never went through the experience you're going through. No wrong or stupid questions, got it?"

"Got it," I agreed.

"You mentioned that you had been seeing things?"

"Yes."

"The other abilities or senses I'm referring to are a sort of second sight that lets us see energy."

"Energy? I'm not sure I follow."

"Everything around us is constructed, in varying degrees, of energy in the form of atoms. This car, the road, those trees, our bodies, everything. Billions of molecules and atoms strung together to make the physical world."

"You're talking about physics, quantum mechanics?" Being a computer nerd, I get exposed to lots of different science concepts and ideas.

"Exactly. Well, with our second sight, we can see the energy emitted by all of these swirling atoms," he explained.

"Shut *up*," I said, awestruck. Elyse snorted, and I saw Mrs. Kelly's shoulders shake from quiet laughter. "Uh, sorry. That's just so epically awesome."

"That's quite all right," he assured me.

"So you, the Society I mean, have, like, an ultimate under-standing of science?"

"Hardly," Mr. Kelly said wistfully. "We are learning all of these things as the world learns them. Throughout our history, we've just called it by its ancient name, magic."

"Magic?"

"Yes. How else would a shape-shifter be explained in, say, the middle ages? Or a person who could look at you and know if you were mad or lying?

"You know if someone is lying?"

"The energy the body gives off, combined with other factors like heart rate and perspiration, are incredible indicators of a person's physical and mental state," said Mr. Kelly matter-of-fact.

I looked over at Elyse, who shrugged, trying to hide a smirk. "You've been able to read me like a book this whole time? Since we met?" I whispered.

"Whispering around shape-shifters, or anyone in the Society, is pretty useless, Orson," Mrs. Kelly said, reminding me of the obvious. She looked back at me and winked.

Every interaction with Elyse and her parents raced through my head. Almost five years of moments, some no big deal, but others . . . oh man, how could I ever look any of them in the face again? I felt my face flushing. I realized that everyone in the car knew exactly what I was feeling and that made me blush even harder.

Mr. Kelly came to my rescue. "You have never done anything to be embarrassed about, Orson. Whatever memory is floating up to frighten you, just remember that we have always invited you into our home and we've never once considered forbidding Elyse to be your friend. You are a courteous, respectful young man that we are proud to know."

Elyse took my hand. Her touch, more than anything Mr. Kelly said, helped calm me. So I was in a car with a family that knew when I was happy or sad, or lying or, heaven forbid, aroused. Oh well. Mr. Kelly was right. If they hadn't kicked me out yet, I guess I was safe.

I croaked out, "Thank you, sir."

I wasn't sure if I was up to more questions just yet. There were a thousand things I wanted to know, but I was still reeling. Elyse helped me out.

"Hey, Dad. Orson asked me a good one earlier today." I looked at her, my eyes wide. I shook my head a fraction, but she didn't stop. "He wanted to make sure I was really eighteen. I assured him he wasn't dating a senior citizen, but then he asked how old *you* were." Holy crap. She had actually said it out loud.

"Did he, now?" Mr. Kelly sounded amused. "Well, Orson, would you be surprised to learn that I was present at the Second Continental Congress?" He locked eyes with me in the mirror.

My breath caught and I felt my eyes bulge. Is it even possible to feel your eyes? Maybe not for regular people, but I was half a superhuman and I tell you, I felt my eyes almost pop out of my head. I didn't remember the exact date of the Second Continental Congress, but they were responsible for the Declaration of Independence, so 1776 figured in there somewhere. Two hundred and fifty years. The Declaration signing had occurred almost two hundred and fifty years ago, and if Mr. Kelly had attended the Congress, then he hadn't been just a kid from the local village, but some kind of delegate or something.

"Breathe, Orson," Mrs. Kelly said. "Richard can be so dramatic. In answer to your question, we are long-lived. Everyone in the Paragon Society is. Richard and I were both born in Ireland in the 17th century."

Over three hundred years. She was telling me they were over three hundred years old. My brain couldn't compute the numbers. It was impossible. But was it any less possible than Elyse turning into a giant cat? Three hundred years. The things they must know. They had lived through the entire history of the U.S. It was unreal.

When all else fails, make a joke. That philosophy has served me well my entire eighteen years, so why not now? "Wow. You guys don't look a day over one hundred," I deadpanned.

The silence in the car was complete.

Uh oh.

Then Mr. and Mrs. Kelly erupted in laughter. Elyse was shaking her head and rolling her eyes. "Honestly, I can't take him anywhere," she said.

"Orson, if you can keep your wits and sense of humor about you in the light of your experiences this past day, you will be okay," said Mr. Kelly..

I spent the rest of the drive asking history questions. It didn't matter that I may be the Ollphiest. It didn't matter that nobody knew what exactly that meant. It didn't matter that I was heading to a remote cabin in the woods where I would turn into some kind of big scary animal. I was getting firsthand stories about Ben Franklin, Thomas Jefferson, and George Washington. I defy anyone to say they wouldn't have done exactly the same thing.

The cabin sat in the middle of four wooded acres. The driveway was a narrow dirt track that wound through the trees. On the road up, I had spotted a handful of other cabins through the forest. Elyse explained that this part of the mountain was a little more private, due to the larger tracts of land.

We rounded the last curve in the driveway and the cabin came into view. It was exactly what you'd expect a mountain cabin to look like, a two-story wood-framed home with a large wrap-around porch. As we got out of the car, I looked around for any sign of neighboring cabins, and all I could see were trees. It was quiet, and the air was fresh and sweet with the scent of pine.

I felt a wave, not of vertigo exactly, but something like it, roll through my body.

Mr. Kelly appeared by my side. He had a hold of my upper arm. His grip wasn't tight, but it was firm enough that I was pretty sure I couldn't break free, even if I wanted. "It's the surroundings, the trees, the mountain air," he said. "Your body is reacting to them on a deep, primal level."

I kept waiting for the feeling to pass, but it never went away entirely. Instead, it became a low undercurrent, a buzzing just below my skin. It was a strange sensation. I would just have to get used to it.

"I think I'm good. It's not gone, but it's manageable," I said.

Mr. Kelly released my arm and gave me a pat on the shoulder. Elyse came around the car and put an arm around me in a half hug. I leaned into her, thankful for her reassuring touch.

"Let's get the car unpacked and give the cabin a quick cleaning before lunch," Mrs. Kelly said. She had the front door unlocked and was holding it open with a hip, her arms full of grocery bags stuffed with supplies. Elyse and I each grabbed bags from the back of the SUV and carried them inside.

The main room of the cabin was large. It had vaulted ceilings and opened onto a good-sized kitchen. The back wall of the main room was almost all windows. The view was of the woods, a peaceful sea of green and brown. A set of stairs next to the kitchen led up and down. I assumed bedrooms were upstairs. I had no idea what would be downstairs. You don't see too many basements in California. Maybe it was a cabin thing to maximize space or something.

"You want a quick tour?" Elyse asked.

"Sure."

"Skip the basement for now," said Mr. Kelly.

Skip the basement? He hadn't said it in an ominous way, but it was a weird thing to say. What was in the basement? More importantly, what didn't he want me to see in the basement?

"No need to worry, Orson. I'll take you down there

myself, as soon as we unpack and dust the furniture," said Mr. Kelly.

Right. Super-senses. I needed to remember that very important fact.

Elyse showed me around. The first floor was comprised of the main room, kitchen, full bathroom, mudroom, and laundry. The stairs led up to a second floor with two large bedrooms, each with its own bathroom.

Being sure to keep my voice low and away from any super-hearing I said, "Only two bedrooms." I grinned. "I guess we'll have to share."

"No such luck, Romeo. You'll be sleeping in the basement."

"The basement? But I got the vibe that there's something . . ." I searched for the right word. "Something different down there."

"Oh, it is different all right," Elyse nodded.

I swallowed, my mouth and throat suddenly dry.

"Come on. The quicker we get everything cleaned and unpacked, the sooner your questions will be answered."

Elyse led me back downstairs. I was put to work vacuuming. With the four of us, the work went quickly. The entire main and second floor were dusted and vacuumed. The beds were made up with clean, crisp sheets. As Mrs. Kelly, Elyse, and I finished upstairs, Mr. Kelly whipped up some grilled cheese sandwiches and a veggie platter with ranch dip.

"So, Orson, there's a few things I want to cover before we head downstairs," said Mr. Kelly.

"Okay," I said, around a mouthful of sandwich.

"The reaction you had by the car, when we first arrived, is something you will need to get used to. Our animal is always with us, just hovering in the background. No matter where we are or what we're doing, you need to remember that.

You're about to get a crash course in something that the three of us have had years to learn—control."

I nodded.

"What you've been experiencing the past few days is your animal trying to break free."

"I have a question about that," I said.

Mr. Kelly gestured for me to continue.

"Elyse's cat form . . . Uh, that's the right way to say that, right?" I looked to Elyse, and she nodded. "Elyse's cat form was much bigger, had more mass, than Elyse herself. The laws of physics say that's impossible."

"Great question. The short answer is that we don't know. In the past we would have explained it away as magic. A term that is overused, by the way. As I mentioned earlier, our researchers are starting to discover insights about our abilities in relation to quantum physics. Do you know what Einstein said about quantum physics?"

"Something about it being 'spooky,' I think?"

"Yes, he did use the word 'spooky,' but he also stated that the laws of physics would need to be rewritten. It is apparent, and becoming more so every day, that magic and science are not mutually exclusive. They may even be opposite sides of the same coin. Does that make sense?"

"Yeah. It's mind blowing, but I get what you're saying," I said.

"Good. The past few days, your body has been in a state of flux. Think about it like flicking a light switch off and on. Your body is not sure what its natural state should be. After your first change, you will be able to distinguish the differences between your human and animal form."

"And I will have control?"

Mrs. Kelly smiled and Elyse shook her head.

"I'm going to say no. Control, and I mean true, absolute control, takes longer to master than just a long weekend."

"That's why Dad had you quit your job," Elyse explained. "You're going to spend your days learning to control the animal side of yourself."

"That's correct. I know you need your paycheck, so I'm going to put you on my company's payroll as an assistant. And you will be doing some assistant-type work, but mostly you'll be learning everything you need to know about being one of us."

"One of you? So you think I may be a cat also?" I hoped that was the case. It would give Elyse and me something more in common. Plus, I wasn't sure how the rules worked. Maybe cat people could only be in romantic relationships with other cat people.

"We don't know. And that's odd." Mr. Kelly's voice remained even and calm, but I could see the worry in his eyes.

"How's that odd?" I wanted to know, but I was also concerned by what the answer may be.

Mr. Kelly and Mrs. Kelly shared a look. Elyse felt for my hand under the table.

"We should be able to smell what you are, but so far we've got nothing," he said.

I leaned back in my chair, glancing at each of them and looking down at the table. "Oh."

"It doesn't mean anything, Orson." Elyse leaned toward me, her other hand under my chin and gently pushing up so that I met her eyes. "No one has ever had experience with someone like you."

"Like me, the monster. I got it." I had successfully been keeping the overwhelming feelings of dread at bay all day long. Since last night really. But how was I not supposed to be completely mental about all of this? Hey, Orson, you're a shape-shifter. Hey, Orson you're probably our version of the monster that lives under the bed. Hey, Orson, we can't even tell what kind of animal you're going to turn into, because you know you may be the boogeyman. With my luck, I would end up shifting into a giant skunk.

"Stop it," Elyse demanded. "We don't know everything, but that doesn't mean we're totally helpless."

"She's right, Orson," said Mrs. Kelly. "We wouldn't have brought you to the cabin if we thought you were a lost cause."

Mr. Kelly pushed back from the table and stood up. "Okay, let's head downstairs. Orson, I need you to try and stay as calm as possible. We use this cabin to help shape-shifters who are having control issues."

"Control issues?"

Elyse, Mrs. Kelly, and I stood up and followed Mr. Kelly to the stairs.

"Yes. Even those of us born with our abilities are not immune to problems. They usually manifest as psychological problems. For instance, an intense traumatic experience could lead to a kind of PTSD that could cause control issues."

"And you bring them here?" I was a little surprised. Yeah, it's a cabin in the woods, but it seemed awfully close to civilization. A cabin located somewhere in the backwoods of Montana or Alaska, or someplace similar, seemed more suitable.

"Don't let the look of the cabin or the location fool you." Mr. Kelly flipped a light switch and the basement stairs illuminated. We descended single file, Elyse keeping a hold of my hand as I trailed behind her. "It is equipped with everything we need."

Mr. and Mrs. Kelly reached the bottom of the stairs and stood off to the side. As I got to the bottom step, my stomach clenched. The basement was one large room with a polished concrete floor and walls of solid stone bricks. The eye catcher, though, was the steel cage in the far corner.

"Um . . . that's a real nice jail cell you guys have . . . here in the basement of your mountain cabin." I couldn't help myself. It was beyond surreal.

Mr. Kelly said easily, "I know it's odd, but you'll soon realize that it's necessary."

"So, I go into the cage." It wasn't a question. This whole shape-shifter thing might be new to me, but I wasn't a complete idiot. I could be the Ollphiest, something even these three-hundred-year-old cat people were scared of. It made sense.

"Mostly for your own safety," Mrs. Kelly said.

"I get it." I gave Mrs. Kelly what I hoped was my best reassuring smile. "I really do."

Mr. Kelly walked into the center of the room. He pointed out the walls and floor. "This entire room is constructed of steel-reinforced concrete and stone. The cell bars are iron and coated with silver."

"Silver?"

"Some of the world's legends and folklore are true," Elyse said.

"I like to think of silver as nature's counterbalance to us," Mr. Kelly added.

"So it, what? Can kill shape-shifters?" I asked.

"In large enough quantities, yes, but here we just use it as a deterrent."

Right. Silver kills shape-shifters. Oh, by the way, Orson, would you mind stepping into the silver-lined cage?

"The bars hurt, a lot, if you touch them. But they won't kill you." Elyse squeezed my hand and gave her dad a please-don't-scare-my-boyfriend look.

Mr. Kelly gestured me forward. He pointed to the floor. The polished concrete had designs inlaid in a darker color. They were faint, but they spread out in front of the cell in an intricate pattern. "Secondary precautions. Warding runes."

"Runes? Like, magic runes?" I bent over to get a better look.

"Exactly."

"So magic *is* real." I looked up at Mr. Kelly. "Not just ancient or misunderstood science? Like we were talking about earlier?"

"What I said earlier is true. Our scientists are finding many correlations between quantum physics and what we've called magic. That said, there is still much that is unexplained. The group we hired to inscribe and power these runes can do things that can only be described as magic."

"What do they do? The runes?"

"They keep the beasts that dwell within us . . . calm. Or calmer." Mr. Kelly walked over to the bars and pointed to runes on them as well. "These are set in such a way that we can sort of turn them up and down as we need them. Quite an amazing piece of spell work."

"How do the spell casters," (There's a word I thought I would never use outside of gaming) "power up the runes? Is it incantations and magic wands? You know, *expecto patronum* or something like that?"

Elyse snorted out a laugh. Even her mom was smiling. Mr. Kelly just looked confused. I guess he wasn't a big reader of magical fiction.

"It's nothing so . . . elaborate or interesting, Orson," said Mrs. Kelly.

Mr. Kelly still looked confused and Mrs. Kelly said she would explain it later. Elyse walked over to me bumping her shoulder against mine. She had a way of making me feel calm and centered. In a way, it was its own kind of magic.

"What's next? Do I just go into the cage and . . ." I stopped.

Mr. Kelly shook his head. He pointed to a seating area opposite the cage. I had to smile. It was patio furniture. It was the fancy kind that looks like wicker and with comfortable-looking cushions, but really was made from sturdy composite and durable water-friendly material. We sold something similar at Costco. Or Costco sold something similar. I had to get used to the idea that I didn't work there anymore.

"That's a nice set. Perfect for easy clean-up," I said.

Mr. Kelly nodded. "Yes. As you can imagine, it can get a tad messy down here sometimes. Let's sit down and we can go over a few more things."

Elyse's parents let us take the two-person love seat. I was thankful they understood that her being close helped my nerves. They pulled the other two chairs up, our knees almost touching.

Mr. Kelly took a moment to gather his thoughts before he began. "You should think of this basement, the cell specifically, as a tool. When a shape-shifter suffers from control issues, containment is key."

""That's understandable," I said. "How does a problem with control become obvious?"

"It doesn't happen often, but sometimes our animal side can become more dominant, and that's a very dangerous thing." Mr. Kelly looked to his wife to continue.

"The biggest problem that arises is the loss of impulse control. For instance, last night, when you were attacked by the blood-mage—"

"Blood-mage? The shark-nurse was a blood-mage?" I turned to Elyse, my eyes wide. "Like a *blood-mage*, blood-mage?"

Blood-mages are a class of character in World of Warcraft. In the game, they are powerful spell-casters that can hand out some pretty serious damage, and Mrs. Kelly was speaking about them as if they were as common as shoplifters.

"It's an ancient term for people who use blood-magic.

That's the worst kind of magic, because it requires human sacrifice. I sometimes think the WoW development team has some inside Society information," Elyse said.

"How do you not just laugh out loud every time we log-on to play? I mean, you're living this stuff for real. Every day." I was in awe. How could I not be? Elyse's main avatar in the game is what's called a Feral Druid, a character that can shape-shift into animals, one of which is a giant cat, to fight the various in-game bad guys.

Elyse shrugged. I shrugged back and made a goofy face. She giggled. Mr. Kelly cleared his throat. Oh, right, it was serious time.

"Sorry. It's just your daughter is one bad Mamba-Jamba."

I could read the question on his face, but before he could ask, Mrs. Kelly spoke up.

"You can Google it later, dear."

I turned my attention back to Mrs. Kelly. "I'm sorry. You were telling me about the blood-mage and loss of control."

"Correct. You witnessed me shift into what we call beast form."

Elyse said quickly, "They don't care that's what it's also called in comic books."

I bit my lip and nodded for Mrs. Kelly to continue, but I would totally be readdressing that item during the question and answer part of this "so you're a superhero now" meeting.

"Beast form is the most dangerous form we can take, and so it requires the most control. Last night, it may have looked like I was raging, completely lost to the instincts of my animal. But I was in total control the entire time. A person with control issues would not have been able to stop chasing the blood-mage until they caught up with it and either killed it or were killed."

"Wow," was all I could manage. My mind was racing. If

Mrs. Kelly *had* continued after the blood-mage, then I'd likely be dead. Note to self, control is very important.

"The loss of impulse control bleeds over to our human life as well. Imagine driving in L.A. traffic without being able to check your anger. Add to that your heightened strength, speed, and other senses, and you can begin to understand why we take control issues so seriously," Mrs. Kelly added.

"That's why we have places like this room. It may seem a bit dramatic. The silver, the magic wards, but all of these things are here to protect the person who needs help. And this weekend they're here to help you."

Mr. Kelly rested his hand on my knee. I felt Elyse tense up next to me. Mr. Kelly was looking into my eyes. Mrs. Kelly was sitting in her chair, but I could tell she was poised to move, her muscles coiled. I sat very still. I wasn't sure what was happening, but they all seemed to expect something.

"Huh?" Mr. Kelly grunted and pulled his hand back. He sat back in his chair and appeared deep in thought. Mrs. Kelly relaxed a little and Elyse eased up.

I glanced around. "What happened?"

"Nothing," answered Mr. Kelly.

"And is that good or bad?" I tried to read their collective expressions with my new-found ability to read body language and facial cues, but all I was getting was confusion.

"It's not normal," said Elyse. "You should have reacted to the touch."

"Reacted how?"

"Angry, threatened. Think of it in terms of two dogs meeting for the first time. If both dogs are dominant, there's going to be a problem until they work out an understanding," Mrs. Kelly said. "You got nothing, Richard?"

"Yeah, Orson doing his best to sit still, that was it. Did either of you sense anything?" Mr. Kelly asked.

They both shook their heads. Great. I was doing something wrong. *Way to go, Reid. You can't even pull off a cool origin story, superhero meeting thingy without screwing it up.*

"Katie, you're sure he reacted last night with the blood-mage?" Mr. Kelly asked, rubbing his chin.

"He lit up like a Christmas tree," she answered, and then turned and explained, "I'm speaking about your aura, dear. Last night, when the blood-mage attacked, your aura was glowing a deep red. That's a clear sign of rage. It's amazing that you didn't shift right then."

I had glowed? I thought about Mrs. Giles and how she had glowed when I caught her out of my peripheral vision. I'd seen her aura. Wild.

"How are you feeling, Orson? Are you anxious at all, maybe a bit afraid of this weird new world that's landed in your lap?" Mr. Kelly asked.

"Um. Not really. I'm just worried that I'm a screw-up because it's not working like it's supposed to."

"So, you're not worried about sitting in what can be described as a magic dungeon with three shape-shifters? You're only worried that you're going disappoint us?" Mr. Kelly's eyes danced with amusement.

"I told you guys," Elyse said. "He's a total dork."

That set all three of them laughing. I shook my head and gave Elyse some side stink-eye, holding back my own laughter, trying to pretend I was a serious dude whose pride had been injured beyond repair. This only made everyone laugh harder. I couldn't help myself and I started to chuckle. I raised Elyse's hand to my lips and gave it a kiss.

That's when I started to convulse and the laughing stopped.

CHAPTER ELEVEN

Calling the mild shiver that ran through my body a convulsion was a little melodramatic—at first. However, it turned quickly into a violent shake. My hand clamped down on Elyse's and I worried I would hurt her, forgetting momentarily that she had super-strength. She squeezed my hand right back, pulling me closer so she could get her other arm around my shoulder to keep me from shaking right off the couch.

Mr. and Mrs. Kelly moved faster almost than I could follow. Both of them stood and kicked their chairs across the room out of the way.

"Katie, get the door," Mr. Kelly shouted.

In a blink, Mrs. Kelly positioned herself at the door of the cell, holding it open with what appeared to be large, leather potholders. Protection from the silver embedded in the bars was my guess.

"Elyse, you have to move aside," Mr. Kelly said, his concern for his daughter clear. "It will be okay, but we need to get him in the cell. Orson, can you let go of Elyse's hand?"

I glanced down at our hands. The veins were popping out

from the strain and pressure, our fingers turning a crazy shade of purple. If we had been normal people, the bones in both our hands would have been crushed into dust. I tried to concentrate on my hand. My vision was swimming in and out of focus, and my head felt like it would explode. The pressure building up behind my eyes was insane.

"You can do it," Elyse told me.

Somehow, I willed my fingers to open just enough so that Elyse could slip her hand out. The moment she was clear, Mr. Kelly grabbed me by both ankles, spinning me off the couch in the classic helicopter move all dads everywhere had perfected. Of course, those dads were spinning a tiny kid, and those kids weren't in the middle of seizure overload. As my head whipped around toward the open cell door, he let go and centrifugal force took over. His shot was straight and true. My body glided, about a foot off the floor, through the door. I skidded to a stop on the concrete before hitting the bars on the far wall, a credit to Mr. Kelly's expert throw. The cell door slammed shut behind me. My body wasn't done seizing. I'm not sure how I avoided seriously injuring myself.

Through it all, I could hear Elyse talking. She kept repeating the same thing. "It's okay, Orson. You're not alone. I'm here. Try to concentrate only on my voice. It's okay. It's okay."

"If he doesn't stop soon, I will have to tranq' him." I heard a click and knew Mr. Kelly had just cocked some kind of tranquilizer gun. He was preparing to shoot me with a dart full of knockout juice.

My convulsions stopped. One second I was shaking so hard it felt like my teeth would rattle out of my head; the next second, complete stillness. The only sound I could hear was my ragged breathing. I just lay there on my back, eyes closed, enjoying the coolness of the concrete beneath me. I slowly stretched myself out, testing my joints and muscles. Everything seemed to be in working order.

"Orson?" It was almost a whisper.

I cracked open an eye. And immediately regretted it. It seemed like the sun was in the room with me.

"It's okay. Keep your eyes shut. Just relax for a minute," Elyse said in her calm, soothing tone.

My breathing was beginning to even out. I could hear Mr. and Mrs. Kelly whispering.

"That was different."

"Have you ever seen or heard of anything like that?"

"No, never. Maybe we *should* tranq' him just to be safe?"

I growled. A deep chest-rumbling growl and it felt fantastic.

I could hear, and somehow even sense, Elyse and her parents freezing in place. It was like I could feel the micro-air currents they made with their bodies, and when they stopped moving, I could sense that too.

That made me smile. Yeah, you better freeze because the Big Bad is awake, and he is not happy.

What?

The Big Bad?

What kind of random thought was that? Isn't that a Buffy the Vampire thing? I'm pretty sure it was. Oh man, I *was* a total dork.

"Orson?" It was Elyse, and she sounded scared.

That wasn't right. I didn't want her to be scared. I did a full systems check. I was pretty sure I could manage to sit up. It was *staying* up that worried me, because leaning back against the magic-zapping bars was out of the question. I took a deep breath. I hoped this didn't hurt or start me convulsing again. I moved, my only goal being not to embarrass myself too much. But I moved with liquid grace. I went from lying flat on my back into a coiled crouch, weight on the balls of my feet, fingertips pressed lightly against the floor in front of me. Whoa. Okay, that didn't seem normal.

I again cracked open an eye. It still seemed super-bright. Light sensitivity had to be a result of the convulsions. My brain had gotten hammered for what had felt like minutes but had probably only been seconds.

"Hi," I croaked. At least my voice didn't sound menacing.

Elyse was kneeling in front of the cage, her face tight with worry. Mrs. Kelly stood next to Elyse, one hand resting on her daughter's shoulder. Mr. Kelly was in shooter's stance, a tranquilizer rifle pointed directly at my chest

"So, on a scale of one to ten, how messed up was that?" I gave a weak smile. "Because from this side of the bars, it totally sucked."

I watched them all visibly relax. The barrel of the rifle even dipped a bit. "Um, Mr. Kelly, I'm pretty sure you're gonna want to keep that rifle pointed directly at wherever it will work the quickest."

The rifle instantly snapped back up.

"Why don't you tell us what's going on, Orson?" Mrs, Kelly said, in her best mom voice.

"First," Mr. Kelly said, most definitely not using his dad voice. "Why don't you get out of that attack crouch, shake out the arms and legs? Just relax a little a bit." It was not a suggestion.

I waited, not long, just a beat or two, before I sat back, resting on my hands, my legs splayed out in front of me. I winked at Mr. Kelly. He did not wink back.

This was fun.

Oh, crap. What was going on? It was like someone was broadcasting weird suggestions straight into my brain, and I was perfectly happy to follow them.

"Mr. Kelly, I'm so sorry. There's something very . . . strange going on inside my head."

"It's okay, son. It's your animal. He is awake, and he's a son of a bitch."

I growled again. I immediately slapped a hand over my mouth. This was not cool. Not cool at all.

Elyse gasped, her eyes wide. Mrs. Kelly tightened her grip on Elyse's shoulder, giving a gentle tug, making Elyse take a couple steps back from the bars.

"Oh, yeah," Mr. Kelly said. "He's awake and ready to rumble."

"What do I do?" I pleaded.

"Right now, your animal is playing peek-a-boo. He's not fully asserting himself, but he's letting us know he's there and can assert himself anytime he wants to," Mr. Kelly explained. I was shocked when he pulled the rifle up and slung it over his shoulder.

"I'm not sure that's a great idea," I said.

"Nope. I don't think so either, but your animal does not like having a barrel pointed at him. It's a peace offering. This is where we start to build trust." Mr. Kelly sat down on the floor, legs folded underneath him. He gestured to Mrs. Kelly and Elyse, who followed his example.

"Orson, are you okay?" Elyse asked. The genuine concern I could hear in her voice put a lump in my throat.

"Yeah. I'm so sorry I squeezed your hand. I didn't hurt you, did I?" It was taking every ounce of control I had to keep my voice from shaking.

Elyse held up her hand. "It's perfectly fine. I'm tougher than I look, remember."

"I'm also, you know, really sorry for scaring the crap out of everyone."

Mrs. Kelly smiled. "I've seen worse." It was a lie. I couldn't tell exactly how I knew, but it was a lie. I appreciated the effort.

My eyes were adjusting. The room didn't seem blindingly

bright anymore. Everything still looked hyper-real though. It was like when you used the HDR setting on your phone's camera app. Colors were bright, details sharp and perfectly clear. I found that I could focus on anything I wanted to and zoom in closer. Seriously, it was like my eyes were two tele-photo lenses. I couldn't help myself. My eyes flicked around the room, zooming in on the chairs, the concrete ceiling, Elyse's legs, and the cabinet where Mr. Kelly had obviously pulled out the tranquilizer rifle.

I went still.

The cabinet door was open, and even though the interior was in shadow, its contents were clearly visible to my new super-vision. A high-powered rifle, Taser guns, what I assume was a cattle prod—having only ever seen one in movies—and lots of silver ammunition. Huh. A rifle with silver ammo seemed a bit more permanent than the tranq' rifle Mr. Kelly was holding. Curious. I decided to see what my other senses could do and opened all of them up wide.

"Orson," said Mr. Kelly. It was impressive that he could sound so calm given the circumstances.

"Yes, sir?" I looked at him, splitting my focus between two tasks. It was so easy I almost laughed.

"Are you doing all right?"

I nodded.

My sense of smell had also achieved the rank of Superman status. I was trying to wade through the sensory overload. Elyse's scent was what my mind seemed to want to focus on. She smelled amazing. But there was also the scent of gun oil, cement, plastic, and floor cleaner. Mr. and Mrs. Kelly each had a unique smell, and they kind of overlapped each other in a complimentary way. It must be a couple thing. There was also an underlying something, a sharp coppery smell I thought I should recognize.

Oh, yes. Blood.

It was blood.

Mr. Kelly tilted his head. "Is there something you want to share?"

"I'm experiencing some sensory overload." I pointed to my eyes and nose. "I can see and hear everything and, wow, you know." I focused on Elyse. "Is this how it is for you? All the time?"

"Yeah. You learn how to filter and it isn't as distracting as you'd think." Her worry for me was pouring out of her in waves. She was literally pulsing with an indigo light. Her aura? It had to be.

The blood kept trying to distract me. Where was it coming from? I was pretty sure it wasn't the blood coursing through the veins of the Kellys or my own blood. It didn't smell that fresh. That's a gross thought. No, it smelled kind of stale. My eyes snapped to the floor. Of course, it should have been obvious. The rifle, silver ammo, and a magic, escape-proof cage. People had died in here. People who couldn't control their animal.

People like me.

I met Mr. Kelly's gaze. "How many?"

"Does it matter?" Mr. Kelly asked.

"You're not sure you can help me, are you?"

Elyse looked at her father. "Dad?"

It was Mrs. Kelly who answered, "Of course, we can help you, Orson."

"Liar!" I roared, springing forward onto my feet. Stopping a fraction of an inch away from the bars.

Mr. Kelly jumped back into his shooter's stance, the gun pointed at me. Could he hit me? With my new abilities, I was pretty sure I could dodge out of the line of fire, no problem. But I would still be locked in this prison cell. I was sure there was a well thought-out procedure for subduing someone just like me.

Mrs. Kelly had jumped up when I screamed. She grabbed Elyse, pulling her back, before she could rush toward the bars.

"Mom. Dad. Please," she pleaded. "It's Orson."

"No. It's his animal," Mr. Kelly said, in a very calm, matter-of-fact manner.

"So, are you going to shoot me or what?"

The movement was so quick I almost missed it. Mrs. Kelly whipped a second tranq' gun into shooting position, this one a pistol, that she must have had tucked in the waist of her jeans at the small of her back. An expert two-handed grip. Feet shoulder-length apart. She exhaled and fired. I could actually see the dart leave the gun. Oh yeah, dodging that slow-moving projectile would be a breeze. I spun to my left and directly into the dart that Mr. Kelly had fired simultaneously. I looked down at the neon orange-feathered dart sticking out of my chest. I heard two more pops and two more darts sprouted from my body, one from my shoulder and the other from my neck.

"Awesome," I said. I fell backward. My head bounced off the floor and then nothing.

The nothing didn't last very long. At least, it didn't seem like it to me. I was still on my back. The Kellys were brainstorming ideas on what to do next. I kept my eyes shut. I wasn't sure if I could fool them for very long, but I needed as much time as I could buy myself. Why was I acting like a crazy person? Mr. Kelly said it was my animal playing peek-a-boo, but I didn't feel different. I felt super-agitated and totally pissed they had shot me, but what other option did they have? Thinking of being shot reminded me I should be unconscious. They hit me with three darts. Darts that I'm positive were loaded with some serious drugs. So why was I awake? Did I even feel groggy? No. I didn't think so.

I concentrated on my body. Did anything feel off?

Of course not, I am Ollphiest.

Oh boy, here come the weird thoughts again.

Stand up and teach these people why their ancestors were correct to fear me.

These people? It was Elyse and her mom and dad. I needed to get a grip.

Enough! It is past time.

I was about to stand up. I didn't want to stand up. Too late.

I stood, moving slowly and stretching as I rose. I noticed the darts still poking out of me. I pulled them out and tossed them aside. The Kellys had gone silent.

"Well, that's unexpected." Mr. Kelly sounded impressed.

"Three darts? That's impossible," said Mrs. Kelly.

"Orson?" Elyse whispered.

"I think I would like to leave the cage now." I grinned and cracked my knuckles. "Please."

Mr. Kelly started to back slowly toward the gun cabinet. The only thing left in there was the Taser and the rifle that shot real bullets. Real silver bullets.

Nope.

What happened next is kind of hard to describe. It was as if all the energy contained not only within the basement but in a five mile radius of the cabin was suddenly, instantly and quite violently sucked into my body. Think of a balloon when you attach it to a water faucet. The second you turn the water on, the balloon expands like ten times larger than its actual size.

I exploded.

Not like a bomb, like the balloon. My clothes shredded off me in puffs of fabric. My entire awareness rippled, for a split second, and then I settled. I was still looking at the world from almost the same height, but I was standing on four legs. Legs that were attached to feet—nope, those were *paws*—with long wicked-looking claws.

"Oh! He's a bear," said Elyse, surprised.

A bear? Really?

I swiveled my head in the Kelly's direction. I opened my mouth to respond to Elyse, and I roared.

It was magnificent. I roared again. It felt good.

Movement caught my eye. Mr. Kelly was pulling the rifle from the cabinet and Mrs. Kelly had shifted into beast form. Oh, so they wanted to play. All right.

"Elyse, get out of here now!" shouted Mr. Kelly.

He was slamming a clip home in the rifle and he'd be ready to shoot any moment. Mrs. Kelly let out a hissy cat sound. I had to get out of this cage. How bad could the magic bars really hurt? Maybe like a magic Taser? There was only one way to find out. I hefted my right paw and swiped at the bars. I braced for some kind of jolt. Nothing. No pain.

The bars, however, reacted the way you would expect iron bars to react when swiped by a giant, pissed-off, super-bear. They crumpled like they were made of Legos. I roared again, this time in triumph. I was the Big Bad and there was no one who could stop me. Mr. Kelly fired. The rifle was a semi-automatic. He unloaded five, maybe six, shots from ten feet away.

I heard Elyse scream.

I felt each bullet hit.

And I felt each bullet bounce off.

I was bullet-proof.

That deserved another roar, but before I could let one loose, Mrs. Kelly pounced on my back. I discovered that even though I was bullet-proof, I was not impervious to her beast form claws. She sank them into my back and it hurt.

A lot.

CHAPTER TWELVE

I roared, but not in the cool triumphant look-at-me-I'm-a-freaking-super-bear way. Nope, it was all pain and rage. I reacted without thought or reason. I stood up on my hind legs, smashing my big stupid bear head into the basement ceiling, cracking the concrete. Mrs. Kelly didn't budge. She hissed in my ear, wrapping her legs around my middle as far as they would reach, allowing her the leverage to reposition her claws in my back.

I didn't care anymore that it was Elyse's mom, one of the nicest people I knew. I would rip her apart. I would dig my claws into her stomach and crush her head in my massive jaws. I was—

Stop.

Just stop. You're Orson Reid.

You don't bite, maul, and kill people—especially not your girl-friend's mom.

But I had to get her off my back. I stopped thrashing for a moment and assessed the situation. I noticed there were still a few of the cell bars intact. I shuffled backward and pressed Mrs. Kelly into the bars. The reaction was immediate. The magic in the bars jolted Mrs. Kelly so hard she dropped off my back and lay semiconscious.

"Katie!" Mr. Kelly yelled, firing the rifle as he ran toward his fallen wife.

Two of the bullets glanced off my skull, the others going wild. It felt like someone had stuffed my head into a bag of dynamite and detonated it. Okay, so I was bullet-proof but not completely impervious. I shook my ringing head, clearing my vision. The door. The stairs were directly in front of me, the passage to the main floor wide open. Upstairs, I would have my choice of windows to crash through and then a whole mountain forest to lose myself in.

I ran, or loped, crossing the room in two quick bounds. I was almost to the stairs when Elyse stepped in front of me. I skidded to a stop, my razor-sharp claws digging into the concrete.

"Orson." It was a gentle plea. Elyse raised her hand in front of her, palm up.

"Elyse no! He'll kill you!" Mr. Kelly shouted.

Kill?

Elyse?

Never.

Elyse didn't acknowledge her dad. She just stared at me, her hand hanging about an inch from my snout. I couldn't hurt her, but I had to get out of this room. My eyes rolled around in my head, my breath puffing from me. Geez, I sounded like a freight train.

I chuffed at her. Not a growl, not a whine, but a kind of grunt. She needed to move. I chuffed again.

"No," Elyse said, her hand not wavering.

I heard cloth ripping. Yesterday I couldn't have told you what would make a noise like that. Today, having heard it twice now, I knew Mr. Kelly had just shifted, shredding the clothes he was wearing.

Great.

There was now a second angry shape-shifter in beast form behind me. My ears flicked around on my head,, trying to pinpoint exactly where he was.

"Dad, stop," Elyse said. "Orson," she repeated, stretching her fingers out just enough to touch my nose.

I chuffed again.

"I said no." Elyse arched an eyebrow at me. She slid her hand farther up my snout, spreading her fingers out on my wide head. She rubbed her thumb in a slow small circle.

I shuddered.

"It's okay. You're okay."

I could finally feel the drugs that my body had somehow automatically quarantined. They slowly released into my system. I wobbled, my eyes drooping. Oh yeah, this was some seriously powerful stuff. I moved forward. Mr. Kelly's warning hiss came from directly behind my ear.

"Dad, stop. Can't you tell he isn't going to hurt me?"

She was right. I just wanted to get closer, so she didn't have to stretch to reach my head. I bumped my nose against her waist, and she brought her other hand up. She buried her fingers under both my ears and gave a scratch.

It was heavenly.

I chuffed again.

"You're such a dork."

With the drugs now coursing through my entire system, and Elyse scratching my ears, I slowly lowered myself to the floor. Elyse followed me down, sitting with her legs under her. I rested my head in her lap and closed my eyes. This was good. I could do this forever. With that content thought, I went to sleep.

I woke up gradually. The first sensation I became aware of was the feel of fabric against my skin. A blanket? Yes, it was definitely a blanket. I would have thought the shocking and crazy violence of my first shift would have brought with it amnesia. You know, how some accident victims only remember driving down the road and then waking up in the hospital. No such luck for me. I remembered, in spectacular detail, every moment from first entering the basement, getting tranq'd, shot with silver bullets, clawed in the back, and finally succumbing to the drugs. And the darkness taking me as my head rested in Elyse's lap.

Elyse.

I could sense her sitting close by. Not only did I recognize the scent that was uniquely Elyse, I could feel the energy of her body. I'd heard about auras even before Mrs. Kelly had mentioned them earlier. I never gave metaphysical things much thought. I was a science guy. If you couldn't test it, measure it, or quantify it in some way, I found it hard to wrap my head around it. Of course, that was before my girlfriend had turned into a giant cat in front of me. Before the shark-nurse blood-mage attack. Before shrugging off enormous, body-crushing pallets of chili. Before I had turned into a raging, rampaging bear.

I had shape-shifted. I had turned into a bear—a giant, claw-wielding, cage-smashing, pissed-off bear.

I did a quick body assessment. Currently I was sprouting only two arms and two legs. My fingers felt normal. I ran my tongue over my teeth; just normal people teeth. I felt no pain. Which didn't seem right? I had been shot, point blank. Yeah, the bullets had basically bounced off my bear hide, but I would expect some kind of bruising. They were bullets fired from a Navy Seal-looking rifle. Also, Mrs. Kelly had given my back the Wolverine treatment with her claws and as far as I could tell my back was intact. The soft cushions, upstairs living room couch maybe, didn't cause my skin any discomfort. Wait. I could feel the cushions against my skin. The blanket was also touching skin. I was naked.

I heard footsteps on the stairs. I could smell Mr. Kelly as he came into the room. Soap, shampoo, clean clothes, with the slight odor of detergent, and those static cling things you put in dryers. He also had a musky undertone. A wild smell my mind immediately associated with dense jungle or rain forest. It was his animal, his second self, his cat. I knew the wild smell would not be discernible to a regular human nose. Huh, a regular human nose. Until yesterday that would have included me. I realized I could also sense his tension and something else . . . was that fear?

"How's he doing?" Mr. Kelly asked.

"With three darts, he'll probably still be asleep this time tomorrow," Mrs. Kelly answered.

Her voice startled me. I'd been so caught up in my thoughts I hadn't realized she was in the room. But now I could sense she was sitting close to Elyse. Not right on top of her daughter, but close enough to grab her if I went all berserker again.

"I don't think so," said Elyse.

I felt her move, her energy pressing deeper into mine. It felt good.

"Elyse," Mr. Kelly grumbled. It wasn't a question, but a warning.

"It's okay, Dad. Really. I can't tell you why, but I can feel it. He won't hurt us."

I felt Elyse's hand close around my blanketed foot and squeeze. "Isn't that right, dork?" I could feel her smile. How was that even possible?

I popped open my right eye. Surveying the room in front of me. I was lying on the living room couch. Elyse sat at my feet, a big beautiful smirk on her face. Mrs. Kelly sat in the matching chair, the high-powered rifle from the basement resting in her lap. Mr. Kelly stood just outside the ring of furniture, body tense, eyes alert for any sign of wrong movement from me.

"Hi, guys. Sorry about the whole ..." I hooked my hands into pretend claws. "You know, bear thing," I said. "I'm kinda starving and kinda naked. Do you think maybe I can get some pants and a sandwich or something?" I smiled. It was the most non-threatening thing I could think of to say or do.

Elyse rolled her eyes. Man, I loved her.

Mr. Kelly laughed. It wasn't one of those slow rolling chortles that builds into a big laugh. It was a full on belly-buster. One moment, he was all serious and silent, and then *wham*—laugh city.

"Orson, you are one amazing young man," he managed to get out between sobbing for air.

"Elyse, go fetch something for Orson to wear. I'll make us something to eat," Mrs. Kelly said, taking charge of the situation. She handed the rifle to Mr. Kelly as she passed him on the way to the kitchen. "And for heaven's sake, Richard, calm yourself."

"Not a word until I get back with your stuff," Elyse told me.

I saluted, which sent Mr. Kelly into another fit of laughter. He flopped down into the chair his wife had vacated. He did not, however, set the rifle down. It stayed expertly cradled in his hands. I held no delusions that, despite his laughter, Mr. Kelly would not hesitate to shoot me in the head if I even looked sideways wrong. I had no idea if non-bear Orson was as bullet-proof as bear Orson, and I didn't really want to find out the hard way.

Elyse came back with a pair of sweats, tossing them at me before asking her mom how she could help. Mrs. Kelly pointed at a tray of meat and cheese. "That'll help take the edge off, while I finish prepping the steaks."

My mouth watered. Steak. I hoped Mrs. Kelly had brought extra, because I was sure I could eat half a cow at this point. Elyse dropped the tray on the table in front of the couch and sat down beside me, taking my hand. I held on and used my other hand to shovel meat, cheese, and crackers into my mouth just as fast as I could chew and swallow.

I decided there was no use in putting off the inevitable. Around a mouthful of food, I said, "So, I'm a bear, how cool is that?"

"Um, you're not just a bear, dude. You're like the king of bears," said Elyse.

"Am I correct in assuming that you remember all that occurred, Orson?" Mr. Kelly asked.

I stopped chewing, swallowing what was in my mouth. I met his eyes, not in a challenging way, just a quick look so he could hopefully see my sincerity. "Yes, sir. I just want to say how sorry I am. I had no intention . . ."

Mr. Kelly said quickly, "Orson, there is no need to apologize. Your animal took over. Even the oldest among us have lost ourselves to our animals in times of trial or when threatened by overwhelming forces."

"That's just it," I looked at Elyse. "It didn't feel like that . . . not at first, anyway."

Mrs. Kelly had stopped to listen. Mr. Kelly looked a bit confused.

I continued, trying desperately to explain. "It was me, but not me. There was this other voice in my head."

"That's your animal, your bear. That's a normal sensation to have at first," Elyse said.

"Okay." I knew I wasn't getting across how it had felt to me. That until Mrs. Kelly landed on my back, I hadn't felt *out of control*. I had been a bit pissed off that they hadn't told me the whole truth about the basement cage and what would happen if I couldn't control myself, but I was fairly certain I had been in control.

"Orson, why don't you start at the beginning? Why do you think that you started to shift at that precise moment?" Mr. Kelly asked.

"I'm not exactly sure." I closed my eyes and tried to focus on that moment. I had felt safe. Things had totally entered weirdville, but I trusted Elyse and the Kellys. I knew they had the experience to help me. "I guess, for the first time since the forklift accident, I felt relaxed. Not stressed. I knew you guys were on top of the situation."

"You felt calm?" Elyse asked.

"Completely." It was the truth.

"That's it," Mrs. Kelly said from the kitchen. "Normally something like the accident or, even more so, the blood-mage attack, would have triggered a shift. Your life was in real danger both times, and yet you somehow avoided shifting while still accessing your power. It's quite amazing, actually. Instead, your body only gave in to the change when you knew you wouldn't be harmed." Having satisfied herself with that explanation, Mrs. Kelly went on preparing the food.

Mr. Kelly considered this, nodding. "It does make sense. And points to an amazing amount of instinctual control on your part, Orson. Okay, so we've established why you shifted. What else can you tell us?"

"So, after you tossed me," I grimaced. "I mean, after I was placed in the cell, that's when the whole two voice thing started."

"And what exactly was your animal saying? I'm assuming he was not happy. Did he want to fight? To attack?" Mr. Kelly sounded like he already knew the answers. Boy, was he in for a surprise.

"Not exactly."

"What do you mean, not exactly?" Mr. Kelly said, leaning forward.

I let out a long breath. "It was like the voice . . ."

"Your animal," Mr. Kelly corrected me.

"Right. My animal. It was like he wanted to come out and play. He saw the whole thing as very . . . amusing."

"Amusing?" Mr. Kelly's jaw clenched. He wasn't happy with that answer. "Your animal. That gigantic bear—a bear impervious to bullets among other deterrents—wanted to kill us, Orson."

"I'm not trying to be difficult, but I'm pretty sure that's not the case." This was not going well at all. "He seemed to think it was all sort of fun, until the end when Mrs. Kelly jumped on me."

"When Mrs. Kelly jumped . . ." Mr. Kelly was trying real hard not to yell. "You mean, when she saved our lives and then you smashed her into the bars so hard she cracked her ribs?"

"What?" I looked over at Mrs. Kelly.

Mrs. Kelly gave her husband one of those wife looks that seem to convey a thousand things at once, the kind of look that a smart husband does not ignore, and Mr. Kelly was a smart husband. She turned her attention to me and she was all kindness and light. "It's okay, dear. I'm fine now. Super-healing, remember? Would you like two steaks or three?"

Huh? Oh. "Three, please."

"Orson," said Elyse. I turned toward her. Her eyes were soft, gentle. "The way you're talking, it seems as though you think that you and your animal are separate?"

"Well, yeah. If you'd been able to hear this voice. He was arrogant and annoying and, you know, kind of a dick." I glanced toward the kitchen. "Sorry, Mrs. Kelly."

Elyse tapped my arm to get my attention. I turned back

and she held my gaze. "Orson, your animal. It's not separate from you. It's just another aspect of you."

"Oh."

That was an idea my brain didn't want to accept. On one hand, it made sense. I was the bear, and the bear was me. On the other hand, it frightened me to my core. I was responsible for all that rage. I considered myself fairly even when it came to emotions. Sure, I could (and did) get mad if the situation I found myself in called for that kind of response. Sometimes you just had to unload on stupid people doing stupid things. There was about a six-month period where I would get in huge flame wars on social media over political opinions. Seriously. I would sometimes find myself physically shaking from the sheer idiocy of comments made about something as ridiculous as supermarkets using plastic bags. I wasted a lot of time and the only thing I learned was that people seldom, if ever, change their minds.

So, yeah, I could get angry, but it wasn't a personality trait I considered dominant. And I'd never felt the kind of rage that had been coursing through me when the Kellys were attacking me.

Whoa, attacking?

No, it was not an attack. They had been trying to help me, while minimizing damage.

Elyse poked me in the arm. "Hey."

"Sorry, I was trying to wrap my head around what you said." I forced myself to look at Mr. and Mrs. Kelly. It was hard because of my embarrassment. No, I was beyond embarrassed. I was ashamed. "I'm sorry. The way I acted . . . you've got to know I don't feel that way." I pointed to my head. "I have nothing but the utmost respect for you both. And Elyse, I . . . the way I feel about her . . ." I dropped my head.

"Hey." Elyse scooted closer against me. "No one thinks

you're bad or evil, or anything like that. Right, Mom and Dad?"

"Of course not," Mrs. Kelly said.

Mr. Kelly finally set the rifle aside, leaning it against the arm of the chair, clearly trying to show he also agreed with Elyse. It didn't escape me, though, that the rifle was still within reach and, with his enhanced speed, still a threat.

No!

Not a threat. A precaution, a safety measure, to not only protect his family, but also protect me from doing anything I would regret.

"Orson, while it's true that we are one with our animals, it takes practice to find balance—the strength of the bear, bound by the strength of your character," Mr. Kelly said. "Our children begin learning this from birth. It is taught, not only by the example of those around them, but also through rigorous training. And after a lifetime of conditioning, you'd be surprised how many of them still struggle with control."

Mrs. Kelly added, "I'm not sure anyone experiencing their animal for the first time, with the accompanying sensory overload, would have been able to stop. What you did was amazing."

Elyse nodded.

"I don't think I was responsible for stopping myself." I bumped my shoulder against Elyse. "It was you. Your voice. Your touch." I raised her hand to my lips and gave it a quick peck. "And the drugs, of course. What's in those darts?"

"It's a cocktail of silver nitrate and heavy-duty animal tranquilizers," explained Mr. Kelly.

"Think elephants," Elyse chimed in.

Mr. Kelly said, "As you've probably guessed, shape-shifter metabolisms are quite robust. The silver nitrate slows our ability to burn the drugs off. But they had no immediate effect on you at all."

"Oh no, they totally did, but the bear . . . or I guess I should say my bear?" I looked to Elyse.

She nodded. "My bear is more correct than 'the bear'. Eventually, you'll get to the point where you won't even differentiate. It'll just be you."

"Hold your thought a minute," said Mrs. Kelly. "I want to get these steaks on the grill."

Mr. Kelly hopped up to help his wife. She handed him a platter mounded with what looked like ten pounds of beef. Mrs. Kelly opened the slider to the patio and they both stepped out into the late afternoon sun.

The late afternoon? "How long was I out?" I asked Elyse.

"Fifteen minutes, tops. You laid your head, which is adorable by the way, in my lap and just kind of slumped over. The moment you went out, you shifted back." She grinned at me.

"Ah. So the truth comes out. All of this was just one giant ruse to get me naked in your lap."

"You wish, Reid."

"All you had to do was ask. I may have even done a little dance for you."

Elyse giggled and pointed to her ears, and then at the open door to the patio.

"Oh, yeah, right."

I let out a huge sigh, the tension in my back starting to loosen up.

"It will be okay. And I'm not just saying that. My parents are experts at this."

I nodded and pointed to the rifle, in a huge sign of trust, left leaning against the chair. "I can tell." I shifted my weight, trying to get a little more comfortable on the couch. The sweats Elyse had given me were feeling a little snug.

"What's up?"

"Feeling a bit constricted in these sweats."

"You will definitely need new clothes. And you will probably need to go to the Big and Tall store."

I laughed. "Right, because I'm so huge."

Elyse leaned back so she could look directly into my eyes. "Yes. You are."

Uh oh, that was her serious face. "Elyse?"

"Orson?" She replied, matching my tone.

"You're kind of freaking me out."

She touched the side of my face, her fingers gentle and loving. "You need to drop the blanket and look at yourself in the mirror." She pointed her chin toward the big mirror over the fireplace.

Okay. With everything that had gone down so far today, I didn't even question why. I stood up, dropping the blanket from my shoulders. I turned toward the mirror and froze. It was me, but it wasn't me. Or better yet, it was the comic book version of me. I looked down my torso and back up at the mirror. I had grown another couple of inches. I was now well over six feet tall. I was also completely ripped. I mean, seriously, I could probably get work as a body double for Dwayne "The Rock" Johnson. My muscles had muscles. I was pretty sure I could enter a body-building contest anywhere in the world and crush the competition.

"Holy fu—"

"Orson!" Elyse cut me off.

My eyes snapped to the patio door. Mr. and Mrs. Kelly were standing there and watching me staring at myself.

"Fudge. Holy Fudge."

Mr. Kelly grinned. Mrs. Kelly pursed her lips.

I recovered quickly. "So, do we have, like, a really excellent excuse for Aunt Tina, because I'm pretty sure this," I spread my hands in front of my body, "can't be hidden by baggy t-shirts and sweats?"

Silence.

I pushed at my massively ripped abs. "Or will all this go back to normal? You know, is this like a Hulk thing, only slower?"

"I don't think so," said Mr. Kelly.

Mrs. Kelly sat down next to Elyse. Mr. Kelly went back to the chair and motioned for me to have a seat. "The conversation we had earlier about physics versus magic, and how our animals have more mass than our human forms . . ."

"Yeah," I said.

"Well, take Katie, Elyse, and me. We are on the larger side of the size scale. We're taller, more muscular."

"We have an athletic build," Mrs. Kelly offered.

"An athletic build, yes. This occurs naturally and all shape-shifters are larger than average. It still doesn't account for the extra mass we add when we shift, but it accounts for some of it."

"Mr. Kelly, no offense, but this isn't an 'athletic build'. I'm freaking huge."

Elyse stifled a laugh.

"Ha, ha. This isn't funny. How am I going to explain this?"

Mr. Kelly rubbed his face and let out a big sigh. "Everything about you is new to us. Your bear . . . it's massive. It's the biggest animal I've come across in three hundred years. It only makes sense that your human form would reflect that. As for how we explain it? I don't know yet, but I'm working on it. I'm sorry. It's the best answer I can give you."

Sorry? He didn't need to apologize to me. I was the one who wigged out and trashed his basement. "You've nothing to be sorry about. You guys have been awesome."

"All right, everyone is sorry, and now we're all on the same page," said Mrs. Kelly in a take-charge, no-nonsense tone. "We need more data. Orson, back to the darts, you said they worked on you. Explain."

"Right. When the darts hit, I could feel the drugs enter my body."

"That's the silver nitrate. A kind of a burning sensation," Elyse said.

'Yes. And I did lose consciousness for a moment, that's why I collapsed. But then, I don't know the best way to describe it . . ." I wracked my brain. "Quarantined, that's it. My body quarantined the drugs together and kept them from spreading through my system. And it happened automatically. Just one more cool super-ability I guess." I smiled at Mr. Kelly, expecting a nod of assurance. Instead, I got a grimace and a slight shake of the head.

"What?" I asked

Elyse answered for her father. "We're strong, fast, we shape-shift into panthers, but we're still limited by physiology. Even in cat form, we're still flesh and bone. Our hearts still beat, blood still courses through our veins. Any of us gets hit with a tranquilizer dart, let alone three, we're down for the count."

"How is it that I can do things you guys can't?" I asked.

"Simple, you're the Ollphiest," said Mr. Kelly.

CHAPTER THIRTEEN

The day's events had wrung me out. Luckily, the steaks were ready. We all grabbed plates and piled them high with steak, mac and cheese, salad, and buttermilk biscuits. We adjourned back to our spots in the living room and proceeded to eat in silence.

As I chewed on my steak, I pondered on all I'd learned in the past few hours. I was a shape-shifter that turned into a giant bear, a shape-shifter who had joined the hidden world of other shape-shifters that included my girlfriend and her family.

Elyse said she was pretty sure I looked like a Kodiak bear. Kodiak and Polar bears tied for the largest species of bear, apex predators both. I remembered reading somewhere that the largest bear ever recorded was a Polar bear that weighed in at over 2,000 pounds. The Kellys told me I was at least that large. This enormous size had spilled over into my human form, and I now looked like a roided-out gym junkie.

In my bear form, I was bullet-proof and somehow impervious to the magic that helped contain out-of-control shifters. Both silver and the empowered mage runes hadn't even slowed me down. Mr. Kelly had not brought that fact up yet, but I'm sure it would be the first subject we tackled after dinner. My new super-senses told me that my ability to shrug off all the control measures had Mr. Kelly worried.

Ollphiest.

I *was* the mythical boogeyman of the shifter world. Continuing to deny it seemed silly. I wasn't ready to share my thoughts with the Kellys just yet, but I think Mr. Kelly was already on that page with me. I was a monster that hadn't been seen in millennia. Why me? Why now? Some would say it was one of those once-in-a-lifetime serendipitous events—a coincidence. Elyse had moved into the neighborhood and we ended up at the same school, end of story. That conclusion was hard for me to accept. I wasn't a destiny kind of guy. I believed you made your own luck and that any achievements were a direct result of how much work you put in. Not anymore. There had to be a reason for all of this, some kind of design. It sounded like hippie mumbo-jumbo, but I couldn't shake the feeling that something was coming.

I was pulled from my musings by the clink of plates. Mr. Kelly was gathering up the dishes. I looked down at my plate, surprised to see I had finished my food.

"Did you get enough?" Mrs. Kelly asked.

"Yeah. It was great. Thank you." I handed over my plate.

Mr. Kelly dropped the dishes into the sink and walked back into the living room. "There's one more thing I'd like to talk about tonight."

"How I managed to ignore the magic wards?" I said. I knew this was a serious situation. The Kellys would have to inform the shifter council, who would then report to the Society itself, and I could guess how they would react, especially with Tommy the Jerk causing problems. It would not be a positive outcome, I was sure.

"Yes. You moved through them as if they weren't even there."

"That's because they didn't work on me, not really."

The Kellys frowned at each other. Elyse was focused on me.

"I could sense the bars. I knew they were there. Kind of like a buzzing in my head, but nothing I was worried about." I shrugged an apology.

"Magic doesn't work on you, you're bullet-proof, you can decide to just ignore tranquilizers — you're unstoppable. This is not good." Mr. Kelly sighed, leaning back in his chair to stare at the ceiling.

"So he's unique? So what?" Elyse said defensively.

"It's a problem," I said, not taking take my eyes off Mr. Kelly. "I'm dangerous, and it appears as if I can't be controlled. That will not sit well with people like Tommy."

Mr. Kelly met my eyes. "So you understand."

I nodded.

"So, we'll figure something out," Mrs. Kelly announced. "We'll start by working on your control."

Elyse wasn't about to let the topic drop. "Wait a second. Dad, you said the Society would give Orson the benefit of the doubt. That you and mom would have time to work with him."

"That was before we knew what he was capable of—"

Elyse cut him off. "Before we knew what he was capable of?" Her voice went up in volume with each word.

Uh oh.

"The world is full of magic . . . magic weirdos." She was shouting now. "Some of whom are crazy dangerous and we're supposed to worry about Orson? Orson, who is the most caring person I know?"

I loved that she was defending me, but what crazy dangerous weirdos was she talking about? Could there be something worse than the shark-nurse? Because that was not a comforting thought.

"Elyse, you know being caring or nice has nothing to do with it. A person's ability to control their animal . . ."

"He controlled his animal just fine!" Elyse jumped to her feet, pointing her finger in Mr. Kelly's face. "After *you* stopped shooting at him!"

I gently on tugged on her arm. "Hey."

"No. It's okay, Orson," said Mr. Kelly. "Elyse may speak her mind." Mr. Kelly stood up to face his daughter. "But she needs to remember I'm on your side. Katie and I will do everything we can to help you and protect you."

A tear rolled down Elyse's cheek and she wiped it away. "I'm sorry I yelled."

"You wouldn't be his daughter if you hadn't," Mrs. Kelly said softly.

Mr. Kelly gave Elyse a one-armed hug, pulling her tight. She gave him a quick peck on the cheek and slid down next to me on the couch.

"So what now? Is there like a training program, or boot camp or something, for people in my situation?" I asked.

Elyse let out a laugh. "You mean like a summer camp for magic kids? Where you can swim and do arts and crafts?"

"Ha-ha." I gave her poke with my elbow.

"Because places like that do exist. I used to go every year. But it's less swimming and hiking, and more guided meditation and combat training," Elyse said.

"Combat training?" That didn't sound like a smart idea. A bunch of hormonal shape-shifter teenagers living together and learning to fight? I couldn't think of a better recipe for mayhem.

"There was no shifting allowed. It was all about control," Elyse explained, sensing my confusion. "Only on the last night did we get to shift and go for a group run. It was pretty cool."

"That's what we should do," Mrs. Kelly said, getting to her feet. "A run. Let Orson experience the joy that shifting can bring."

"Katie, I don't know—" Mr. Kelly began, but Elyse was already jumping up.

"That's a great idea. Dad, you know Mom's always right about these things."

"Thank you, dear." Mrs. Kelly gave Elyse a wink. "Richard, we're in uncharted territory. Orson would never hurt Elyse. He proved that earlier. We know he doesn't react well to bars, tranquilizers, and guns, so I think a run is exactly what he needs."

A run?

That's exactly what I wanted to do.

Now.

Immediately.

I tensed, because those weren't my thoughts. It was him —the bear. He wanted out, he wanted to run. I noticed that Elyse and her parents had become still. They were all watching me. Elyse tilted her head in an unspoken question. Of course they could feel my tension, it probably freaked them out. Everyone being able to sense my feelings or change in mood—that would definitely take some getting used to.

"Sorry. My bear got a little excited about going for a run."

The Kellys relaxed. Elyse just gave me a smile.

"It's settled. A run it is," Mrs. Kelly said.

Mr. Kelly shook his head. "Okay, but we will need some ground rules. And that's not up for debate," he said, stopping Elyse's protest before she could even begin.

"Um . . . I think a run sounds cool and everything, but I'm not sure I can, you know, shift at will," I said.

"Nonsense. Richard will guide you through the process. It's much easier after the first time," Mrs. Kelly said.

"Orson, are you sure you're up to this?" Mr. Kelly asked.

"Of course he is." Elyse held out her hand, and I took it and stood.

"Yeah, let's do it," I said.

"The rules are as follows. One," Mr. Kelly held up a finger. "I decided the path we run. Two, we stay together at all times. Three, if I decide Orson is having difficulties, we stop and return to the cabin immediately." Mr. Kelly looked at each of us until we nodded.

Mrs. Kelly began to strip. I felt my face flush and looked everywhere but directly at her. Elyse giggled.

Mr Kelly said, "First lesson, nudity among shifters is common, for obvious reasons—the cost of replacing clothes among them. We're not nudists, we don't look for reasons to be naked, but nudity is necessary sometimes."

"Imagine going on a run with twenty or thirty others. It would take forever if everyone had to go into separate rooms to change," Elyse added.

I gave a weak smile and a nod. So, yeah, Mrs. Kelly was completely naked and damn was she hot.

No.

Stop.

I started a silent chant in my head, *my girlfriend's mom, my girlfriend's mom, my girlfriend's mom.* And then Elyse pulled her top off, and I lost all train of thought. I did my best not to stare, just quick glimpses from the corner of my eye. Yes, she had pulled her clothes off at my house last night, but that was a much more stressful situation. Here, in this cozy cabin in the woods, it was a much more vivid experience. Both Elyse and her mom weren't being sexy in the least. They just clinically removed their clothes so they could shift. But I'm an eighteen-year-old guy and, well, boobs were boobs.

"Orson," Mr. Kelly said, bringing my attention back to the matter at hand. "Your sweats." He pointed at my legs.

"Right. Sweats," I stammered.

Oh man.

This was nuts.

Here goes nothing. I pushed the sweats down over my hips and let them slide to the ground. I was naked, so very naked. Mr. Kelly quickly undressed. I could only hope to look so good at the ripe old age of three hundred. He crossed over to the patio door and slid it open. Mrs. Kelly and Elyse filed out. I followed, trying to play it cool and not cover my junk with my hands.

I watched in awe as both Elyse and her mom shifted. It was fluid; graceful, even. There were no jerky motions or popping noises. Elyse and her mom both fell forward, and in the time it took them to reach all fours, they had shifted. There was only a whoosh of air to signal the change. Amazing.

Elyse's coloring, the black fur with the light red under-coat, matched Mrs. Kelly's. The only difference was in the pattern the red made against the black. They were beautiful. Elyse padded over and nuzzled my hand. I stroked her head, giving her ears a scratch.

"Okay, Orson, let's get started." Mr. Kelly kneeled down on the patio deck and motioned for me to join him.

Elyse and her mom settled down a few feet away and watched with inscrutable cat eyes.

"Close your eyes and start taking in deep breaths. Fill your lungs as much as you can and then let the air out slowly, completely emptying your lungs before you take another breath."

I did as instructed and took in a long breath. The smells of the forest overwhelmed me and I started coughing. Not this again.

A sputtered, "Whoa," was all I could manage.

"That's all right. Your senses are adapting to all the new input they are receiving. Just breathe through it." Mr. Kelly continued to deep breathe allowing me all the time I needed to calm myself.

I got my coughing under control. With every breath I took, I could smell the surrounding forest. And not just the expected foresty pine scent, but everything—everything growing and living in the forest. The trees, plants, animals, it was a whole new world, and I was experiencing all of it.

"Good. You're doing real good." Mr. Kelly was speaking in a low, deep tone. It was soothing. "Now stretch out your feelings. Visualize the energy emanating from your body. See it being gently pulled, like taffy, in long tendrils stretching out to meet the energy of the forest, the sky, the setting sun. Now, allow your energy to mix with that wild energy."

I could feel it. My body was completely relaxed, but my energy was a spinning ball, moving around me in a whirl. I could sense the places where my energy and the forest's energy were touching. The forest was alive, its power was wild, ancient, and in some way I couldn't comprehend, tied to all the other forests of the world.

Magic.

I was sensing the magic that was an innate part the planet.

And it was huge.

I almost cried out in delight. How could we, as inhabitants of this planet, miss this powerful force? It was everywhere, in everything.

"Orson." It was Mr. Kelly. I had almost forgotten he was there. "As you connect to the energy, the magic, try to concentrate on your bear. When he comes into focus, imagine merging with him and you will. It's that simple."

Really?

I focused on the feelings I'd had earlier in the basement—before things went south. I recalled the exhilaration that had flowed through me and the power of that first roar. Oh yes, I wanted out. I wanted to run and run, and never stop.

I was Ollphiest.

Calm down! I shouted at the crazy thoughts running through my brain.

I am vengeance, I am the Big Bad and I will not—

I said shut the hell up!

I could feel my body starting to do the vibrating thing from earlier. Nope. Not this time.

"Orson?" Mr. Kelly sounded worried.

I couldn't blame him. The bear shouting weird stuff in my head was a part of me, and I was worried I wouldn't be able to control him. I forced my hand up in a wave I hoped conveyed that I was good and just needed a minute. Of course, that wasn't true. I wasn't doing well and in the next few minutes things were either going to go my way or the bear's way. But at the moment, all I could manage was the gesture.

Let me loose, boy.

Nope.

Trust me, it's the only way.

Nope.

Let me loose!

Something wet touched my arm. It sent a jolt through my body. Elyse, it was Elyse. She had nuzzled my arm. I could do this.

I concentrated on the voice in my head. I knew the bear wasn't separate. He was me, at least a part of me, but it was easier to think of him as a passenger in my head. And so I spoke to him as such.

Listen up. This is how it's going to be. We will go for a

run with the Kellys and you will behave yourself. You will not be a dick. Got it?

Fine. Have it your way. But there will be a time when you will unleash me.

Maybe, but that day is not today.

My body slowly stopped its shaking.

I took a deep breath.

I shifted.

It wasn't the violent explosion like the first time. But it also wasn't as fluid as Elyse and Mrs. Kelly. For me, it was more like melting in reverse. My body shimmered and warped, building upon itself until my human form disappeared, leaving only bear. I shook my massive head and sneezed. The force of the sneeze made the patio deck shake. I was a walking earthquake. I was a force of nature and it was intoxicating.

I roared. It wasn't a super-loud roar, I was just going for a 'hey world here I am'. But from the Kellys' response I may have over done it. Mr. Kelly took a few steps back and Mrs. Kelly switched into a defensive stance, tail twitching. Only Elyse stood her ground. She stared me right in the eyes and chuffed. Even in cat form, she could call me a dork.

I immediately sat back on my rump, my front paws in front of me as close to folded as bear paws could get. I was doing my best Yogi Bear impression and I hoped it looked as non-threatening as it felt. Elyse chuffed again and sat down next to me.

"Excellent," Mr. Kelly said, before quickly shifting. His cat was the same size as Mrs. Kelly and Elyse, but his coloring was black with a blue-grey undercoat. He looked wicked-cool.

Mr. Kelly and Mrs. Kelly touched noses and then took off into the woods. Elyse bumped me and ran after them. She stopped at the edge of the trees and looked back to make sure I was following.

Two days ago, I was worried about my class schedule for the fall—would I get the classes I needed, would my student loan fund before the tuition deadline? Now I was a giant bear, about to go for a romp in the forest with my girlfriend and her parents, who were giant cats.

Yeah, life had definitely taken a hard turn into the strange.

CHAPTER FOURTEEN

I was in Heaven. I had been worried that the Kellys' cat form would be faster than my bear, but I should have known better. I kept pace without even breathing hard. My breath sounded like a steam engine, my heart like a pile driver. Mr. Kelly must have been holding back at first, probably to assess how I was doing, because he suddenly kicked it into another gear and tore up the mountain. I grunted and poured on the speed. It felt like I could run like this for hours, maybe even days.

The connection I had made to the magic in the world remained. It swirled around me in rivers of energy and light. It flowed from the trees, the ground, the very air itself. I started to understand that my energy and the magic surrounding me existed in a kind of symbiotic state. The magic fed me and I, by using the magic, gave it purpose. I know that sounds ridiculous, but the magic seemed to be its own thing, a sentient being that derived pleasure and purpose from my utilization of the power it provided.

It's an out-there kind of thought, but I was pretty sure I was on to something.

Eternal wisdom, maybe?

Ha!

Who was I kidding? I had been a shape-shifter for one whole day, and already I thought I had some kind of esoteric understanding of existence—what a nerd.

Elyse helped break me out of my deep thoughts by starting a silly game of tag. She crisscrossed in front of me, almost causing me to stumble or crash into her, but always putting on a burst of speed at the last moment and avoiding a collision. As she moved to make another pass, I changed direction, sure she would miss, but instead of running in front of me, Elyse leapt over me, tagging my back with her paws as she sailed over.

Elyse let out a series of chuffs, very proud of herself. I grunted back, she was a goofball, and I loved it. As we gained elevation, the trees grew more numerous and their size doubled, then tripled. The cooler air must be better for their growth. All the large trees gave me an idea. Elyse was setting up for another pass at me and I would need to time this just right. She switched her direction, cutting in on a path that would was going to lead her straight toward me. She was going to try for another jumping tag —perfect! As Elyse made her leap, I made my own, soaring over her back. I landed on the side of a nearby tree, my claws digging in to keep from falling back to the ground. Elyse spun around in mid-air when she realized I wasn't under her. She landed in a skid, whipping her head around looking for where I had gone. I made a noise that wasn't quite a roar or a growl. It was more of a stuttering, clicking chuff. I like to think it was laughter.

When Elyse looked up and spotted me, I jumped to another tree, still making my new bear laugh sound. I jumped from tree to tree with more agility I thought my bear form could muster. I clicked at Elyse, hoping she got the game. She needed to try catching me. Cats, even big cats, can climb trees, so I was sure she would give chase. Instead, when I looked around, I found Elyse following me slowly from ground level.

Mr. and Mrs. Kelly emerged from the trees ahead and watched our progress. I jumped to a few other trees before I realized something was up. Elyse and her parents were standing close together, watching me.

Not again.

I don't know what I was doing, but from the vibe I was getting from the Kellys, I had done something I shouldn't have. I jumped to the ground and landed on two feet.

Two feet?

I looked down. Holy shape-shifter, Batman. I was in beast form. Two legs, two arms, and lots of fur and claws. I looked up as all three Kellys shifted back into human form. Without even giving it a second thought, I immediately followed their lead.

"How did you do that?" Elyse said, awestruck.

"I don't know. I didn't even know I had changed, morphed, shifted, whatever. I was just playing around . . . you know, Tarzan Bear."

"Orson, the hybrid form is very advanced." Mrs. Kelly said carefully. I could see concern in her eyes.

"It's also a form that takes a long time to master," added Mr. Kelly. "It also has only one purpose—battle."

"I didn't know. I'm sorry." I kept doing things that totally freaked them out. I didn't know how much more they could take before they decided I was a lost cause.

"It's not your fault," Elyse tried to reassure me.

"I also noticed you had no trouble shifting back to human form just now," Mr. Kelly said. "Impressive."

"I wasn't thinking about it. I just did it. You know how that goes?" I smiled, trying my best to convey that even though I was apparently the weirdest shape-shifter they had ever encountered, I was also just me, Orson.

"I think it's time to get back to the cabin." Mr. Kelly glanced at his wife, and she nodded. "Orson, why don't you shift first, just in case you need some extra time or help."

I nodded. I knew it wasn't about extra time or help, Mr. Kelly was worried again. Not only was I impervious to magic and other normal control measures, I could shift into beast form. Even I knew that was bad. In movies and comic books, it was the stronger, meaner, nastier form, only used in times of extreme necessity, because it was usually harder to hold onto your humanity. It was a berserker form, a killing machine. And I had used it to play tree tag with Elyse.

I would worry later. Right now, they were waiting on me to shift. It seemed so simple now that I had a better understanding of the magic. It was really as normal as walking. I shifted into bear form, quickly and fluidly. Mr. and Mrs. Kelly gave each other one of their looks. Elyse shifted and padded over to stand by me.

That's when the forest exploded.

CHAPTER FIFTEEN

It wasn't an explosion in the normal sense. There was no giant fireball. It was more of a concussive wave. Tree limbs shattered like wooden grenades, sending pine-scented shrapnel in all directions. And I was hit with what felt like a speeding invisible semi-truck. Even in my gigantic bear form, I was lifted off my feet and tossed through the air like a cartwheeling piñata. I sailed end over end until a rather large tree got in the way.

Ugh.

I may be a huge badass mega-bear, but I'm not going to lie. It was painful. My massive body snapped the top of the tree off, leaving a ten-foot stump in its wake. I thudded to a ground-shaking stop about a hundred feet from where I had been standing. I stood and shook myself out. Nothing broken, just a couple of sore spots.

Elyse.

I focused on the rivers of energy flowing around me, and relying solely on instinct, I tapped into one. It allowed my senses to flow out around me, expanding what was visible to me through my natural senses. I found Elyse, she lay crumpled in the opposite direction. She was breathing heavily and unconscious. I moved toward her, keeping my crazy, magical spidey-sense thing up, searching for Mr. and Mrs. Kelly.

I found Mr. Kelly first. He was dragging himself forward, one of his legs seriously broken—I'm talking bone popping through skin, leg twisted into an unnatural geometric shape kind of broken. He was dragging himself toward Mrs. Kelly, who looked dazed but seemed to be physically okay. She was shakily getting to her feet.

What the hell had hit us?

Now that I knew the Kellys were safe, or at least not dead, I cast around, searching for the source of the attack. Attack? That's all it could be. There was no other explanation that made sense. Somebody had hit us with a very powerful magic missile.

There. Three people, two women, one man, dressed in black hoodies—how original. The hoods were up and I couldn't make out faces. But my new magical sight gave me loads of information. An oily black and red mist surrounded all three. Nothing the natural eye could detect, but it was there. It coiled around them, pulsating in and out of their mouths and eyes.

Blood-mages.

I don't know how I knew it; I just knew it. But why were they here? Had they been hunting us? It seemed ridiculous to think the three of them had just been out for stroll through the forest at the exact moment that the Kellys and I decided to go for a run.

No. They were hunting us.

Which led to the next question. How did they know we'd be here?

"Orson." It was Mrs. Kelly whispering my name. Have I mentioned how totally cool super-hearing was?

Mrs. Kelly whispered again, "Orson."

I turned my head slightly so that I could see her, but still keep the blood- mages in my peripheral vision. I was close enough now that we could make eye-contact. I nodded my giant bear head.

"Richard's hurt, the kinetic spell was a direct hit. I'll need to carry him. You must get Elyse, but you will have to slow them down first. Do you understand?"

So, the blood-mages had targeted their spell on Mr. Kelly, probably assuming he was the biggest threat to them.

They were so wrong.

And they would pay for their mistake.

I blinked an okay at Mrs. Kelly and turned my attention to our three attackers. They had been moving steadily toward the Kellys and were now only about thirty yards downhill. The nasty black-red stuff was swirling faster around them. It looked like they were powering up for another attack.

I roared.

The blood-mages froze.

Every other creature in the forest fell silent. The only noise was the soft rustle of the wind through the upper boughs of the pine trees.

Rage filled me.

Time to unleash hell.

Yes! My inner voice shouted with glee.

I moved like lightning. I could imagine how terrifying I looked, a bear the size of a Volkswagen, speeding forward in a blur. The blood-mages didn't even have time to spread out before I slammed into them. My jaws clamped down on the first one I reached, one of the women. My teeth sank deep into her shoulder and upper arm. The other two were knocked to the ground as I smashed through the group. I didn't slow down. I had the blood-mage locked between my teeth and I carried her like a ragdoll about fifty feet beyond her fallen comrades.

It seemed far enough. I skidded to halt in a puff of dirt and pine needles. I turned to make sure the other two blood-mages were watching. The mage hanging from my mouth was screaming in pain and fear. She punched at my head, flailing her arms in a useless attempt to get free. My eyes locked on the other two attackers. I positioned the woman in front of me, violently shaking her when she wouldn't comply. Then, using my front paws as leverage, I pulled my head back and methodically ripped her in half.

Blood and gore showered down on the green and brown of the forest. It was violent and disgusting, and I didn't care. In fact, I received pleasure from it. I knew it was a non-human, monstrous response, but I couldn't help myself. These people had attacked Elyse, her parents, and me—death was the only answer.

Then something happened that I wasn't expecting at all. Apparently, blood-mages can store power within their bodies, some kind of evil back-up battery system. Because, as the woman came apart, this stored power popped like a burst water balloon. I could feel it hit me like a spray and sizzle where it landed on my fur. But instead of just dissipating, the extra power was absorbed by my body and it was a rush.

I felt supercharged. The power surged through me, ramping up my rage and the desire to destroy the people who had dared attack us.

I am Ollphiest. There is none who can stand against me.

Geez, corny much?

But that inner voice had a point. The other two blood-mages needed to be dead.

Now.

With the blood of their friend dripping from my jaws and fur, I charged. They stood their ground—impressive. Stupid, but impressive.

The second female mage let loose with some kind of magic whammy with enough power to force me to a stop. The more I pushed forward, the more an invisible force pushed back. My cool new magical sight revealed the same black and red oily mist that surrounded the mages was now enveloping me. I also realized I could taste the magic infusing the spell, and I gagged a little, because it was like rancid meat and vomit.

Gross.

The spell slithered over my body trying to penetrate my thick hide. No such luck. I shook myself, breaking up the mist and the spell's hold on me. Head down, teeth bared, I stalked toward the blood-mage. I was close enough now that I could see the panic in her eyes. She let loose with the same exact whammy, but knowing now what it looked like and tasted like, I was able to push through it quickly. Awesome. It seemed I could adapt to magical attacks on the fly. Nice to know.

The third blood-mage stepped in to help his companion. Good. It would save me the trouble of hunting him down. Unfortunately, he had also been watching the fight and adapting his fighting style also. He didn't waste his time on another direct attack on me. Instead, he fired some really nasty-looking green fiery stuff at the Kellys.

Mrs. Kelly had Mr. Kelly slung over her shoulder in a fire-man's carry and was moving quickly away from the battle, but that green stuff had a range on it and hit her in the legs. Mrs. Kelly cried out in pain and toppled over, spilling Mr. Kelly to the ground.

I roared, and the forest shook.

Yeah, that got their attention.

I rushed to put myself between the blood-mages and the Kellys. If they were going to attack again, it would have to be through me.

It was time for these two losers to learn exactly whom they were dealing with.

Hey! Time to wakey wakey! I yelled at the big bad nasty that lived inside of me now.

Yes?

Beast form, now.

All you had to do was ask.

I shifted from giant-killer-bear to taloned-nightmare-beast. Part man, part bear, all monster.

The fear emanating from the blood-mages was intoxicating. I threw my head back and roared again, because it was quickly becoming my favorite scare-the-bad-guys bear move. But the sound that came out wasn't a roar, and it shocked even me. Instead of the deep, rumbling, make-them-poop-their-pants roar I had intended, I emitted a higher-pitched wailing shriek. Both blood-mages dropped to their knees, hands covering their ears, pain etched across their faces.

My beast form roar—or shriek really—was a weapon, and not just a single target weapon. Nope, it was the equivalent of a SWAT team's flash-bang grenade. An AOE blast, as we gamers liked to call it.

The two magic assassins writhing on the ground in front of me were in so much trouble.

When I finished shrieking, the blood-mages didn't waste any time. I didn't see them saying anything or signal each other—some kind of telepathy maybe—but as one they attacked. The female mage decided to go with the "nuke the site from orbit" philosophy and set the forest on fire. And not just a couple of trees, she unleashed an inferno. Walls of fire sprang up around me. The male mage, not to be outdone, used the same kinetic spell from their initial attack, only he was targeting the nearby trees. I was suddenly in the middle of an active minefield. The trees exploded, again sending spiked wooden shrapnel everywhere. The shrapnel had no effect on my thick hide, but the concussive waves from the multiple explosions slowed my progress. I was getting battered from every side. It was only making me angrier, but smoke and heat from the fire was playing havoc with my senses. I leapt in the direction I was sure the blood-mages were attacking from. Nope. Just more smoke and exploding trees. I let loose with another shriek, hoping to disrupt their spell-casting, but that didn't work either. They must be retreating and laying down mayhem to cover their tracks, but which direction?

"Orson!" It was Mrs. Kelly again, her voice coming from somewhere in the smoke to my left. "Get Elyse and run. The fire is out of control."

Never.

I don't run.

I rip. I eviscerate. I kill.

Elyse.

No.

Yes.

I struggled with the blind rage that consumed me. It was hard, but I concentrated on Elyse, her eyes, her laugh, and her strength. I thought about the way she made me feel. Complete was the best way to describe it. I beat the rage into submission, locking it away. I spun in circles, searching for Elyse, but the smoke was too thick. I couldn't see her or smell her.

Elyse. I closed my eyes and reached out through the rivers of energy. There she was, behind me and to the right. She was still unconscious and the fire was almost on her. Eyes closed tight, I jumped through the smoke, trusting the magic to lead me to her.

I found her in moments. The fire raged all around us. A nearby tree exploded, signaling that the blood-mages were still flinging mojo. It was definitely time to leave. I scooped

Elyse's cat body up, placed her around my shoulders, and ran.

I let my magic sense spread out wide around me. The blood-mages weren't giving chase, so that was good. But the fire was now a bona fide Southern California wildfire, and it was racing in all directions. I needed to get us off this mountain. I was already running faster than any animal in the world, but I dug down deep and sped up just a bit more. My senses caught a tingle of Mr. and Mrs. Kelly. They weren't that far ahead of us. I focused on their location and kept running.

I was relieved when I finally cleared the smoke. It seemed the fire was heading in a more northerly direction, and the Kellys and their cabin were to the south. We were going to make it. With nothing dangerous currently threatening to kill me, my mind started to organize everything that had just happened. The blood-mages had been looking for the Kellys and me. It was that simple. Or they had been lying in wait, which made more sense, because even though I wasn't certain, it was pretty good bet blood-mages didn't have the ability to keep up with four full-grown shifters running at top speed.

So, the question was: how did they find us? Was it the shark-nurse? She had tracked me down at my house, but of course that wasn't super-hard when she had access to my medical record. Plus, she wasn't one of the three who had attacked us, and she hadn't seemed like the type to call up the local blood-mage union and turn me in. No, she was a greedy little shark-nurse who wanted me all to herself. So where did that leave us?

Tommy.

That rat-bastard, two-faced . . .

There was nobody else who knew where we would be. Nobody else who could have turned us in. It had to be him.

Tommy didn't know it yet, but he was in for a world of pain. He was going to—

Ow!

Elyse was awake and clawing at my chest. I tried to lift her off my shoulders, but she was in too much of a frenzy and her claws were sharp, so I dumped her off my back. She landed in an attack crouch and hissed at me. She was adorable. I lifted my wicked beast-form claws in what I hoped was an 'aw shucks' gesture and attempted a chuff, but I quickly discovered beast form vocalizations all sounded like some kind of death threat.

Elyse stopped hissing. That was a promising sign, her initial shock and confusion seemed to be clearing. She sniffed the air and sneezed once. I couldn't blame her, because the forest fire smell was very overpowering. She must have been satisfied that it was me, because she shifted.

Oh boy, naked girlfriend time. Okay, I can handle this. I just faced down three blood-mages. I shifted. We stood there for a moment, naked, silent, and then she ran into my arms.

Whoa.

A naked girlfriend hug was not fair at all.

"What happened?" Elyse asked, thankfully stepping back so that our bodies were no longer mashed together.

"Blood-mages. Three of them."

"Mom and Dad?" Her lip trembled.

"Oh, they're fine, they're good. Well, your dad's leg is kind of messed up, but I'm pretty sure it's nothing he can't handle. They're just ahead of us."

"You were in beast form again?"

"Um, yeah. Like I said, three blood-mages and ... you know," I pointed behind me. "A forest fire. Beast form seemed like the prudent choice."

"You are amazing, Orson Reid." She stood on her toes and gave me a quick kiss.

Every ounce of control I had at my disposal was currently being used to keep my stupid man body in check.

Elyse turned in a circle. "The fire is totally messing with my sense of smell. Which direction do you think the cabin is in?"

"Yeah, smelling our way is out of the question. I'm using my cool new spidey-sense magic river thing to guide us," I said proudly.

"Your what?" Elyse looked confused.

"You know? I'm dipping into the rivers of energy, the surrounding magic, to pinpoint your mom and dad."

Elyse raised both eyebrows.

I knew that look.

"Let me guess. That's not a regular everyday shifter ability, is it?" I asked, letting out a huge sigh and shaking my head. I couldn't win. Every time I turned around, I displayed another thing that marked me as different. That marked me as the Ollphiest.

Wonderful.

"Nope. We can see the magic spectrum, things like auras, but nothing like you're describing. Like I said, Reid, you're amazing," Elyse said, as she re-mashed her naked perfection against me and gave me a kiss that in no way can be described as a peck. She then gave my butt a smack, adding, "And you're all mine. Now which direction is the cabin?"

I pointed. Elyse shifted and ran in that direction. When I could finally breathe again, I shifted into bear form and ran after her.

CHAPTER SIXTEEN

As the cabin came into view, we could see Mr. Kelly standing on the patio deck scanning the tree line for us. He waved when he spotted us.

"Quick. Katie's grabbing our stuff and packing the car. We need to leave now," Mr. Kelly said, tossing us our clothes as we shifted back to human form. He was looking pretty good for a guy who had a mangled leg not too long ago. All that was left of his injury was a nasty bruise. His entire lower leg, below his knee, was a dark angry purple, but other than that, his bones seemed to be back where they belonged and the leg was holding his weight. He had a slight limp, but I guessed that by tomorrow he wouldn't even be limping anymore. Accelerated healing. You had to love it.

Mr. Kelly locked up behind us as we headed through the cabin and out the front door. Mrs. Kelly was just shutting the rear door of the Range Rover. She gave her daughter a hug and my hand a quick squeeze.

"Everybody in. The police just rolled by and this entire side of the mountain is being evacuated," Mrs. Kelly told us.

"What about the blood-mages?" I asked, concerned about another attack.

"Sweetie, I think you scared the living hell out of those blood-mages."

Elyse and I shared a look. Mrs. Kelly was not a fan of cursing, so she must really be freaked out.

"Mom, such salty language," Elyse said.

"Yes, dear. Get in the car, please," Mrs. Kelly said, all business.

Mrs. Kelly slid behind the wheel, another sure sign that Mr. Kelly's leg was still healing.

"How's your leg, Dad? Orson said it looked horrible," Elyse asked.

Mr. Kelly turned in his seat so he could face us. "I've had worse. Orson, I need to thank you for protecting my family."

"Always . . . I mean you guys are—you know . . . like family to me," I said, trying to convey how much they meant to me.

Mr. Kelly was quiet for a moment, his eyes searching mine. He gave me a nod, a grunt, and turned back to watch our progress through the windshield.

Elyse squeezed my knee.

Mrs. Kelly made excellent time—with shifter reflexes speeding was no problem—that is, until we hit the main road leading down the mountain. A single line of cars snaked down the street, disappearing behind a curve in the mountainside. The fire had become a full-blown disaster. Mr. Kelly switched on the radio. The announcer confirmed that mandatory evacuations had been ordered, and fire officials were very suspicious because of the explosive intensity of the blaze. The fire department captain being interviewed confirmed that, in her experience, some sort of accelerant must have been used.

I huffed. "Yeah, a psycho blood-mage accelerant. I can't

believe they would burn down an entire forest just to get at us."

"It makes no sense. How did they even find us?" Elyse said.

Mr. and Mrs. Kelly remained silent, but the tension in the car spiked. Elyse frowned at me and leaned forward in her seat.

"Dad? What's up?"

"We'll talk about it when we get off the mountain. Let your mom concentrate on her driving," Mr. Kelly said.

"It had to be Tommy," I said, my anger clear.

Boom.

It was as if I'd dropped a bomb.

Mrs. Kelly's hands tightened on the steering wheel. Mr. Kelly stiffened in his seat. Oh yeah, a direct hit.

"Uncle Tommy? Orson, there's no way—" Elyse began.

"I said *no* talking," Mr. Kelly snapped.

"Dad?" Elyse said, surprised by his outburst, but Mr. Kelly had gone silent, his jaw throbbing from how hard he was clenching it. "Mom?" Mrs. Kelly glanced at her daughter in the rearview mirror.

I rested my hand on Elyse's shoulder and shook my head quickly. Elyse waited a moment longer to see if her parents would respond—nothing. She slid back against the back of the seat and leaned against me. I put my arm around her and she sighed.

The drive down the mountain became a two hour marathon. Two hours of tense silence, only broken when Mr. Kelly called Elyse's sister Jenny to let her know we were all right. He also told her to take Kevin, leave the house, and check into a hotel, and he would contact her later. Jenny didn't ask questions or argue. She just immediately agreed, and knowing all of us could hear her side of the conversation, she told us to be safe. The realization of what life must be like, day to day, as member of the Paragon Society was becoming clear to me. On a moment's notice the world could flip upside down and how you reacted was very important. I was so thankful that I had Elyse and the Kellys on my side to help guide me through the crazy.

Mrs. Kelly exited the highway as soon as she could and pulled into the drive-thru of an In-N-Out Burger. We ordered enough food for ten people and then parked in the lot of a huge Mega-market, as far from any other cars as we could get.

We still didn't speak. The four of us were starving. The run up the mountain and the fight with the blood-mages had exhausted us and we were all a little cranky. Mr. Kelly passed out the food and we all chowed down in silence.

I was working my way through my third Double-Double when Mr. Kelly broke the silence with a long, chunky burp.

"Richard!" Mrs. Kelly admonished.

Elyse and I burst out laughing. Luckily for me, I had just swallowed a large mouth full of burger. Elyse wasn't so lucky. She had been taking a swig of Dr. Pepper, which shot out of her nose as she snorted at her dad.

"Ugh, gross," Elyse, sputtered.

This only made me laugh harder, which got Mr. Kelly laughing and even Mrs. Kelly was trying hard to stifle a chuckle.

"Ha-ha, you're all hilarious." Elyse was not amused.

The tension was broken and everyone relaxed, enjoying the last of the fast-food feast.

"So, those were blood-mages, huh? Bunch of pussies if you ask me," I said lightly.

This got Mr. Kelly laughing again.

Elyse slapped my knee, "Orson," she hissed, nodding toward her mom.

"That's okay, sweetie. I have to agree with Orson. They were kind of pussies," Mrs. Kelly said.

"Mom!" Elyse said, shocked.

Mr. Kelly and I both started laughing again and couldn't stop. Mrs. Kelly smiled, proud of her ability to crack everyone up. Elyse just shook her head and threw a French fry at me.

After the laughter died down, Mr. Kelly gathered up the garbage and tossed it in a nearby can. When he got back in, he sat sideways in his seat. Mrs. Kelly also turned around.

"Let's start at the beginning," Mr. Kelly said.

"The initial attack was, what, a kinetic spell?" Elyse asked.

"Yes," Mrs. Kelly answered. "And I believe it was meant to kill all of us at once. I think the blood-mages gauged the distance incorrectly. That was the only thing that saved our lives."

"Why was I the only one knocked unconscious?" Elyse said.

"Dumb luck. You went head-first into an outcropping of rock," Mrs. Kelly said, her voice thick with emotion. "I thought you might have broken your neck." Elyse patted her mom's arm.

"Orson, you seemed to recover fast. Did the spell even slow you down?" Mr. Kelly asked.

"Yeah, I got tossed through a tree, but no real damage was done."

"So, then your . . . charge at the blood-mages . . ."

"Wait," Elyse interrupted. "You charged three blood-mages? Are you crazy?"

"I was kind of pissed at that particular moment. It seemed like attacking was the best thing."

"Blood-mages are super-dangerous. They could have killed you," Elyse scolded me.

"That's the thing. They *did* try to kill you. That second spell they attacked you with, I've seen it used before and it's instant death," Mr. Kelly said.

All of my super-senses were tingling. Mr. Kelly was trying real hard to cover up the fact he was wigging out. "What?" I asked, *instant death* ringing in my ears.

"What?" Elyse echoed.

"It's a nasty and rare bit of blood-magic," Mrs. Kelly added.

"You mean, it's like a real life 'avada kedavra'?" I was stunned. On one level, I had accepted magic was real, but on another level I never imagined a straight-up killing curse. And if Mr. Kelly had seen the death spell used before, that meant he had been in some 'Thunderdome' kind of fights.

"I don't know what that means. Is that even English?" Mr. Kelly asked, confused.

"Yes, Orson," Mrs. Kelly answered for her husband. "It's exactly that, an instant spell to murder people."

"Oh," I muttered.

Mr. Kelly wouldn't be deterred. "Orson, my question is . . . how come you're not dead?"

"Dad!"

"Damn it, Elyse, the question has to be asked. He was targeted and hit with death magic—*death magic*—and all it did was slow him down momentarily. Please, Orson, help us understand."

I realized something at that moment. Mr. Kelly was afraid. The idea that I might be the Ollphiest had intrigued him when it had just been a theory, an abstract idea. But now he was facing mounting irrefutable evidence that I was the monster that his people feared. And, unfortunately, there was nothing that I could do to help calm those fears, because I was exactly what he thought I was. My only course of action was the complete truth.

I took a deep breath. *Here goes nothing.* "It's because I *am* the Ollphiest."

Mr. Kelly's eyes went wide. I think he was surprised at my

honesty and maybe he had been holding out hope for another possible answer, one that didn't involve his daughter being in love with the boogeyman. Mrs. Kelly let out a small gasp. Wow, being faced with the reality of the Ollphiest really freaked them out.

Elyse was the one to speak first. "So what? Hadn't we already figured out Orson was special?"

"I think the actual reality of it is a bit unsettling," I said.

"Yes. Yes, it is." Mr. Kelly let out a big sigh and ran his fingers through his hair.

"Orson, there was a kind of ripple in the magic spectrum when you dispatched the blood-mage. Do you have any idea what that was?" Mrs. Kelly asked, giving me a reassuring mom smile.

Complete honesty.

Right.

"Yeah, she had some stored-up magic, like a reserve." I looked to Elyse for confirmation. She nodded.

"That's right. All mages can store some magical energy internally."

All mages? How many kinds where there? There was so much I didn't know about this world. I was in serious need of a 'Magic History and You 101' YouTube video series or something. "Well, her magic reserves sort of popped when she died and I . . ." Oh boy, this would not be information they would be happy to hear. "I kind of absorbed it."

Elyse gave a low whistle.

"Oh, I see. Thank you for explaining," Mrs. Kelly said, looking at Mr. Kelly, eyes full of concern.

"All right. It's time for a recap of everything we know," Mr. Kelly announced. "Orson, please let me know if I've missed anything," I nodded. "You are impervious to the following items—silver, powerful rune magic, mundane weapons like guns, bullets, and knives. Also, having just learned how to shift into your animal form, you have also gained the ability to shift into battle form or beast form, if you prefer. And to top it all off, death magic is only a nuisance to you *and* you can absorb the magic of your fallen enemies. Did I miss anything?"

"Um, well, there is one more thing," I hesitated, but Mr. and Mrs. Kelly were on my side and they needed to know everything.

"You're kidding me?" Mr. Kelly sounded exasperated.

"Dad, be nice," said Elyse.

"I'm sorry. Orson?"

"I can tap into the magical . . . I guess the best word is spectrum," I said quickly.

"That's something we can all do," Mrs. Kelly assured me, letting out a sigh of relief.

"That's not what Orson means," Elyse tried to help.

Mr. Kelly rubbed his face. "What exactly is it that you can do?"

"Not only can I can sense the energy, the surrounding magic. I can also tap into it and . . . do stuff. For instance, earlier, I was able to locate Elyse through the fire, even though I couldn't see her or sense her in any normal way. I could see her through the magic."

Mr. Kelly made a face. "I now see why the legends surrounding your kind are filled with blood and horror."

My kind? I thought we were all shape-shifters.

No.

We are Ollphiest.

All others kneel before us.

Not you again. Please shut up.

Elyse, my fierce protector, came to my defense. "What do you mean 'his' kind? He's a shape-shifter, like us. He's just got some extra abilities. Who cares?"

"Everyone," Mr. Kelly breathed. "Everyone will care.

Orson is a threat to the balance of power. He changes everything."

It was all becoming very clear. I was something that nobody had counted on. The Paragon Society ruled the magic world, they had the most powerful shifters, mages, and other magical beings on their side. Their rule was absolute. Until now. My very existence would threaten that rule.

"Is that why Tommy sent the blood-mages?" I asked.

Mr. Kelly's eyes snapped to mine. "We don't know if that's what happened."

"Orson, Uncle Tommy hates blood-mages. There's no way he sent them," Elyse said, pulling on my hand trying to get me to look at her and stop the staring contest with her dad.

Not this time. I would not look away again. Mr. Kelly needed to understand I would not turn a blind eye to the obvious fact that Tommy had tried to kill us.

"I'm on your side, son."

"At the moment, it doesn't really feel like it."

Mrs. Kelly slammed her hand down on the horn. The piercing sound shattered the quiet of the car. Elyse jumped in her seat, and both Mr. Kelly and I looked toward Mrs. Kelly at the same moment. Crisis averted—for now.

"Knock it off, both of you," Mrs. Kelly said, taking charge. "Orson, we will do everything in our power to help you. I promise." I nodded in acceptance. "But you have to remember we've been around a long time and we know how to play the game. Okay?" Then she turned to face her husband, reaching out to stroke the side of his head. "And you need to keep an open mind. I've known Tommy as long as you have, but if it wasn't him who betrayed us, it was someone close to him. Someone in his inner circle, and that's just as dangerous."

Mr. Kelly placed his hand over his wife's and turned his head so he could kiss her fingers. "You're right, as always."

"Is everybody finished?" Elyse asked. "Do you think maybe we could leave this lovely parking lot now and go home? I seriously need a shower."

"Of course, sweetie," Mrs. Kelly said, starting the car and heading back toward the highway.

CHAPTER SEVENTEEN

I had a lot to process. I was something that nobody alive had ever encountered. And that was saying something, because apparently Society members were all very long-lived. Just the possibility of me being the Ollphiest was threatening enough that someone had ordered up a blood-mage death squad to take me out. I could only imagine how everyone would react when their worst fears were confirmed.

When we were back in Pasadena and off the freeway, Mr. Kelly turned in his seat again to talk.

"Orson, I think you should stay with us for the rest of the weekend. Your aunt isn't expecting you back for another two days, and we can continue to brainstorm ideas. What do you think?"

"That'd be great. Thanks." The mention of Aunt Tina reminded me I should have sent her a text hours ago. "I forgot to text her earlier today. Let me check in with her real quick." I pulled out my phone and sent her a quick message. She didn't immediately respond, but that wasn't weird. She was probably in the middle of doing something. Hopefully, she was out on a date. I was always telling her she should go out more.

Mr. Kelly said, "Also, we'll need to think more long-range. You may have to get out of L.A. for a while."

Mr. Kelly told Elyse, who bristled at that idea, "Elyse, he's hot as hot can be right now. The blood-mage attack proves that there are those who want Orson eliminated, no questions asked. On top of that, the Society itself will demand an official investigation and want immediate action taken to ensure the status quo. Things are going to move quickly. We need to prepare ourselves and stay ahead of any knee-jerk reactions."

"Where would I go, and what about Aunt Tina?" I asked.

"I'm thinking the compound that Katie and I used to run up north. It's remote and easily defended. As to your aunt, I'm still thinking about that," Mr. Kelly said.

"The compound?" Elyse sounded surprised. "Is that possible? Would the council allow it?"

"I know it seems surprising to you, but your old dad still has a lot pull with the council," Mr. Kelly teased her.

Elyse stuck her tongue out, and he winked back at her. I was glad the Kellys thought so highly of the compound, but to me it sounded like a prison and I was about to be sentenced to an indeterminate sentence with my only crime —being born.

Mrs. Kelly navigated through the winding streets to their house, but she rolled to a stop at the bottom of their driveway. I looked up from checking my email and saw the problem. We had a welcoming party waiting for us.

"What is going on here?" Mrs. Kelly asked.

"Maybe you should just keep driving," said Mr. Kelly

That sounded like a great idea, but just as soon as he made that suggestion, two cars raced up, blocking the street in both directions. We were trapped.

I growled.

"Orson, please try to stay calm," Mr. Kelly said, pulling out his cell phone. He pressed a number on his speed dial. Thanks to super-shifter hearing, everyone in the car could listen to both sides of the conversation.

"Hello, Richard." It was Tommy, his voice as clear as if he was sitting in the car with us.

"Hi Thomas, is there a reason why you have a small army standing in my driveway?" Mr. Kelly asked.

"You took the boy up to the cabin, and now the mountain is on fire. Richard, if the boy is being hunted by blood-mages, that changes the situation. We think it prudent the boy—"

"His name is Orson," Mr. Kelly cut Tommy off.

"Fine. We think it's prudent that Orson be taken into protective custody." Tommy must have put his hand over the phone, because his next words were unintelligible, but the two cars boxing us in backed up. They were still close enough to cause trouble, but it was obvious Tommy was trying to get us to trust him.

Fat chance, dickhead.

Mr. Kelly hung up on Tommy and spoke in low tones, wary of all the shifter ears around. "I think we need to see how this plays out."

"Dad! No way."

"It's either get out and try to talk this through, or a car chase through the streets of Pasadena. I vote for the more sane option." And then Mr. Kelly earned a ton of points in my book when he added, "But I'll leave the decision to you, Orson."

I so didn't want to get out of the car. I respected the Kellys, but they were too trusting of Tommy, the Shifter Council, and the Society. They were basing all of their decisions on past experience and they probably truly believed that we had a chance of talking through this and cooler heads prevailing. I, on the other hand, knew that this would only end one way—in blood. Maybe it was another Ollphiest ability, but I could almost smell the carnage to come.

Bring it.

Hey, no comments from the corporeal challenged.

You waste time debating.

Yeah, it's called logical reasoning.

We must . . .

I said 'no comments,' so shut up.

"Although a *Fast and Furious* style car chase sounds cool and all, I think we should go with your gut feeling," I said.

Mrs. Kelly relaxed, probably happy that she would not have to engage in a car chase. Elyse sighed and snuggled a little closer.

"Good." Mr. Kelly looked relieved, and I felt bad that I was about to crap all over his good mood.

"But there is one thing that isn't up for debate." I locked eyes with Mr. Kelly, willing him to see my resolve. "I will *not* be taken into custody by Tommy or *anyone* else."

A quiet stillness settled over the inside of the car. Mr. Kelly and I stared at each other for a moment. I opened up my magical sight and Mr. Kelly's energy pulsed a bright blue. I would need to figure out what all the stupid colors meant, because his just being blue wasn't helpful.

Mr. Kelly reached out and grasped my knee. "I understand. And if it comes to that, I'll stand with you."

"We all will," said Mrs. Kelly.

"Damn straight," Elyse added.

"Elyse."

"Sorry, Mom."

Mr. Kelly called Tommy back. "We're coming up, but nothing happens until we talk. Understand."

"Sure."

"I'm serious, Thomas. This is a tense situation and

everyone needs to relax. We don't want an incident. My neighbors are nice people, but they will not hesitate in calling the police."

"I got it."

Mrs. Kelly slowly drove the Range Rover up the driveway to the front of the house. I counted a total of seven people standing in the Kellys' driveway and front yard. Tommy, his son Kyle, and five other henchmen types. I reached out through the magical spectrum and four of the henchmen— well, two henchmen and two henchwomen—were shifters. That was to be expected, they were probably all members of the local Shifter Council. The fifth person was a surprise. She didn't emit the telltale red-black oily energy of a blood-mage, but she was definitely some kind of spell-slinger. Her aura was like a mini-sun, bright and churning with power. I knew there were other kinds of mages, the Kellys had alluded to as much, but I had yet to encounter one. I think that was about to change. Lucky me.

I pointed to the small group. "Those four are shifters," Mr. Kelly nodded. "The last one, the woman in leather, she's a mage right? But not a blood-mage?"

"Correct. She's a battle-mage, and she's bad news," Mr. Kelly answered, exasperated. "Thomas, what were you thinking?"

Tommy heard this and stiffened at the mention of his name. He glanced at the battle-mage and then turned his attention to Mr. Kelly, stone-faced and unapologetic.

Mrs. Kelly moved to turn off the car, hesitated, and then left it running. Good choice. A faster getaway, but somehow I didn't think we'd be leaving in the Range Rover. The four of us sat in silence for a moment.

"Okay, everybody get out on the passenger side and stay close together," Mr. Kelly said, feeling no need to whisper when everybody could hear us anyway.

We piled out the passenger side doors. Mr. Kelly and I stood in between Mrs. Kelly and Elyse. I stretched my sight out further, checking for any surprises. There was nobody hiding in or behind the house. The only other shifters were the two guys waiting in the cars down on the street.

I scanned the seven people spread out before us. I sensed no conventional weapons. Of course, each of them individually was more deadly than a truck full of bazookas. I paid particular attention to the battle-mage. She was medium height, short black hair, and dark piercing eyes. She was dressed in head-to-toe black leather, maybe she was a fan of the Underworld movies. The energy coming off her was intense. It was gold with purple streaks, and it swirled around her like a tornado. The mage's eyes narrowed, a frown forming on her face.

"I thought I was the only mage you called," the battle-mage said to Tommy.

"Yes, that's right, but that's not important right now," Tommy hissed.

"Something's wrong. There is magic here I can't account for," the mage persisted.

"Richard?" Tommy asked.

Mr. Kelly spread his hands wide. "Nobody here but us."

"I'm telling you, something's wrong." The mage reached behind her and pulled two really long, nasty-looking daggers from sheaths that must have been secured to her back. I couldn't help it, the gamer in me was in nerd heaven. The blades were double-edged and had runes etched in the steel. The handles were some kind of polished wood and fit the mage's hands as if crafted specifically for her. Oh, and they also glowed with an eerie light in the magic spectrum. They were wicked-cool. Unfortunately, they were pointed in my direction.

"Lucy, stop being ridiculous and put those away," Tommy demanded.

"No, I don't think I will." The mage, Lucy, had her dark eyes locked on me. "There's something odd with this one."

"So this is how it is, huh, Thomas?" Mr. Kelly said to Tommy, but never taking his eyes off Lucy. "You show up with a Society battle-mage and let her start making threats."

Lucy's eyes flicked from me to Mr. Kelly. "Nobody *lets* me do anything. I decide when and if I need to take action. And I'm telling you, there is something off here."

Things were spinning out of control fast. I was trying to watch everyone at the same time. Tommy, Kyle, and Lucy the angry battle-mage were standing toe-to-toe with us. The two shifter henchwomen and one of the shifter henchmen took up positions behind Tommy, spreading out in a menacing manner. The fourth shifter crony was creeping around to the left of where we were standing. We looked like two rival gangs ready for an old-fashioned rumble.

I didn't know how Mr. Kelly was going to talk us out of this one. Lucy, in particular, looked like she wanted to bash skulls, starting with mine. I was shocked when it was Tommy who tried to diffuse the situation.

"Lucy," Tommy spoke out of the side of his mouth. "Orson only shifted for the first time earlier today. That must be what you're sensing."

Lucy didn't sheath her daggers, but the tension in her shoulders relaxed a bit. "Okay. I'll play along. Why would that matter? Shifter magic is shifter magic."

"Yes, but when a person shifts for the first time, it plays havoc with the magic spectrum. Granted, it's probably not on the level of Orson here, because our kind begin shifting at a much younger age."

I watched Lucy process this information. Tommy's explanation must have made sense, because her daggers disappeared in a blur of motion. She folded her arms, but never stopped staring at me, her dark eyes seeming to see right through me. With my super-senses, I could see that her skin was flawless. In any other situation, I would have grouped her in the totally hot category, but with the murderous glare she was giving me, not so much.

Elyse moved closer to me and wrapped her hand in mine, matching Lucy glare for glare. Lucy smirked in response. I felt Elyse tense up, and I gave her hand a tug. I appreciated the sentiment, but we didn't need things to escalate. Elyse squeezed my hand in acknowledgement.

"Tommy, I'm curious as to why you thought that this rather large homecoming party was necessary?" asked Mrs. Kelly.

Tommy snorted. "He set a mountain on fire."

"No, the blood-mages set the mountain on fire," Mrs. Kelly corrected. "In fact, if it wasn't for Orson, we all may have ended up in a bad situation."

"Now, Katie, you know—" Tommy began, but he was cut off by Lucy.

"Blood-mages? Nobody mentioned anything about blood-mages." Lucy turned, directing her murder stare toward Tommy. It was much cooler when focused on someone else.

Tommy held up his hands. "There was an altercation up at the cabin. But . . ."

"An altercation?" Mr. Kelly tried to keep his voice calm, but the stress of the day was getting the best of him. "It was an ambush. They were waiting for us, Thomas. Three powerful blood-mages—*three*—tossing around death magic like it was nothing."

"That is unfortunate, but the fact still remains—" Tommy wasn't interested in facts—man, he was a dick.

This time I cut him off. "Hey, Tommy, how did they know we would be there? Or even at the cabin at all?" I asked in a quiet but threatening tone. All eyes turned in my direction. Oh yeah, I had their attention now. Yesterday, I wouldn't have even thought it possible that I could sound threatening. What a difference a day makes. Letting my inner Ollphiest peek out and play was a definite party-stopper.

"Orson." Mr. Kelly conveyed the *shut the hell up* with just my name.

Nope, sorry Mr. Kelly, Tommy's attitude was pissing me off. Plus, the jerk had shown up with henchmen, actual henchmen, and a very twitchy battle-mage.

Do they really think they can stand against me?

Really? Dude, you need to calm down, we want to get their attention, not start a war.

Strength is all their kind understands. And we are the strongest of all.

Just stop. Let me handle this, and if it doesn't work . . . well, then, maybe we can try it your way.

The only response I received was a chuckle. If you've never had the voice inside your head chuckle at you, just know that it's totally creepy.

"Sorry, Mr. Kelly, but I think Tommy needs to answer the question. He was the only one who knew where we were going."

"Is that right, Tommy?" Lucy asked, taking a step backward. It was a small gesture, but it was clear she wanted him to answer.

"This is ridiculous." Tommy was getting flustered, but his eyes betrayed him when they quickly darted toward Kyle and then just as quickly snapped back to Lucy. "I don't answer to him or you," he snapped at Lucy.

Why had Tommy given Kyle the side-eye stink? Was Kyle the one who had sent the blood-mages? If so, it seemed to be news to his dad. Well, this was an unexpected turn of events.

Lucy wasn't missing any of the unspoken shenanigans. She

took another step backward. I had just met the lady, but even I knew that Tommy's snapping at her had been a huge mistake. My magical senses started tingling again. I reached out, letting my awareness flow around the driveway and front yard. Lucy's aura was buzzing. The rivers of magic were to be pouring into her.

She was powering up.

I could also sense that Tommy's henchmen down the street had vacated their cars and were shifting into animal form—giant wolves. The three behind Tommy and the guy who had been moving to our left weren't shifting, but in the magical spectrum I could see their energy pulsing. They were prepped and ready for a fight. Even if they didn't shift, with their enhanced speed and strength they could cause a whole bunch of damage.

I wish I could say I was surprised when Kyle who spoke up, but some clichés only exist because they're true. "This ends now. I'm sorry, Dad." Kyle nodded toward the henchman on the left.

The muscle-bound tough guy didn't shift, but moved with lightning speed straight for me in an NFL lineman tackle position. Elyse was standing beside me and the idiot made a huge mistake when he put his hands on her to shove her out of the way. Elyse was fast, stepping back and striking out with her fist, smashing the guy's nose. His face exploded in a shower of blood as he stumbled into me. I used his own momentum, adding a substantial boost from my own strength, and tossed him head-first into what I assumed was Tommy's car, a shiny cobalt-blue BMW. The front end of the car crumpled like tinfoil, and the sickening crunch of the guy's skull fracturing sounded like a gunshot. Even with his shifter healing, he was going to feel that in the morning.

The two wolves from the street came scrambling up the

driveway, taking up positions on either side of us. The Kellys and I all dropped into defensive stances. Nobody else shifted.

"Kyle, what's going on?" Tommy demanded.

"He," Kyle pointed at me, "is being taken into custody. Now."

"I don't think so," I growled.

"Kyle, why are you doing this?" Elyse asked.

"He's dangerous. How can you and your parents be so blind?" Kyle shouted. Then, his focus never leaving us, he spoke to Lucy, "The Society has seen the evidence and made their decree. Now do your job."

Lucy let out a sigh. "That was before I heard about blood-mages starting forest fires."

"That is a separate matter that can be discussed at later time. Right now, you have a shifter standing in front of you that wasn't born, but made. Something unheard-of for centuries. Take him, or I will."

"Kyle, please." Mrs. Kelly tried using her best mom voice, but Kyle shook his head.

Lucy huffed again and pulled what looked like a dog collar from her pocket, a silver dog collar, a silver dog collar that lit up the magical spectrum like a flashlight. Magic handcuffs, or would that be neckcuff? Lucy held the magic dog collar casually in one hand as she assessed my neck, probably trying to figure out if the stupid thing would fit.

Oh, hell no.

"He's right. I've got to take you in, and we'll sort everything else out later," Lucy said, moving toward me as if I would actually let her put a dog collar on me.

"Thomas, you need to stop this now." Mr. Kelly stepped in front of me. "Orson, please remain calm."

Lucy stopped. A perplexed look on her face, she was surprised that Mr. Kelly would try to stop her. "Richard, you know me. I've got a legal decree from the Society. I'm taking him."

Okay. This had gone on long enough. Tommy looked constipated, staring from Kyle to Lucy, not sure how he'd lost control of the situation. Kyle had a look of pure hatred on his face, and it was quickly becoming obvious to me that he was a couple sandwiches short of a picnic. Daddy issues? Unrequited love for Elyse? Both? It didn't really matter. It didn't seem like a far leap of logic that he had sent the blood-mages and that meant he was my enemy.

Destroy him.

Yeah, this time I think you might be right.

But first, I had to deal with Lucy the battle-mage. What did that mean—battle mage? If her power was similar to the blood-mages, she shouldn't be too much trouble. It appeared, however, that she was some kind of cop or enforcer for the Paragon Society and that was problematic.

I said mildly, "So, Lucy, nice to meet you, by the way. I feel very confident that Kyle here is the one who sicced the blood-mages on us. Which, I'm sensing from your tense vibe, is a huge no-no." I nodded, seeking her agreement. Lucy didn't nod back, but she was listening. "I bet if you ask Tommy, he'll confirm that only he and his mini-me knew where the Kellys and I would be for the weekend."

Kyle, who had bristled at the mini-me comment, started to turn a nasty shade of red. "Shut. Him. Up. Now!"

Lucy hesitated for a moment. I could see her struggle with the facts. It was clear Kyle had an ulterior motive, but she had a job to do and that won out.

"Like I said, we'll sort all that out later," Lucy said, moving toward me once more.

"If you try to put that thing on me, we're going to have ourselves a situation." I tried so hard to keep my voice calm and passive, but once again I failed. My inner monster wanted blood.

Mr. Kelly's shoulders slumped. He knew what was coming.

"Whatever you're thinking, son, it's a bad idea," Tommy said to me under the mistaken impression that he could still control the situation.

"Don't call me son."

Kyle leapt at Mr. Kelly, who had anticipated the attack. Mr. Kelly caught the younger man and threw him into the wolf that was charging from the right. Elyse and her mom had intercepted the wolf on the left. Mrs. Kelly grabbed a back leg, causing the wolf to stumble and Elyse let loose with a monster kick that sent the yelping beast into the bushes.

In one fluid motion, Lucy dropped the collar and flung some battle-mage mojo directly at me. Now, I hadn't had time to test out the extent of my new, fancy Ollphiest powers. I knew I was impervious to magic when in bear form, but I had no idea how my human form would handle it. I closed my eyes tightly and gritted my teeth, expecting the worst. I felt the spell hit me and, just as in bear form, it slithered around me, looking for a way through my natural defenses.

It didn't find one.

I opened my eyes and smiled.

Lucy was stone-faced. Her eyes held no shock or anger, just cool calculation. She was dangerous.

"Ollphiest!" Tommy screamed.

The Kellys' driveway erupted into a shifter-fest. Mr. and Mrs. Kelly went full beast form. Tommy and Kyle—Kyle had untangled himself from Mr. Kelly's initial throw—also shifted to beast form. Luckily for us, it seemed that all the all the extra muscle Tommy had brought with him could only shift into animal form. Don't get me wrong: six massive, snarling wolves were scary as hell, but considering what we could've been facing, it was a blessing.

Elyse, in cat form, was pressed against my side and hissing at the wolves surrounding us. I was the last to shift, choosing beast form because of the shock factor. I wasn't disappointed. As my clothes ripped off of me and I reached my full man-bear hybrid height, Tommy and his wolves paused at the sight of me.

Lucy whistled. "You're one ugly son of a bitch."

As if her words had been some kind of pre-ordained signal, Tommy, Kyle and their wolves attacked as one. It should have worked. They had the numbers. But, instead, it ended almost before it started.

Tommy and Kyle jumped straight for me, but Mr. Kelly caught Tommy and they tumbled away in a ball of growls and snapping jaws.

Mrs. Kelly tackled Kyle midair, and maybe it was his life-long relationship with her, but he didn't immediately try to claw or bite her. Instead, he kind of grappled with her, trying to get her off-balance and throw her to the ground.

Elyse had decided to take on two of the wolves by herself and whatever crazy shifter jujitsu fighting techniques she had learned at that shifter summer camp were helping her kick the crap out of those two.

That left three wolves and, of course, Lucy the battle-mage for me to deal with. The wolves were almost embarrass-ingly easy. They attacked together, hoping to overwhelm me. No such luck. I was faster, stronger, and because of the Ollphiest in my head, a lot more vicious. I ripped through them, leaving them broken and bloody. The monster in me wanted to kill them, pull their hearts from their bodies and take their heads as trophies. But he and I were starting to build a working relationship, one where I let him out to kick ass, but with the understanding that I would always retain control. These wolves were just following orders. I know that's one of the worst excuses in the history of armed combat, but they were raised to think of someone like me as the boogeyman, someone to be feared, a monster to vanquish. As far as they understood, they were the good guys.

Another spell hit me. It packed a much bigger punch than the first one. It actually sizzled on my fur a bit before it dissipated. I turned my attention to Lucy and growled.

The stunned look on Lucy's face said it all. She was surprised the spell hadn't done more damage. She recovered quickly and pulled her daggers. I reminded myself that she represented the Society and that she was in possession of what must pass for an arrest warrant in the magic world. The only problem was that the warrant was based on incomplete information. I needed to put her out of commission, but I had to be gentler than I had been with the wolves. I didn't know the healing capabilities of battle-mages.

Lucy had different intentions. She moved just as fast as the wolves. Super-speed? Impressive.

I prepared to catch and body-slam Lucy into the driveway. It seemed like the most non-lethal thing I could do. At the last minute, she dropped to her knees in a power slide underneath my claws. She was still moving fast and slashed out with both blades. They sliced across my belly as she tucked into a roll and came up onto the balls of her feet behind me.

Ouch.

My stomach was on fire.

She had actually cut me. Bad.

Witch.

I think the politically correct term is battle-mage, but yeah, she did some damage. What's up with that? I thought we were the Big Bad?

Witch. We must destroy her now.

Hold on. We're not destroying anyone.

I spun, ready to parry Lucy's follow-up attack. Unfortunately, I had not spent my summers at Camp Shifter and my fighting skills were limited to stuff I had picked up from online gaming and late night cable marathons of Kung-Fu Theater. It would not even be nearly enough to beat Lucy, who was moving like Neo from the *Matrix* trilogy.

Lucy was twirling her blades, dancing from foot to foot in some serious martial arts badassery. I would be super-impressed, if she wasn't trying to gut me.

I could feel the cuts on my mid-section bleeding freely. My cool man-bear fur was getting all matted and gross. I could also feel a kind of void in my energy—my aura. I think Lucy's daggers had cut a hole in my Ollphiest magic shields. It was a small hole, but I bet if Lucy flung any more mojo my way, it wouldn't just slide off me. It would find the hole and proceed to magic my butt into submission.

Never.

Yeah, well, I don't think this is the right time to test our limits.

But it was time for my newly discovered beast mode AOE roar.

Lucy attacked with a tricky spinning-leg thingy.

My roar caught her mid-spin and she dropped like a stone. Her hands covered her ears, her eyes wide in pain and shock.

Everybody else on the driveway also dropped. I felt a twinge of guilt that Elyse and her folks were getting dosed with my super-roar, but the professional battle-mage who had been kicking my butt took precedence over their momentary discomfort.

I ended the shrieking roar and moved in before Lucy could get her focus back. She struggled to her feet, swaying slightly. Wow, she was tough.

Gut her.

What? No. There will absolutely be no gutting.

She would show you no mercy.

Yeah, well she's supposed to be one of the good guys, so no gutting.

Instead, I backhanded her. My hand felt a momentary resistance and then the telltale pop of magic discharging. A shield. Lucy had a shield spell and I'd just punched through like it was paper. Her eyes went wide again. The back of my fist connected with the side of her head. I made sure to pull back on the force of my blow, not wanting to crush her skull. I guess I needed a bit more practice because the hit sent her flying backward into the side of the house. I winced—well, the beast form grunt that served as a wince—when she hit. Her eyes rolled back into her head and she collapsed in a heap. In the magic spectrum, I could still see her life force pulsing strong, so I hadn't killed or damaged her too much.

A snarling growl, followed by a hiss of pain, brought me back to the fight. I spun and quickly assessed the status of the Kellys and our attackers. The stun from my roar had worn off, and the fight was getting back into full swing. Unfortunately, the temporary lull in the fighting and the assistance he was receiving from his dad had helped Kyle get the upper hand with Mr. Kelly. Tommy had hold of Mr. Kelly's arms, which had allowed Kyle several free swipes at Mr. Kelly's unprotected torso. The result looked like something out of a slasher movie—deep ragged cuts crisscrossed Mr. Kelly's chest. There was a ton of blood. I had no idea how Mr. Kelly still had any strength to struggle against Tommy. Kyle let out a satisfied grunt and moved in for what looked like a killing blow.

Not going to happen. I let the Ollphiest out.

Yes.

I leapt at Kyle, moving faster than fast. I struck out, lightning quick, with one of my monster-clawed hands.

Kyle lost an arm at the elbow and received a vicious slash

across the face. He fell back, shifting back into human form as he hit the ground. He held his amputated arm out in from of him and screamed like a madman. Tommy let Mr. Kelly go, shifted to human, and rushed to his fallen son.

I made sure Mr. Kelly was good and then quickly dispatched the other shifters. I moved through them like they were standing still. A slash here, a bite there, bone-shattering punches to faces everywhere; I was a force of nature. I was surprised that the Ollphiest side of my *persona* wasn't killing anyone. Ripping, shredding, and maiming, yes, but no killing. Interesting.

You expressed your desire for no death.

Yeah, but I thought you'd just ignore me.

WE are Ollphiest.

Right. There was no 'he' or 'I,' just *we*. And we had just kicked the crap out of Tommy's little army of henchmen.

The driveway was littered with bleeding bodies. All the henchmen had shifted back to human. They were in various stages of messed up. Kyle was still screaming. Geez, what a drama queen. He's lucky all he lost was an arm. He deserved to have his throat ripped out.

Tommy had used some torn clothing to create a tourniquet for Kyle's arm. He cradled Kyle in his arms and sobbed, "My son. My son."

I felt a slight ripple in the magic flowing around me. I looked over at Lucy. She was regaining consciousness. I watched in fascination as one of the rivers of magic diverted from its natural course and sort of dipped into her before resuming its normal flow. She was healing. I was sure of it.

Tommy started shouting in some other language. Irish, maybe? He sounded really pissed. He was gesturing at me, while looking over at Lucy.

Mr. Kelly shifted back to human, kneeling down in front of Tommy and Kyle. "Thomas, he was going to kill me."

Tommy just yelled louder. I wasn't sure why everybody seemed so distressed. Yes, I had done some damage, but shifter magic would have everyone back in shape probably by tomorrow. I looked around at my handiwork. Well, maybe not tomorrow, but soon.

"Elyse, take Orson and go. Now," said Mr. Kelly, never looking up from Tommy and Kyle.

Mrs. Kelly, still in beast form, let out a clicking noise.

"Katie, they have to go before Lucy wakes up." Mr. Kelly sounded pained.

What was going on? Kyle had way overstepped his bounds and been slapped down. So what? I was about to shift and ask just that question, when Elyse nudged me toward the back of the house. I looked over at Lucy again. Her eyes were fluttering. I received another more demanding nudge from Elyse. I huffed and shifted into bear form. Elyse rubbed noses with me and ran around the side of the house. I gave one more glance at Mr. Kelly. This time he met my eyes. He was afraid.

For me?

For his family?

Or for all of us?

He flicked his eyes toward the side of the house where Elyse had run. I got the message and ran.

CHAPTER EIGHTEEN

Elyse led me into the hills behind her house. With our unnatural speed we were far from suburbia in minutes. I could still smell the city, but it was just a small undercurrent. Elyse had been running these hills for years and she knew every trail and pathway.

I had questions about what just went down, but Elyse kept moving, so I'd have to wait until she decided to stop. She led us down into a deep ravine that, in human form, would have been near-impossible to get into, but in animal form it was no problem.

When we reached the deepest part of the ravine, Elyse sniffed around, stopping under a California Oak. She started to dig.

Okay.

She stopped digging and chuffed at me. I looked from her to the small hole she had already dug out. I blinked at her and snorted. I padded over and started digging alongside her. Our giant paws were not exactly designed for digging, but they still made quick work of our task. The hole was about four feet deep when my claws clicked against something hard, something man-made from the smell of it.

Elyse shifted and gestured for me to do the same.

She pulled me into a fierce hug.

Oh boy, here we go again, naked soft girlfriend parts mashed into my dumb man parts.

Thankfully—but not really—she pulled away.

"How is your stomach?" she asked, bending over to inspect the cuts Lucy's daggers had left. She gently prodded the skin around the wounds. I sucked in some air. They were really tender.

"How bad is it?" I asked.

"The wounds have already closed up, but you may be sore for a couple of days."

"What did she cut me with, anyway? They were like magic Ginsu knives or something."

"Not sure. I've never seen anything like them before. But they seem like they may be your Kryptonite."

I thought about that. It made a kind of sense, that there would be something to balance my powers. So far, in my day-long career as the Ollphiest, those daggers were the only thing that had actually hurt me. I wondered where Lucy had picked them up? Was there, like, a battle-mage Walmart where nasty things were sold over the counter? I sure hoped not.

Elyse kneeled down to clear away the last of the dirt from whatever was buried under the tree.

"She also hit you with some serious magic."

"Oh. Yeah, that . . . well, I'm pretty sure magic is more of an annoyance to me more than anything."

Elyse paused her digging, shook her head and smiled at me. "Amazing."

"So what've you got down there?"

"Emergency supplies, clothes, some money. We have

several stashes like this around here and up north. It helps for situations just like this."

"You mean being on the run from Tommy and his merry band of shifters is a regular thing?"

Elyse rolled her eyes. Having cleared away enough dirt, she heaved out a large, plastic, waterproof case and popped it open. It held several pairs of sweats, yoga leggings, and t-shirts. Elyse dragged out a pair of leggings and a t-shirt for herself. She also pulled out a rather large medical hygiene kit. I was thankful when she handed me some antiseptic body wipes. I gave myself the once over, removing most of the dried blood from my body.

"Dig in. There should be something that will fit you. May be a bit snug, but it's better than running around naked and scaring the neighbors," said Elyse. "And no, by situation, I don't mean being on the run. I mean out in the open with no clothes. It doesn't happen often, but it's the shifter version of a flat tire, except there's no roadside service we can call."

I found a pair of black sweat pants that didn't cut off my circulation when I put them on. I added a blue t-shirt and poked around in the case.

"No shoes?" I asked.

"No, too many sizes to deal with. We'll pick some up as soon as we can."

Elyse dug around under the clothes and pulled out a Ziploc bag containing money, a credit card, and surprise, surprise . . .

"Is that a burner cell phone?" I asked.

"Yep. When you've been alive as long as my parents have, you always plan ahead."

"How Jack Bauer of them." More seriously, I asked, "Your parents will be cool right? I mean, they're not going to get put in magic jail are they?"

Elyse snorted. "No. They'll be fine." She dropped the case

back in the hole and started shoveling the dirt back in. I bent down to help.

"So, why did your dad seem so, I don't know, worried? It seems like we can prove that Kyle sent the blood-mages. Heck, he pretty much admitted it. So that means Tommy overreacted with his goon squad. We were only protecting ourselves. The Society will see it that way, right?

Elyse let out a deep sigh and stopped. "I don't know. The Society, they're really old school. You saw how Lucy responded—act now and ask questions later. People like my parents have been trying to get the Society to change their ways, but traditions get ingrained, especially over centuries."

"So, we're in trouble?"

"Let's just say it will take some time to clear up."

I absently pushed dirt into the hole. "Why did Tommy freak out so bad there at the end? I mean, I know I jacked his kid up, but with shifter healing I figure . . ."

Elyse rested her hand on mine, stopping me. "You took Kyle's arm off, Orson. No amount of shifter magic can heal that."

I rocked back, shocked. "What?"

I didn't like the guy, but taking his arm . . . oh jeez.

"Hey." Elyse tapped my chin. "Look at me. Kyle wasn't pretend-fighting. He would have killed my dad. You did the right thing."

Had I done the right thing? The day had spun out of control so fast. I had *killed* a person up in Arrowhead. Sure, she had been an evil blood-mage trying to kill the Kellys and me, but she was still dead because of me. And now Kyle was down an arm for the rest of his life. I closed my eyes. It was all too much. I needed to just stop. I wished I could just go home, curl up in my bed, and sleep for a couple of days.

My pity party ended with Elyse's soft lips touching mine. I didn't open my eyes. I just kissed her back, slowly at first, and then with more passion as my mind quieted and I focused on what my mouth was doing. I pulled her in close, my hands twining through her hair. She kissed me until all my worries melted away. Oh, we were still very much in a bad situation, but with her kiss I was able to put everything in perspective. She pulled back a little, our noses still touching.

"Better?" she whispered.

"Much." I opened my eyes and we gazed at each other for a moment. Then she smacked my butt.

"Let's get moving, dork."

I followed Elyse through the foothills of Southern California. We stayed in human form, but we were still super-fast. Whenever we sensed day hikers or campers, we would give them a wide berth to avoid any witnesses who might report the location of the two weird, shoeless people smashing through the underbrush.

The burner phone was a great resource, or rather, it would be as soon as we could get it charged. That's the problem with our tech-dependent world. It only worked if we had the juice to keep things humming. Elyse was leading us toward a gas station and truck stop. There was a small café where we could grab some food and charge the phone.

I have to admit the run through nature had a calming effect on me. I was able to think a bit more clearly about the events of the last couple of days. Two days ago, the biggest decision I had been facing was how early I should schedule my first class. Did I go for sleeping in, or getting my classes over and done with by the afternoon so I could enjoy the rest of my day?

Now, I wasn't even sure if I would be able to start school in the fall. I was sure the two classes I was currently enrolled in to get ahead of the freshman curve were done. How was I supposed to show up for class tomorrow, or even the next couple of weeks, when I had Tommy and possibly other

Paragon Society members gunning for me? It seemed the most likely scenario would be me going into hiding while Mr. Kelly tried to smooth things over. And if that wasn't possible, then I didn't know what would happen. Would I have to run for it? Was that even possible when the people looking for you could conjure some kind of locating spell? Was a locating spell even a real thing?

I realized again how much I didn't know about this new world I found myself in.

And Elyse? If I had to go on the lam, would she want to go with me? I, of course, would love that, but how could I ever justify putting her in that kind of danger?

I also thought about the violence of the past few hours. I now understood that if I was pushed to protect myself or those I cared for, I would—and I could do so with extreme prejudice. I think most sane people consider their capacity for violence, maybe not all the time, but in the face of mass shootings, terrorist attacks, and full-on street riots, the thought of 'how far would I go?' is normal.

And, it turned out I would go as far as I needed.

Maybe that realization should have given me more pause, the fact I would kill to defend me and mine, but it didn't. Was it the Ollphiest polluting me? Were these thoughts and feelings me, or were they the 'me' before I became a shape-shifter? Would I have ever let anyone hurt Aunt Tina? I didn't think so. With or without my new monster alter-ego, I was fairly confident I would always do whatever was needed to stop bad guys from doing bad-guy stuff.

Elyse slowed the pace and I matched her. She came to a stop and checked our surroundings. I knew she was using more than just her sight. She was also smelling and listening, taking in all the sensory input our abilities gave us. I did the same. I could smell the truck stop: gas, people, and fast food. I could also hear the freeway with the high buzzing sound of small cars and the load roar of semi-trucks. I have to admit I was already addicted to and completely dependent on my super-senses.

Elyse waggled her fingers at me. "Are you picking up any magical presence with your Ollphiest radar?"

I let my senses expand even further and the magic spectrum popped up, almost like a 3D overlay of the surrounding terrain. No signs of any magic other than the natural rivers flowing around us.

"Nope."

"Good." She pointed. "The truck stop is just on the other side of the next hill."

"What's the plan?"

"The Society has people everywhere. There are members in every branch of government, including law enforcement. My dad has probably been able to stop them from putting out a full-on all-points bulletin on us, but people may still be on the alert. We need to be inconspicuous."

I glanced down at our appearance. Yoga pants, sweats, t-shirts, bare feet and assorted pieces of nature clinging to us.

"Well, we look like a couple of meth-head tweakers. We should fit right in at roadside truck stop."

"You're a comedian. We need to clean ourselves up as much as we can. I'll go down first and make sure there aren't any cops. I'll buy us some flip-flops at the mini-mart so they'll at least let us into the café. Give me about five minutes and meet me at the edge of the parking lot closest to the back of the buildings."

"Got it." I pulled her close and brushed her lips with mine. "Be careful."

"Always."

Ten minutes later I was sporting brand new flip-flops and a turquoise California baseball cap. Elyse had also purchased a large shoulder bag and filled it with water and other snacks, just in case we needed to head back into the hills while her parents came up with a plan. We entered the café and picked a booth as far from other people as possible, but that didn't stop the stares at my new over-sized frame. I tried to project my best nice guy vibes.

The whole place looked like it had undergone renovations recently, everything was still shiny and new-looking. Lucky for us, the renovation included adding charging plugs at all the tables. Elyse plugged in the burner phone. The waitress raised her eyebrows when we ordered half the food on the menu.

"We've been fasting for religious reasons," I tried to explain.

The waitress just nodded and smirked. Oh yeah, she was sure we were coming off a drug-fueled bender and needed to stuff our faces. That wasn't too far from the truth, shifting was a kind of high, the way the world snapped into a brighter, louder, and sharper focus. I'm sure it rivaled any drug experience.

After the waitress dropped off our water and large sodas, Elyse picked up the burner and dialed her mom's cell. I could easily follow both sides of the conversation.

"Are you safe?" Mrs. Kelly got right to the point.

"Yes. We're at that truck stop off the Five. You know the one, the last exit before the Grapevine." Elyse spoke quietly to avoid being overheard by any of our fellow diners.

I glanced around the small restaurant. The other customers were what you'd expect to see at a truck stop diner, a mix of long-haul truckers looking bleary-eyed as they sucked back cups of coffee and steak sandwiches. Mixed amongst the truckers were families on the road to visit grandma or some other kind of road trip. Interstate 5, or 'the Five' as Elyse and every other native Southern Californian called it, ran the length of the West Coast. It stretched from

Mexico to the south all the way to Canada in the north. If you were heading anywhere in the north west, 'the Five' was how you got there and the Grapevine was a particular steep, winding part of the highway. Some considered it the gateway to Southern California. If we needed to get out of town, this was a good spot to start from.

"Good," Mrs. Kelly said, talking fast. "Stay put, I'm in the car, and I'll be there in thirty minutes."

"Mrs. Kelly," I kept my voice low also, knowing Mr. Kelly would be able to hear me. "I'm so sorry."

"Nonsense. You did nothing wrong, Thomas should have known better." Even through the phone I could detect an edge of worry.

"Is Dad with you?" Elyse asked.

"No. Tommy called an emergency meeting of the entire council. Your father is there trying to diffuse the situation."

Elyse and I looked at each other. An emergency meeting didn't sound good.

"We'll talk more when I pick you two up. One last thing, Orson. I need you to start thinking of a way to tell your aunt about your new abilities," said Mrs. Kelly.

"What?" I was shocked. I thought regular people weren't supposed to know about the whole magic, shape-shifter world.

"Why, Mom?" Elyse seemed just as confused.

"I can't explain everything right now, but we're going to need to leave L.A., and for her safety we need to take Orson's aunt with us. I'm hanging up now. I need to make several more calls. I will be there soon."

Mrs. Kelly clicked off. I sat staring at the phone in Elyse's hand, stunned. Leaving L.A. and delaying school was one thing, but now I had to burden Aunt Tina with the knowledge that magic and monsters were real? I looked up into Elyse's eyes.

She pulled me into a hug. "We'll think of something. I promise," she whispered.

We ate our food in silence. Elyse was awesome, giving me time to organize my scattered thoughts. The only way I could see of convincing Aunt Tina that I wasn't insane or brainwashed by a cult was to shift into bear form in front of her. If that didn't cause her to run screaming from the house, or keel over dead from a heart attack, I was pretty sure I could convince her of the danger we were all in. There was no way to avoid the guilt I was feeling. Aunt Tina's life was about to be blown apart by choices I had made.

The burner phone rang. My head snapped up, my body ready to fight. Elyse patted my hand and I took a deep breath.

"I'm exiting the freeway. Meet me out front," Mrs. Kelly said.

Elyse dropped enough cash to cover the bill with a generous tip, and we moved quickly outside. It was summer and even though the sun was setting and had passed behind the mountains, the sky still glowed with an indigo light. The Kellys' Range Rover pulled into the parking lot, tires squealing. Elyse jumped into the front seat and I climbed into the back. Mrs. Kelly hugged her daughter, giving her the once-over to check that Elyse was undamaged. Satisfied, Mrs. Kelly reached back and touched my knee.

"Have you heard from Dad?" Elyse asked immediately.

"Yes. Tommy is doing everything he can to brand Orson as a renegade."

"Well, that doesn't sound good," I said.

"A renegade? He just shifted for the first time yesterday, and he hasn't killed anybody except for the blood-mage, who was trying to kill us. Which is perfectly legal," Elyse said.

Mrs. Kelly didn't respond. She looked at me in the rearview mirror.

"It's Kyle, isn't it?" I didn't like the dude. I was pretty sure he had tried to have me killed, but I hoped he wasn't dead. "Is he dead?"

"No. But he might die."

Elyse let out a small noise. It wasn't a gasp or whimper, but it was a sad sound. I couldn't blame her. She had known him her whole life. They had dated. Even if he had grown up to be a total tool, they had a history.

"I'm sorry." I seemed to be saying that way too much the past twenty-four hours.

"He didn't really leave you much choice. If he had attacked anyone other than Richard, it would have ended in death, no questions asked. He was in the wrong, and Tommy knows it, but—"

"Kyle's his son. I get it. Elyse, I know you guys are friends, that you—"

"Stop," Elyse cut me off, turning in her seat to face me. "Kyle made his choice and I've made mine." Elyse sat there, glaring at me, daring me to contradict her. She was tough, loyal and sexy as hell.

I nodded.

"Dork," she added.

CHAPTER NINETEEN

It was after nightfall and still Mrs. Kelly was an absolute speed demon behind the wheel. Intellectually, I understood that her heightened senses gave her the ability to weave in and out of traffic like a Formula One driver, but that didn't stop me from cringing when she zipped across three lanes, slotting the Range Rover in between two semi-trucks.

I also worried about the CHP. The California Highway Patrol were notorious for handing out maximum penalty traffic tickets, and with her aggressive style of driving, Mrs. Kelly ran the risk of being arrested for drag racing, which in our current situation would be disastrous.

I tried to broach the subject as tactfully as I could. "Mrs. Kelly, do you have the traffic app on your phone that gives a heads-up about police?"

Mrs. Kelly laughed, and even though I couldn't see her face, I knew Elyse was rolling her eyes.

"Smooth, Orson. Real smooth," Elyse said.

"Orson, there is no need to worry. Shifter senses are very versatile. It's easy to track the anxiety level of the drivers ahead and behind. A much more accurate warning system than an iPhone app."

"Really?" I hadn't thought about using my super-senses in that manner.

"Yep," Elyse answered. "It works the same way as being able to tell if someone is lying or angry. Their aura puts off telltale signs. You just have to expand your range a bit further."

I was impressed. My brain started running through all the everyday encounters this kind of ability would come in handy for. Any type of interpersonal relationship—family, romantic, business—would have a totally different dynamic. I thought about Mr. Kelly at the council meeting and wondered how something like that would work with everybody being able to read each other with just a glance. Wouldn't all the council members know Tommy was a lying douche-bag?

"So, how does Tommy expect to get away with his plans? I mean, if everyone can tell what everyone else is thinking?"

"You already know the first thing shifters learn is how to control their ability to shift. The second thing they learn is how to mask their auras," Mrs. Kelly explained.

"That's possible?"

"Yes, and an absolute necessity. Could you imagine how hard life would be if everyone knew exactly what you were feeling?

"Um, I don't have to imagine it. I guess I'm an open book right now." It kind of creeped me out to know I couldn't hide my feelings. I would have to start training on that ability immediately.

Mrs. Kelly surprised me when she said, "Actually, you're not."

"Huh?" Time for me to be confused again.

"I think it might be another of your innate Ollphiest abilities. You're a blank slate. You have an aura, but it always looks the same, just a calm, peaceful glow. At least, when you're in human form."

Elyse had spun in her seat again. "Yep. Even when your aura should be raging, there's not even a ripple. Then bang." Elyse smacked the seat headrest. "You shift and then it's all explosive, red, rage machine. It's crazy-weird."

"Crazy-weird." I repeated and dropped my eyes to my hands. Wonderful. One more thing to mark me as different, as dangerous. I didn't want to be crazy-weird.

"I said, 'it's crazy-weird', not *you're* crazy-weird."

I nodded. Elyse knew me all too well. She didn't need an aura to know I was feeling sorry for myself. She tangled her fingers in my hair. "Hey, it's okay. You're just able to do something naturally the rest of us have to work real hard at. Like some people are naturally good at sports or art, or bowling."

I couldn't help myself. I let out a small chuckle. "Bowling?"

"Yeah, you know . . ." Elyse dramatically pantomimed a person bowling.

My chuckle turned into a laugh. Mrs. Kelly smiled at me in the review mirror.

I had a thought and tried to put on my serious face. "So, young Miss Kelly, before yesterday and my unique transformation, you could read me like a book?"

Elyse's answer didn't matter, because I got the reaction I was hoping for when she blushed. Watching her blush was now a full sensory display. I watched as her cheeks became rosy, but I could also hear her heart rate speed up and her breathing increase. And her aura lit up like a Christmas tree. She was beautiful.

"Oh-ho. Busted," I said.

"It's not something that can be controlled. We can't turn off our senses," Elyse insisted.

I waggled my fingers at her. "Keep spinning, Miss Kelly,

keep spinning." I was going to enjoy this. She was cute when she was flustered. "All those times over the years," I glanced at Mrs. Kelly who was still smiling. "When I noticed that you were a girl and not just my best friend. You knew."

Elyse folded her arms and tossed her head. "I will not apologize for something I had no control over."

"And you knew, when my feelings changed . . . at Prom."

"They didn't change, you just finally accepted them." Elyse said. She was correct, of course. I had been falling in love with her for at least a couple of years. I had just been in denial.

"Dork," she added, sticking her tongue out for emphasis.

"Mrs. Kelly, I don't want to make you uncomfortable, but I would really like to kiss your daughter right now."

"Please, dear, pretend I'm not here."

I leaned forward and kissed Elyse. It wasn't the kind of kiss I wanted to give her, but hey, her mom was sitting two feet away from us. Still, I think it conveyed everything I wanted her to know and understand. I sat back satisfied.

"Sorry to be the one to break the mood, but we're almost to your house, Orson. Do you know what you will say to your aunt?" Mrs. Kelly was back in her no-nonsense mode.

"I've been wracking my brain, but there is no way to ease someone into this situation. I think I need to go in by myself at first and, I don't know, soften her up. I don't have anything prepared. Aunt Tina would spot that from a mile away. I'm just going to have to wing it, and trust in my super-spidey senses to get a feel for how she's accepting what I'm telling her."

"Okay. We'll be right outside waiting for your cue. Call us in when you think the time is right."

"Will do."

Mrs. Kelly turned onto my darkened street. I'd only been

gone for a day, and yet it seemed different somehow. I'd lived here with Aunt Tina for most of my life. I'd ridden my bike, played tag football with the neighborhood kids, and skinned my knees on this street. It was a symbol of my childhood and of a normal life of which I was no longer a part. A part of me was saddened by that thought, saddened by the loss of plans and life-goals that would go unrealized. But another part of me was excited by the new world I found myself in, a world of magic and limitless possibilities.

Even with Tommy and the Paragon Society breathing down my neck, I couldn't wait to see what this new world had to offer. I wasn't naïve. I understood I was in serious trouble and had, by extension, pulled in the Kellys and Aunt Tina, but if and when I got this all cleared up, life was going to be a wild ride. And I like wild rides.

Mrs. Kelly slowed as she approached my house.

"Okay, you two, I need some help. Do either of you feel or sense anything out of the ordinary?"

I reached out with my magical sense, but didn't pick up on anything odd. It was my good old-fashioned human sense of sight that spotted the problem. Tony's pickup truck was parked under a streetlight across from my house.

I pointed. "That's Tony's truck."

"Tony?" Mrs. Kelly asked.

Elyse said, "Tony worked with Orson at Costco. He was the other guy in the forklift video. He must be a lot more upset than we thought."

"This complicates things." Mrs. Kelly tapped her fingers on the steering wheel. "Okay, instead of waiting in the car, we will go in with you and help get this Tony to leave, quickly. And then you do whatever you think best—even shifting if necessary—to get your aunt to come with us. We'll follow your lead."

I nodded. I was the Ollphiest, the Big Bad, and yet my stomach was doing flip-flops. The thought of how Aunt Tina would react had me jumping out of my skin. I knew she loved me, and our bond was more like mom and son than aunt and nephew, but I was about to ask her to accept a whole bunch of crazy.

We left the Range Rover. I took Elyse's hand. I was glad she would be standing next to me when I dropped the truth bomb on Aunt Tina. I moved swiftly toward the front door, figuring that dragging my feet would only prolong the tension.

I froze halfway across the lawn. I had been so distracted by Tony's truck that I'd missed some very quirky ripples in the energy flowing around my house. It was definitely some kind of residual effect from magic use.

Mrs. Kelly and Elyse were instantly alert.

"What?" Mrs. Kelly asked.

"Mage mojo, but weak. I'm not sure, maybe it's old, left-overs from the shark-nurse?"

"I don't think a magical signature would last that long. A few hours maybe, but not longer, certainly."

Okay, so a mage had been active in or around my house in the past few hours. "Unfortunately, I can't tell if it's blood-mage magic or someone like Lucy."

"At this point, it probably doesn't matter. Both scenarios would be equally bad," Mrs. Kelly said wryly.

I closed my eyes and really concentrated on opening up to my surroundings. There was nobody hiding in the front or back yard.

Wait.

What was that?

It was faint, an underlying vibration being masked by the residual magic.

Blood.

Aunt Tina.

"There's blood." I let go of Elyse's hand—I had to get inside now. I moved with shifter speed, but Mrs. Kelly was faster. She blocked the front door.

I growled.

"Orson, we have to be smart, not just rush in. It could be a trap. Do you sense anything else?" Mrs. Kelly spoke in her calm mom voice.

I tried to slow my mind. It was hard, because visions of Aunt Tina broken and bleeding kept trying to flood my mind. Elyse placed a hand on my shoulder. I searched once more, following the residual magic like supernatural breadcrumbs, but there was nothing else. No breathing, no heartbeats, no energy signatures signifying people—it was just blank.

"There's nothing. It's almost like the entire house is a giant black hole of energy."

"A shield spell."

"A shield spell?"

"Yes. It's warding magic. It's blocking your abilities."

"That would be a first. He's been immune to every other kind of ward magic." Elyse didn't sound convinced.

"Agreed. It may be a proximity thing. Maybe you have to be closer to the spell for your defenses to kick in? We need to be smart about this."

"Mrs. Kelly, I respect you a whole bunch, but my aunt could be inside, she could be hurt or . . ." I couldn't say *dead*. I couldn't let myself go there.

"I understand. I didn't say we weren't going in. I just want as much information as possible first. You should go around the house and come in through the back door. Elyse and I will enter here and we'll take care of the situation."

Take care of the situation. Mrs. Kelly could make even the most dangerous scenarios sound like a cookie bake-off.

"Mom?" said Elyse, her worry evident.

"It will be fine." She patted Elyse's arm. "But I suggest cat form for you, and if you can manage it, Orson, beast form."

I nodded.

The moon wasn't up yet, so the night was extra dark, which would give us more cover when we shifted. I left Elyse and her mom on the front lawn. They had moved behind a hedge to undress. We would need our clothes after, plus I still had neighbors who would be suspicious of two women getting naked outside. I moved quietly to the back of the house. I tried to peer in the windows I passed, but nothing was visible. Part of the shield spell, I imagined.

When I reached the back door, I quickly undressed and easily shifted to beast form. My worry and anger for my aunt fueled my ability. The plan was for Elyse and Mrs. Kelly to wait for the signal—me smashing through the back door—and then to break through the front door. I figured a few broken doors would be a small price to pay for the element of surprise.

I let out a window-rattling shriek and jumped through the door. The wood was pulverized into nothing bigger than splinters. Inside the back door, I could see it. A bubble of energy filled the entire house. The shield spell.

I ripped at with my claws. I watched, amazed, as the energy shredded beneath my strikes like sticky taffy. After several swipes the bubble popped, releasing a burst of magic that shook the house. I heard the front door crash open. Elyse and her mom were inside.

With the shield spell gone, the smell of blood became overwhelming.

It was the stench of death.

I roared again.

Kill everyone.

This time, the beast inside me had the right idea.

Everyone who had dared enter my house and attack my aunt was toast.

An explosion of the magical variety ripped through the front of the house and shattered all the downstairs windows. I entered the living room and into a scene straight out of hell. Tony was a crumpled, bloody ball. It looked like all of his blood vessels had ruptured, a look of pain and fear frozen on his face. The walls and floor were splattered with what I assumed was his blood. Aunt Tina was bound to a dining room chair. She was bleeding freely from several cuts on her face and arms. She was alive, but terrified.

Elyse and Mrs. Kelly were fully engaged in battle with the surviving female blood-mage from Arrowhead. I assumed that meant the dude blood-mage was somewhere close. I sensed him right before he attacked. He had been hiding in the downstairs bathroom and let loose with a fully charged whammy. It could tell it was a slice and dice spell, because the floor and walls got chewed up as if multiple invisible chain-saws were flying through the air toward me. I instinctively held up an arm to protect my face. I had only been the Ollphiest for a day and it was going to take longer than that to overcome a lifetime of self-preservation instincts. The spell, like all the others so far, just kind of slid around me.

Oops. The blood-mage paled.

I bared my teeth—all of them.

My turn.

I rushed him. I have to give him credit. He stood his ground and shot the same nasty fire spell that they had used to set the forest on fire. The flames erupted around me, setting the living room on fire. I was barely singed. He tried one more spell, the kinetic kind. I was starting to recognize the unique energy signatures associated with each spell. It was also useless against me, but the blast wave caused the fire to explode even wider. I was pretty sure the house was a goner. I needed to get Aunt Tina out of here.

The blood-mage suddenly split into three separate blood-mages, all running in separate directions.

Huh?

This was new.

I've played a ton of video games and immediately recognized this as a diversionary tactic. Defensive magic. Two of the three retreating blood-mages were illusions, meant to confuse me so the real blood-mage could get away. Unfortunately for him, I could see magic. I ignored the two distractions and grabbed the real blood-mage by the face, my claws digging into his skull.

He screamed.

I popped his head like a ripe watermelon.

It was messy.

I felt the same odd sensation as I absorbed his magic.

Aunt Tina! Everything was on fire and the smoke was thick. Aunt Tina's eyes went wide as I materialized from the smoke. She whipped her head back and forth, trying to shout through her gag. I was scaring the crap out of her. Oh well, I thought, no time like the present, and I shifted to human form.

Aunt Tina's eyes went even wider. I bent over and snapped the ropes holding her, freeing her from the chair.

She pulled the gag from her mouth. She touched my face as if for confirmation. "Orson?"

"Hi. I promise it's going to be okay, but we need to get out of this fire, like now."

Aunt Tina nodded.

"I think it'd be better if I carry you, we may have to, um, use an alternate exit."

"Okay." She held out her arms for me to hoist her up. No questions, no second-guessing, just pure trust—one of many reasons why I loved this woman. I shifted back into beast form and picked her up, careful to not cut her with my claws.

Elyse roared. It wasn't a triumphant I-just-kicked-your-ass roar. It was a roar filled with pain. I whipped around and through the smoke I saw the female blood-mage towering over Elyse, pummeling her with kinetic whammies. Elyse's cat body was beyond strong, but the blows were taking their toll. She was struggling to get her paws under herself, to gain some leverage, but the blood-mage was not giving her an opening.

I needed to get Aunt Tina to safety, but I just couldn't leave Elyse. The smoke was becoming unbearable. Aunt Tina coughed uncontrollably into my chest, trying to use my fur as a smoke filter. I kicked an overstuffed ottoman and sent it flying like a football directly at the blood-mage's head. Without breaking her unrelenting attack on Elyse, she flicked one of her hands and the ottoman reversed course. I spun in place and crouched over to protect Aunt Tina as much as possible. The blood-mage had spelled the flying piece of furniture, because when it reached my back it exploded like a giant wood and fabric grenade. My iron beast form skin deflected all the shrapnel, but the force of the blast knocked me forward and Aunt Tina was thrown from my arms. I couldn't grab for her, afraid that my claws would slice her up.

Then something happened that almost caused my brain to short-circuit. A kid—well, a guy a few years younger than me, maybe sixteen—materialized out of thin air. One second, Aunt Tina was falling toward the floor, crying out in fear, and then—*blink*—this redheaded kid in glasses, jeans, and a hoodie appeared and did a horrible job of trying to catch Aunt Tina. They both collapsed to the floor in a jumble of arms and legs.

The kid untangled himself, pushed his glasses back up his nose, gave me a quick smirk and said, "Sorry, dude."

I was so stunned that I didn't react fast enough.

The kid grabbed a hold of Aunt Tina and *blink*, they both disappeared.

Gone.

I swiped the air where they had just been and nothing, zip, nada.

Teleportation?

Was that even a thing?

In this new insane world I found myself in, I don't know why anything surprised me, but this did. Who was the kid and where the hell had he taken Aunt Tina?

My fur was starting to smoke from the blast-furnace heat surrounding me. I turned back to Elyse just in time to see Mrs. Kelly, in full beast form, slam into the blood-mage. Mrs. Kelly sunk her claws deep, carrying her screaming victim through the glassless front window, taking a large chunk of the front of the house with her. The sudden influx of extra oxygen caused the fire to whoosh, the flames becoming walls of super-heated death.

I didn't care if I got burned; that's what super-healing is for. I leapt through the flames toward the last spot I had seen Elyse. My fur was on fire now. Elyse was on her feet, a bit wobbly, but she seemed good. I touched her and she chuffed back, turned, and jumped through the hole her mom had just made.

A monster battle royale was taking place on my front lawn. Mrs. Kelly and the blood-mage had each other in a death grip. Mrs. Kelly's claws were buried knuckle-deep in the blood-mage, but the blood-mage had transformed into some kind of scary-looking gargoyle thingy. Elyse waited for her moment and then attacked the blood-mage from behind, meaning to pull her off Mrs. Kelly. However, the blood-mage had set some kind of shield, because Elyse not only bounced off, but also received a blast of energy for her trouble. The force of it flung Elyse into the bushes that separated my yard from the neighbors.

Some Ollphiest whammy-protection would be necessary to get through the blood-mage's defenses. I charged the blood-mage and tore at the protective magic shield. She let out a shriek and, gripping her fists tight, released a powerful slice and dice spell. Mrs. Kelly's body erupted in blood and she went limp.

Elyse roared.

I got my claws on the blood-mage. Her shield was no match for my claws. I didn't kill her, but I removed both of her hands and then tossed her to Elyse. Elyse didn't waste any time removing the blood-mage's head from her body.

We'd won, but the house was a raging inferno, the lawn was slick with blood and gore, and three shape-shifters were out in plain sight of every neighbor on the street.

The Paragon Society was going to have kittens.

Elyse shifted to human form and knelt by her mother. I was going to follow her lead, but I figured I needed stay ready to rumble, because I assumed this was far from over.

"Mom?"

Mrs. Kelly's eyes flickered.

"Orson, there's too much blood," Elyse cried.

Screw it. I shifted.

I joined Elyse. She was right. Her mom didn't look great. We needed to get her help, fast. I wasn't sure I should pick her up though. It looked like her body would fall apart. There were just too many cuts and slashes. That last blood-mage spell looked like it had blown Mrs. Kelly up from the inside.

Nasty.

I could hear sirens, maybe a few blocks away. Someone had called the fire department. My only hope was that they could stabilize Mrs. Kelly until her shifter healing could catch up to all the damage.

Mrs. Kelly let out a sigh and shifted to her human form.

"Mom?

Mrs. Kelly managed a weak smile.

"Mom, help's coming."

"I don't think so, honey," Mrs. Kelly whispered, before a coughing fit wracked her body, blood oozing from her mouth and ears.

"Mom, please," Elyse pleaded.

Mrs. Kelly went very still, got her cough under control, and opened her eyes. "You'll have to help your father. Promise me, Elyse."

Elyse was crying. I placed my hand on her shoulder. Tears welled up in my own eyes. Mrs. Kelly couldn't die. She was a three hundred-year-old badass shape-shifter.

"Elyse, promise me," Mrs. Kelly insisted.

"I promise. I swear it."

Mrs. Kelly tried another smile, but she was too weak. "Tell your brothers and sisters that I love you all forever."

Elyse let out a sob and touched her mom's matted hair.

"You need to run. Now," Mrs. Kelly said.

Elyse bent down to kiss her mom's cheek, and when she pulled back I could see that Mrs. Kelly was gone, her eyes staring, vacant.

Elyse let out a wail of grief. I pulled her into hug. She was trembling.

The sirens were close. We needed to move.

"We've got to go," I said, as gently as I could.

Elyse nodded into my shoulder.

"Tina?" Elyse asked.

"I don't know, she's not here. Someone took her."

I thought about my aunt as I gazed down at Mrs. Kelly's broken body and the rage that filled me was complete.

Yes.

Now you understand.

We will destroy them all.

Sounds good to me.

I stood and pulled Elyse up with me. I glanced around. Everyone was out in the street. The flickering light of the fire gave the scene on my front lawn a surreal nightmarish quality. I spotted more than one cell phone pointed our way. Everything was being recorded. I couldn't worry about that right now. Elyse and I needed to get gone.

"Let's get to the back yard, away from all the cameras. We can shift and run for it."

Elyse nodded, but didn't move, her eyes still on her mom.

"Hey, are you with me?"

Elyse shook herself and took a deep breath. "Yes."

A few of the braver neighbors called out to me. They wanted to know if I was okay. Elyse and I were standing, bloodied and naked, in front of my burning house with two dead bodies and I was fairly certain everyone had seen us shift—and they wanted to know if I was okay. The human brain's ability to adapt to the most outlandish situations is truly amazing. Maybe the Society could spin this fustercluck somehow after all.

We ignored the shouts of people trying to get our attention and ran for the back yard. The sirens were almost on us. We were both about to shift when—*blink*—the redheaded kid was back.

He was sitting on the back fence and he was alone, Aunt Tina nowhere in sight.

"Hi, again." The kid gave us a little wave.

I growled. My shifter speed propelled me toward the fence in a blur, but he was no longer on the fence.

"Dude, really? The cops are, like, right down the street."

I swiveled my head. Redheaded boy was now standing across the yard from me.

"Where's my aunt?"

"It's cool, she's totally safe. I swear," Red said, holding up the three fingers of his right hand in the Boy Scout salute.

"Where. Is. She?"

Elyse streaked toward Red, while I had his attention.

Not even close.

My eyes never left him and even with my super-senses I didn't see him move. He was there and then he wasn't there.

"Guys, you're not going to catch me, seriously. So, please, just listen, okay?" Red was now sitting on a large branch of the Elm tree at the back of the yard. With my abilities, I knew I could make the distance in one jump, but I believed the kid. We wouldn't catch him.

"All right," I conceded and waved Elyse over to me.

"Like I said, your aunt is fine. We're not going to hurt her. We just thought it best that she get pulled from that blood-mage death-match." The kid winced and then looked at Elyse. "Hey, sorry about the death-match thing and your mom—really, I'm so sorry."

The sound of sirens, tires squealing to a stop, and doors slamming filled the air.

He told us quickly, "We're out of time. Everything will be explained, but you need to come to the old boarded-up UA Movie Theater in North Hollywood. Got that? The old UA movie theater."

"I got it."

"And only you two. No one else. Now get out of here."

Blink.

He was gone.

This time, I was monitoring the magic spectrum and caught just a hint of a power surge when the kid disappeared.

"I didn't know society members could apparate like Dumbledore," I said, just a tiny bit amused. The kid was likeable.

"As far as I know, they can't," Elyse responded, before shifting.

They can't? That wasn't the answer I expected. If the kid wasn't a Society member, then who was he? Where did he come from, and more importantly, whom was he working for or with?

Elyse bumped my hand to get my attention and vaulted over the back fence. I shifted into bear form and followed.

CHAPTER TWENTY

North Hollywood sounds much more glamorous than it actually is. It isn't, as the name implies, the north part of Hollywood. Instead, it's a small city located within the San
Fernando Valley. There are a couple of movie studios located
nearby, so maybe that's why the original citizens tried to cash
in on the Hollywood mystique. Unfortunately, North Hollywood had slowly evolved into a lower income area and that
brought with it all the associated problems—gangs, drugs,
and crime in general. There were still pockets of really nice
homes, but much to the owners' dismay, they were
surrounded by some very rough neighborhoods.

There were entire blocks of North Hollywood where
businesses had closed up shop and all that remained were the
empty husks of buildings. The UA movie theater was located
in one of these sections. The theater's parking lot was a
cracked, weed-filled wasteland. Its front windows were
boarded up and covered in spray-painted street art and gang
graffiti.

The run from my house had been swift. We had used the
interconnected series of what L.A. liked to call rivers but

were actually just giant cement storm-drainage channels. They crisscrossed the Valley and Los Angeles basin and were perfect cover for a couple of shape-shifters trying to cross the city.

We cautiously approached the theater. We were both very aware this could be a trap, but we didn't really have another choice. The last we heard, Mr. Kelly was at the Society council meeting and surrounded by people who wanted me taken into custody or terminated.

I reached out with all of my senses, magical and non-magical. The parking lot seemed clear. The theater was another matter entirely. It was lit up like a Las Vegas casino in the magic spectrum.

I slowed, trying to discern what all the swirling light might mean. I so needed a lesson in magic color association —if such a thing existed. Elyse and I would need to shift if we wanted to talk, and that could be dangerous. The redheaded kid made our decision for us.

"Hey, guys, you made excellent time," Red shouted from his perch on the roof of the theater. "The board on the far left window opens like a door. Come on in. There's water and clothes so you can clean up. See you inside."

Blink.

He was gone.

I led the way to the window the kid had indicated and pushed on the board with a paw. It swung open, smooth and quiet. I poked my giant bear head through—it had proven indestructible so I wasn't too worried. The interior of the theatre was gloomy with lots of dust and cobwebs, but no one waited to attack us. I caught Aunt Tina's scent and that convinced me. It may still be a trap, but my aunt was inside, and I wasn't leaving without her.

I shifted. "Aunt Tina's somewhere in this building."

Elyse shifted. We both looked like hell. Which made

sense considering we'd been fighting bad guys for almost twenty-four hours.

"Are you ready?" I asked.

"Let's do it."

We stepped through the door and into the lobby of the movie theater. It was covered in what looked like a decade's worth of dust and grime. The once-multicolored carpet was worn and faded. The concession stand was a long rectangle against the far wall, an ancient popcorn machine still standing sentinel behind it. I counted six doors leading to what I assumed were the individual screening rooms. A single movie poster had survived the ravages of time mostly intact—Lethal Weapon—so this place must have closed down in the late 1980s.

A folding table was set up just to the left of the door and, true to the kid's word, we found water, baby wipes, and clean clothes—gym shorts and t-shirts with the Burbank High School logo on them. Interesting. We cleaned ourselves up as best we could and waited.

One of the screening room doors cracked open and the kid called out, "Are you guys decent?"

"Yes. Thanks for asking."

I shrugged my shoulders at Elyse. The kid was polite.

The door opened wide and Red waved us over. The screening room beyond was well lit. Aunt Tina's scent was much stronger here. Elyse tapped my hand with her fingers. She had picked up the scent as well. I scanned as much of the area as I could. It seemed my aunt was in there alone—which made no sense.

"So, where's the rest of the welcoming committee?" I asked.

"They'll be here soon." Red waved us in. "Come on inside. Your aunt is kind of a basket case. She doesn't believe me that you're okay."

"I don't know your name," I said.

"Oh, yeah. Wyatt, my name is Wyatt." He stuck his hand out. He was a real piece of work. I took his hand. I didn't get any kind of magical, psychic, Ollphiest insight, no sense of impending danger. He was just a kid.

"How old are you, Wyatt?" Elyse asked, as she shook his hand.

"I'll be seventeen in four months." Wyatt bristled, a slight frown threatening his perpetually happy demeanor.

"So, sixteen then," I said.

"Yes, I am sixteen, but don't let that fool you."

"I've seen you in action. I would never let your age *fool* me."

"Good." Wyatt seemed satisfied. He waved us into the screening room. Rows of chairs had been removed from the back third of the auditorium. In their place were two old sofas, a few folding chairs, and a couple of mismatched dining room tables.

Aunt Tina was sitting on the edge of one of the sofas, looking stressed. She jumped to her feet when I walked in, rushed over, and pulled me into a hug. After a moment, she reached out and pulled Elyse in with us.

"I'm so glad you two are okay." Aunt Tina's voice cracked. She was trying real hard not to cry. "Let me look at you." She pushed Elyse and me back to arm's length and gave us the once-over. Satisfied that we had no mortal injuries, she pulled us back into a hug. "Elyse, honey, I'm so sorry about your mom. Wyatt told me what happened."

I felt Elyse stiffen at the mention of her mom, but she didn't pull away. She let Aunt Tina console her, relaxing into the embrace. Then I could feel Elyse shaking as she began to cry again. Aunt Tina gave me a squeeze, let me go, and turned all her attention to Elyse.

Wyatt wasn't sure where to look. He knew this was deep,

personal family stuff, and he wasn't family. I gave him a nod to let him know that it was okay.

Aunt Tina led Elyse to one of the sofas and they both sat down. She cradled Elyse in her arms, stroked her hair, and let her cry.

Wyatt pulled a bottle of water from an ice chest and offered it to me, pointing at Elyse. I took it from him, cracked it open, and knelt in front of the two women I loved. I touched Elyse's arm. "You want a sip?"

Elyse nodded, wiped her eyes and took the bottle, giving it a long pull before handing it back. Elyse took a couple of deep breaths to calm herself. "Sorry about that. Thank you."

"No sorry needed, ever." Aunt Tina kept an arm tight around Elyse's shoulder.

I have to admit Aunt Tina's calm state was surprising. She had been attacked by blood-mages, had probably watched poor Tony die, and witnessed her nephew shape-shift from a monster bear-man into human form, then back again. I would have expected a little more anxiety on her end.

"So, Aunt Tina, you doing all right?" I asked tentatively. "The past few hours must have been . . . well you know . . ."

"Different?" Wyatt offered.

I rolled my eyes at him. "Sure. Different is one way to describe it. A horribly understated way to describe it, but yeah, let's go with different."

She said, "I'm doing all right. I've mostly been worried about you."

"I'm sure you have questions. Ask me anything . . ."

"I think we should wait on the questions," Wyatt interrupted. "Sorry, I'm just thinking it will all make more sense, maybe, if we wait."

Wyatt's cell phone rang, and he answered it. He had experience with shape-shifters, because he didn't even try to walk away or speak in whispers. Smart kid.

"Are you almost here?" Wyatt asked.

"I'm pulling up now." The voice was female, that's all I got before she disconnected.

"Can I use your phone, please?' Elyse asked. "My dad's probably heard about my mom and he'll be really worried about me."

I could see the conflict on Wyatt's face. He was a nice kid who wanted to help, but knew he probably shouldn't. I watched the battle rage across his freckled features and could pinpoint the instant he decided to hand Elyse his phone.

"What's going on?" a woman's voice demanded. We all jumped, because she hadn't made a sound. Even my super-senses hadn't picked up anything. I turned. Standing in the screening room doorway was Lucy, the battle-mage.

Well, crap.

Wyatt recovered and said, "She needs to call her dad. You know because the . . . thing."

"Oh. Sure, but can I ask that you not tell him where we are just yet?" said Lucy.

I was floored.

Compassion.

Lucy wasn't instantly flinging spells or throwing magic daggers. She was offering to let Elyse call her dad. This was a very unexpected turn of events.

"If you go down toward the front of the theater, you'll have some privacy. But with all the enhanced hearing in the room, complete privacy isn't possible, sorry." Lucy shrugged. It was such a normal person thing to do, and it seemed so out of character. The first time we had met, the interaction had lasted for less than five minutes, but in those few minutes she had attacked me with absolutely no mercy. So this kinder, gentler Lucy was freaking me the heck out.

Elyse stood, took Wyatt's phone, and walked down to the front of the theater. I could hear her dial, the phone ringing, and her dad answering. Mr. Kelly sounded horrible. When he realized it was Elyse, he started shouting into the phone. Elyse kept speaking in soothing tones until he calmed down.

"We should try to give her privacy, no?" Lucy asked.

"Yes, of course," I did my best to tune out Elyse's conversation.

"It's so cool that you guys can hear that." Wyatt was bouncing on the balls of his feet. "I can't hear anything except, like, a low murmur. How about you, Tina? Can you hear anything?"

Aunt Tina shook her head and smiled at Wyatt's enthusiasm. I could see how it would be contagious. The kid just had one of those personalities that could brighten even the darkest mood.

"We should sit," Lucy said.

I took the spot next to Aunt Tina. Wyatt plopped down on the other sofa and Lucy spun a folding chair around, swinging a leg over to sit backwards, her elbows resting on the back of the chair. She stared at me, a frown of concentration on her face.

"What?" I asked.

"You look normal. Even in the magic spectrum, you're like a regular person. It's the most complete camouflage I've ever encountered. It's scary."

"Scary?"

"Yeah, you're invisible to people like me and that's dangerous."

"Dangerous for you maybe, but for me, well, I consider it protection."

Lucy folded her arms and continued to stare at me.

I ignored her and turned my attention to Aunt Tina. "Are you sure you're doing all right? I know all of this must be confusing, and if you're freaking out, I understand."

Aunt Tina patted my arm. "I'm okay, really. Now that I know you're safe."

"Your aunt isn't as innocent as you think she is," said Lucy.

"I don't think you know as much as you think you do," I snapped back.

Aunt Tina shocked me when she said, "Orson, she's not completely off-base."

"Huh?" What could Aunt Tina possibly know about shape-shifters and secret societies?

Lucy said, "I think we need to wait for your girlfriend. It sounds like she's just finishing up her conversation."

I stood up as Elyse hung up with her dad and handed the phone back to Wyatt.

"Thanks again," Elyse said to Wyatt and Lucy.

"No problem. Everyone has a dad," Lucy said, smiling. Again with the compassion. It was bizarre.

Elyse and I sat down next to Aunt Tina.

"How's your dad?" I asked.

"He's a mess," Elyse said. "He's trying to put up a strong front, but I can hear it in his voice. He's devastated. He kept demanding to know where I was."

"You didn't tell him?" Lucy asked abruptly.

"No, I didn't tell him, but we need to finish whatever this is, so I can go hug my dad."

I looked at Lucy and Wyatt expectantly. This was their show, but I felt reluctance from both of them. Wyatt was fidgeting, crossing and re-crossing his legs. Lucy picked at the chipped finish on her folding chair.

"Well? Why did you kidnap my aunt? Why are we here?"

"Dude, kidnap is, like, a really strong word," said Wyatt. "In a way, you can say that we helped keep her safe. Those blood-mages were blasting everything in sight."

"You're kidding me, right?" I was incredulous. As far as I

understood, Lucy and Wyatt were members of the opposing team. Maybe not total bad guys, but they had definite bad guy tendencies.

"Maybe you should start at the beginning?" Aunt Tina suggested to Lucy. "The internal problem at the Society."

Elyse and I both stared at my aunt, our mouths hanging open in disbelief.

"Excuse me? The Society?" I stared at my Aunt Tina.

She knew.

She knew about the Paragon Society. If she knew about the Society, then did she know about my potential to become a shape-shifter? Why hadn't she ever said anything?

"Aunt Tina?"

"I told you she wasn't as innocent as you thought," Lucy said.

I stabbed a finger in her direction. "Shut up, please." My anger was stirring.

Lucy stiffened at my rebuke. Her eyes blazed.

Wyatt spoke up, doing his best to diffuse the situation. "Whoa. Hey now, everyone just calm down. Tina, maybe you could tell Orson what you told us earlier?"

Aunt Tina gently took my pointing finger and pulled my hand down against her chest. Elyse touched my thigh. I waited for Aunt Tina to speak. Waited for an explanation. And it had better be the most awesome explanation ever.

"My great uncle, your great-great uncle, was like these two." Aunt Tina waved at Lucy and Wyatt. "He could do magic, real magic. He never did anything as crazy as Wyatt here, no teleportation, at least I don't think so. He was just a funny old guy who occasionally did something really weird and unexplainable. And as far as I understand it, he was member or had been a member of this Paragon Society. Beyond that, I knew very little—about the Society, I mean. I don't know much more even now, just what Wyatt has told me while we were waiting."

Elyse let out a sigh of disbelief. I couldn't do anything except stare at my aunt. I thought maybe if I stared long enough, her words would begin make more sense. My world had been turned upside down, and she had known all along that our family had a history with magic.

As if she was reading my mind, Aunt Tina said, "I swear, Orson, I didn't know you would have any kind of latent abilities. Uncle Jacob didn't have any kids, and none of his nieces and nephews, including my dad, showed any magical ability. Needless to say, I don't have any special abilities—except never losing when I play the slots in Vegas," she added, trying to lighten the mood.

"Actually that's probably magic-based," said Lucy.

We all turned to stare at her and she shrugged. "I'm just saying—extraordinary luck is a very weak, magical ability."

"Orson, I watched you like a hawk growing up, looking for any signs that you had inherited any kind of ability. You were just a normal kid."

"Well, he's not normal anymore, is he?" Lucy said dryly.

Elyse shot Lucy a withering look. I pulled my hand back from Aunt Tina and sat back against the couch, staring at the ceiling. I had been worried how I was going to tell her about what had happened and was still happening to me, and as it turns out I had stressed over nothing. I couldn't really be angry with her. What was she supposed to have done? Tell me that her uncle was a magic-wielding member of a secret society? I would have thought she was crazy.

This new information also meant that I hadn't inherited my ability from my dad like the Kellys theorized ... had that only been this morning? It seemed like a lifetime ago. I had to admit that I'd liked the idea that my dad and I shared something. It had made me feel connected to a man that I'd only seen in pictures.

I took Aunt Tina's hand. "I get it. You didn't know what you didn't know, so how could you warn me?"

Aunt Tina's eyes welled with tears, and she hugged me hard and long. Wow, she had really been worried how I'd react. I hugged her back and whispered, "I love you."

Wyatt rubbed at his moist eyes. "You guys are awesome."

Lucy rolled her eyes. I guess compassion time was over. "If you're done with the family therapy session, I've got more info on crazy, ol' Uncle Jacob. The reason nobody in the family inherited his ability is because he wasn't your great uncle, he was your great-great-great ... oh, I don't know how many greats—the guy was old even by Society standards. And according to Society records, he was supposed to have died during WWI."

"World war one? He wasn't that old." Aunt Tina looked at each of us. "Are you trying to say he was immortal or something?"

All I could do was shrug.

Elyse stepped up to explain. "Society members, people who have magic, they—*we*—live for a long time."

Aunt Tina was stunned. "You're telling me he was, what, over a hundred years old?"

"More like four, maybe five hundred years old," Lucy said in her no-nonsense tone.

It was Aunt Tina's turn to sit with her mouth open wide in shock. I understood the feeling. I was still getting used to the idea that there were people walking around that pretty much were going to live forever, and that I could now count myself among those ranks.

"What do you believe happened to dear Uncle Jacob?" Lucy asked.

It took Aunt Tina a moment to find her voice, but she managed a weak, "He died in a plane crash."

"A plane crash? I highly doubt that," Lucy scoffed. "He probably faked his death and is still walking around. Interesting."

I said, "Okay, so we know there's a Society member in my family tree. Would that result in what's going on with me?" I needed answers. I'd accepted I was a shape-shifter and even the Ollphiest, but I needed more specifics. Could something as simple as a make-out session with my girlfriend really be the cause?

"That's an excellent question," Lucy said. "The problem is that we don't know exactly what you are. That idiot, Tommy, keeps shouting about legendary monsters. And your dad, Elyse, is doing some real fast talking about how Orson is just a shape-shifter who had a delayed onset of ability." Lucy looked between Elyse and me, hoping for a reaction, but we kept our poker faces on, so she added, "I think we all know that's complete BS. So, Orson, what are you?"

This was one of those moments you read about on Facebook. A moment that could, depending on what I said in the next few minutes, become life-altering.

"I'm the Ollphiest."

"The all-feast?" Wyatt tried to get his mouth around the word.

"Ollphiest," I corrected.

"What the hell's an Ollphiest?" Lucy asked.

And so I explained. Elyse helped me keep the story as fairly linear and concise as possible. Lucy, Wyatt, and Aunt Tina listened without interrupting even once. There were a couple of times when I thought Lucy was going to say something, but instead she would just grip her chair a little tighter. The story didn't take long. It had only been a day—and I didn't know much of the legend myself—and I finished with the blood-mage attack at my house. I took Elyse's hand when I mentioned her mom.

"Holy crap," said Wyatt.

"Yes, indeed." Lucy stood abruptly, pacing around the small sitting area. "You're impervious to even death magic? You're absolutely sure?"

"Yeah, pretty sure."

"I can see why the shifters want to keep you a secret—well, with the exception of Tommy. You're a game-changer."

"Why? What does that even mean? I'm willing to live by the Society rules or laws, or whatever?"

"Your aunt alluded to it earlier. There's a rift in the Society. A separatist group, a cabal, is trying to take control of the ruling council. There have been random attacks, just like you described, that can only mean the cabal has aligned itself with blood-mages. Some fear this will lead to an all-out civil war within the Society."

"Can't the Society just arrest or, I don't know, take out the cabal members?" I asked.

"Um, the definition of cabal means secret," Wyatt said.

"You're telling me there's a secret society within your secret society?" I threw my hands up in exasperation. "Fantastic."

"Are you saying that Tommy and Kyle are part of this cabal?" Elyse leaned forward. "Do my parents . . . does my dad know about this?"

"Nobody outside the ruling council knows. They've recruited a few trusted people." Lucy nodded at Wyatt. "But someone is leaking information. It seems the council itself may have been compromised. As far as Tommy and Kyle, I don't know."

"So what now? If the Society isn't safe, what options do we have?"

Lucy stopped pacing. "We have each other."

I was startled. "Each other? Are you saying you believe us, and even more importantly, that you trust us?"

"You could have killed me earlier, easily. Why didn't you?

"I don't know? Instinct? I had the thought that you're supposed to be one of the good guys."

Lucy smiled at me. "I am. We *are* the good guys, and we need your help. Will you help us?" Wow. Lucy sounded almost vulnerable. It seemed under the tough, leather-clad exterior there was a real person.

"If you're right and the Society is compromised, how would this work?"

"After the events of the past day, the cabal will have to lie low for a while. There are still those we can trust within the Society. I want to take you in, and we'll need an excellent story because we can't tell them the entire truth. But I still suggest we work from inside the Society. They have resources we'll need. What do you think?"

"We get a vote?" I asked. Lucy just kept surprising me.

"Of course you do. We're a team now."

I turned to Elyse, and she nodded. I wasn't sure what we would do with Aunt Tina. She had no super-powers to protect her, and it seemed she would become a target of anyone trying to get to me.

"My aunt?"

"I can take care of—" Aunt Tina started to wind up into mom mode, but Lucy cut her off.

"She goes into the Society's version of witness protection."

"Is that safe, with the whole cabal thing?"

Aunt Tina jumped up, standing between Lucy and me. "Now wait just one minute."

Lucy just went on. "Absolutely, it involves a spell that I'll cast myself that will render her invisible to the Society. I'd be the only one who can find her."

Aunt Tina poked my chest. With all the height I'd gained, she had to stand on her toes. "Orson, damn it, stop ignoring me."

I grabbed her gently by the shoulders. "Aunt Tina, this is beyond our control. I can't stop being who I am, what I am. If we're ever going to be safe, I have to fight, and I can't do that if you're constantly in danger."

Aunt Tina's eyes welled with tears. "I'm supposed to protect you, not the other way around."

I pulled her into hug. "I know, and you've been the best mom I could ever have hoped for, but it's time for me to take care of you now."

I looked at Lucy over the top of Aunt Tina's head. "What do we do first?"

CHAPTER TWENTY-ONE

Lucy convinced us we needed to report to the Society immediately and that it would look better if we walked in of our own accord. She and Wyatt would give testimony on our behalf, and she was fairly certain she could sway the council to her way of thinking.

"Fairly certain?" I didn't like the sound of that. *Fairly certain* left a whole lot of room for uncertainty.

"You will have to trust me. I know two of the seven council members are completely trustworthy. They will keep control. And we know if any cabal members have infiltrated the council, the last thing they will do is draw attention to themselves."

Elyse and I talked it over for a minute. Her dad was still at the L.A. Society headquarters, so we'd have another ally on our side as we made our case.

Aunt Tina would have to stay at the theater. Lucy was convinced the council would let us plead our case, but their patience had its limits and waltzing into Society headquarters with a mundane, even someone with Aunt Tina's unique history, would push them over the edge.

It took some convincing. I didn't want to leave Aunt Tina alone and unprotected.

"I warded this building myself. It is the safest place, not only in Los Angeles, but in the entire SoCal region."

"If I've learned one thing in the past day, it's that wards can be broken with little effort."

Lucy's mouth snapped shut and her jaw flexed. Oops, I think I had hit a sore spot.

"Yeah, Orson, dude, that's not a *normal* thing," Wyatt said lightly. "Breaking magical wards usually takes multiple mages working together, and even then they aren't always successful. I think your ..." he hooked his hands into claws and growled, "Ollphiest thingy has given you a skewed idea on how powerful magic really is."

"I'd say so," Lucy said, through gritted teeth.

"Well, I'd still feel more comfortable if Wyatt stayed with Aunt Tina." I looked at Wyatt, my eyebrows raised in hope.

"If that will make you feel better, then I'll stay, no problem. Lucy?"

"Fine. But if the council demands to hear your testimony, you'll have to come immediately," Lucy said.

"Absolutely." Wyatt beamed at Aunt Tina. I think the kid genuinely like my aunt.

"Aunt Tina, you good with this?"

"Yes, I'll be fine. Go, please."

"Okay."

"Excellent," Wyatt said, giving me an enthusiastic high-five.

That's how Elyse and I found ourselves folded into Lucy's car, a tiny convertible Mini-Cooper. With my new super-sized body, I would only fit in the back lying across the seat, my knees pulled in tight to my chest. Even Elyse found the car uncomfortably tight.

Los Angeles is infamous for its traffic. It is almost

constant and always relentless, except for the middle of the night or the early predawn hours. So, with the roads clear, the trip from North Hollywood was quick, especially since we were only traveling to Downtown, a trip of less than twenty miles.

"How is it that the headquarters for a secret society is located in one of the largest metro areas in the country?" I asked, as Lucy pulled onto the freeway.

"Where should it be located?"

"I don't know? It just seems that Downtown isn't that secret."

"Magic, Orson. Remember they're protected by magic," said Elyse.

Even with the knowledge of where we were going, I was still shocked when Lucy pulled into the parking garage of a large, modern, glass and steel building.

"You're kidding me?" I said. "This is it? This looks like a tech company or something."

"What did you expect, Hogwarts?" Lucy smirked at me in the rearview mirror.

I grinned. I was kind of impressed that she could pull off a pop-culture reference, because up until that moment she had been so stiff and serious.

I let my senses open up and the magic hit me like a tidal wave. The building was a fortress. I watched as Lucy drove down the ramp into the garage. Intricate warding magic opened like a series of gates, one after the other. I glanced behind us and they all slammed closed in sequence.

Oh boy.

There was a welcoming party of a dozen people, who could only be guards, waiting at the bottom of the ramp. I scanned them: no shifters, all mages, and from the energy swirling around them, they were juiced up and ready to rumble.

"Um, Lucy."

"Stay calm. It's protocol."

"Everyone got the memo, right? They know we come in peace?"

"Of course. We wouldn't have made it as far as the front of the building, let alone into the garage. It's cool, really," Lucy said. "Just don't get twitchy and we're golden."

Lucy parked and we pulled ourselves out of the ridiculous-sized clown car. I groaned as I stretched and popped my back. Our welcoming party spread to let us through to the underground entrance. There were two elevators waiting for us: s. Six of the guards stepped into an elevator with us and the other six took the second one..

Lucy acknowledged none of them, so Elyse and I kept quiet also, but we did clasp pinky fingers in solidarity. The elevator rose, swift and smooth, to the top floor. The doors slid open and I felt Elyse's finger tighten on mine. Yeah, it was quite a sight.

The doors opened onto one vast room. It was cavernous. The entire thing was covered in marble—floors, ceiling, walls —and intricately carved columns were spaced evenly around the perimeter. Those were more than decoration; they looked structural. The columns were also covered with inscribed runes that were more than just ornamental. They literally glowed with power. I've never been to Rome or Greece, but I had taken an Art History class and this room would rival anything those ancient civilizations built.

In the center of the room was the largest table I'd ever seen. It looked like it was carved from one massive piece of wood, a redwood tree, maybe. There were seven people standing around the table—the council, obviously. I was a little bummed out they weren't all dressed in robes like Dumbledore or the Volturi. Nope. Expensive business suits all around. They looked like hedge-fund managers.

Or, even worse, politicians.

Now that I thought about it, that's exactly what they were —the executive, legislative, and judicial branches of the magic world, all rolled into one ruling body.

Scary.

Movement caught our attention. It was Mr. Kelly hurrying toward us. Elyse released my hand and rushed to meet her dad. They both sobbed as they came together and my heart hurt for them. They whispered to one another. I would've expected an echo in a chamber this size, but I realized, even with my enhanced hearing, I couldn't hear their words.

Interesting.

It must have been some kind of warding spell, so that people could have private conversations if needed. I wondered why it was working on me with my unique abilities. I reached out around me, searching the rivers of energy, wondering if I could pinpoint that specific ward and disable it. As if it knew I was looking for it, the energy strand representing the sound-dampening ward—what else was I supposed to call it?—became discernible from all the other magic swirling around. I poked at it with my energy and realized I could disable it if I wanted.

"What the hell are you doing?" Lucy whispered out of the side of her mouth.

I stopped poking at the strand and pulled my energy back in. "Sorry, I was just looking."

"Well, knock it off."

I had to control myself, to consciously will my body not to react when I saw Tommy walking toward Mr. Kelly and Elyse. He was making like he wanted to console Elyse also, but his eyes kept flicking toward me. I didn't need my magic spidey-sense to see the malice in them.

Elyse pulled back from her dad and even though I

couldn't make out what she was saying, it was clear she wasn't happy. The three of them huddled together for another moment, their angry whispers sounding like buzzing insects.

One of the council members, a tall woman with dark hair, had had enough. "If you please, we would like to get started, now."

The ward must be of the customizable variety, because her voice carried around the chamber like she was using a megaphone. She was definitely the grand poo-bah, or whatever the Society council called their leader, because her tone conveyed that she was in complete control and would be obeyed immediately. And sure enough, Mr. Kelly, Elyse, and Tommy stopped arguing and turned their attention to the council table.

Mrs. Grand Pooh-Bah motioned for us all to come forward. As we approached, I noticed that the table rested on a giant map of the world inlaid on the floor. It was highly detailed and I realized that parts of it were in motion. I had a momentary sensation of vertigo as lines moved across the map in some kind of pattern that obviously meant something to the council but wasn't immediately discernible to me. The table stood in the space that would be the Atlantic Ocean, giving an unobstructed view of the world's land masses.

I couldn't help myself and I took a quick peek at the map in the magic spectrum, wow. Lucy bumped my arm and I focused all my attention on the people in front of me. My first assessment remained, the seven council members looked like politicians. The council was comprised of Mrs. Grand Poo-bah, three other women, and three men. All of them were staring intently at me. I didn't verify with my own senses, but I knew they were inspecting me with all the mojo they had at their disposal.

Get a good look and beware, the Ollphiest is among you.

Mrs. Grand Poo-bah turned to Mr. Kelly and Tommy, and asked, "This is the young man you've been telling us about?"

"Yes, Cynthia. This is Orson," Mr. Kelly said.

The suit standing next Mrs. Grand Poo-bah, er, Cynthia, a steel-haired man with a square jaw spoke. "I must be getting old, because I see nothing special about him. Maybe his aura is a little on the active side, but nothing to worry about, I would think."

"That's what I've been trying to explain," Tommy said, annoyed. "His ability to cloak himself is absolute."

"That's ridiculous," Square-jaw said. "In this chamber, something like what you suggest would be impossible."

Interesting, so the room was warded against what I assumed was the use of magic. The problem for them was that I wasn't performing a magic spell. I was just *me*. I didn't think the council would react very positively when they discovered their magic romper-room didn't work on me.

"That's the power of the Ollphiest—" Tommy tried to argue, but was cut short by another council member, a blonde woman with super-creepy eyes. They were a silvery color and seemed to shine almost cat-like when the light hit them just right.

"Thomas, we've been through this. The archives have been searched. There is nothing to suggest that the Ollphiest was ever a real being. It is much more likely that it was a construct to explain certain combined abilities of ancient enemies."

Enemies?

Uh-oh.

There is danger here.

Now is so not the time.

We must lay waste to all in this chamber of lies.

Whoa. Whoa. Whoa. There will be no 'laying waste' of anything.

You are a fool.

Hey, I thought we had come to an understanding. We need to be patient and see where this leads. Now, pipe down.

I waited for a response, but my inner nasty had gone silent again. Even though I didn't want to *lay waste*, I was very concerned with the term *enemies*. It may have been against protocol or whatever, but we were here to discuss me, so I was done being quiet.

I raised my hand in the international gesture of 'I've got something to say'. Grand Poo-bah Cynthia tilted her head at me, as if she just noticed I was there.

"Hi, nice to meet everybody. Great room by the way," I said.

Lucy looked over at me, her eyes wide in disbelief.

I continued, "I just wanted to assure everyone I'm not an enemy. I heard that word and it kind of freaked me out, you know? I just wanted you all to know that I'm all-in, totally on board. That's all."

Well, that had sounded completely idiotic. The council members didn't look amused. Except Grand Poo-bah Cynthia. I couldn't be sure, but I thought I detected a quick micro-grin.

I looked over at Elyse and Mr. Kelly, hoping for some support. Mr. Kelly was a blank slate and he didn't meet my eyes, just staring at the floor. Elyse had an arm locked around her dad almost like she was keeping him from tipping over. She gave me a weak smile. Tommy was radiating rage in waves. No surprise there.

Lucy spoke up. "If I may address the council?"

Grand Poo-bah Cynthia nodded at Lucy.

"Orson is a shape-shifter," Lucy said. "But he is unique."

Several council members turned their attention to me again, no doubt looking for the telltale magical signature that marked all shape-shifters. Good luck with that.

Lucy played to their egos. "As you can all obviously see, he doesn't have the aura of a shape-shifter. But as you all know, there are clear precedents of unique abilities. Wyatt is the perfect example."

Wyatt? His ability was unique? Now that I thought about it, I hadn't noticed the same energy around him that was practically bursting out of Lucy. Was he not a mage? And if he wasn't a mage, then what was he?

"This is nonsense!" Tommy snapped. "He is the Ollphiest. I witnessed it with my own eyes. Lucy's magic didn't so much as singe his fur."

"Lucy, is this true?" Creepy-eyes asked.

I held my breath. This was the moment of truth. Was Lucy on my side, or was she about to rat me out?

"No, Thomas is mistaken," Lucy lied.

"Mistaken! My son is crippled for life because of him." Tommy was going apoplectic.

"As unfortunate as that is, it is an internal shifter matter and has no bearing on these proceedings," Grand Poo-bah Cynthia said.

Tommy wasn't done. He stepped toward the table, his body shaking with rage. "Unfortunate? Is that all my son and I get after decades of loyalty? Mere words?"

"The council hasn't heard my full report yet," Lucy said.

Full report? This should be good.

Lucy told them, "There is mounting evidence that Kyle French colluded with blood-mages to attack the Kellys and Orson, not just once, but twice. The last attack resulted in the death of Katherine Kelly."

Tommy roared, running at Lucy. He wanted blood. He didn't shift—I think the chamber's magic prohibited that—but he still had super-speed and strength and could do some serious damage. He was a blur and I wasn't sure if Lucy's magic worked in the council chamber. I looked at the council members, but none of them moved to intervene. They didn't seem worried in the least.

I, however, wasn't going to take any chances. I could easily track Tommy even at the speed he was moving. The moment he was in range, I backhanded him across the face. The crack of bone on bone was like a gunshot.

Tommy was a powerful shape-shifter who was centuries old. He would have been a match for any ten shape-shifters. But I was the Ollphiest.

Tommy's limp body sailed through the air and crashed against a pillar. I could hear his heart beating, he wasn't dead, just unconscious. I rubbed my hand. Even with super-strength, that had stung a little. The chamber's mojo swallowed the echo of the crack and Tommy's body falling to the ground. Nobody spoke. The silence was complete, and it was eerie.

I glanced around. I had finally gotten Mr. Kelly's attention. He stared at me and he looked kind of pissed. Oh well. Elyse had a stunned look on her face. She kept looking from me to where Tommy lay. Lucy kept her attention on the council, who were all staring at me.

I broke the silence. What did I have to lose? "Sorry about that, but you guys know him. He's kind of a dick."

This time, Grand Poo-bah Cynthia didn't hide her smile. She laughed out loud. I could feel Lucy relax next to me. A few of the council members were smiling, but the others, like Square-jaw, were frowning. They spoke among themselves for a moment. Several guards went and stood over Tommy, who was stirring.

"I could've handled him," Lucy whispered to me.

It was the best I would get from her, so I took it. "You're welcome."

Grand Poo-bah Cynthia turned to address us. She didn't look happy now. That didn't bode well.

"The council has decided," she began in a clipped tone. Yeah, she was not happy about something. "We will accept your word on this matter, Lucy, if you agree to re-assert your testimony, including that of Orson's ability, under oath."

That was it? So, Lucy would tell a little white lie, she could cross her fingers, and ask for forgiveness at a later date. Then I noticed Square-jaw smiling. He seemed overconfident, and I started to get a bad feeling.

Lucy took a deep breath. "I understand. I am ready for the oath."

I was missing something.

"Do you, Lucy Newton, accept the oath of truth upon pain of death?"

Death? Holy shit. These people where psychotic. A death sentence for lying? I looked at Lucy, but she refused to meet my eyes. What was she doing? If she told the truth, we were sunk. But if she lied, she ... what, dropped dead on the spot? Who even got to decide if what she said was the truth?

I raised my hand again to speak.

Grand Poo-bah Cynthia shut me down. "Orson, you will remain silent."

Lucy nudged me.

This was going sideways fast. I didn't care if I set off some kind of magic alarm system. I reached out with my magic spidey-sense. If we needed to fight our way out of here, I wanted to be prepared.

The entire council raised their arms and began chanting something in a language I didn't understand. I watched, fascinated, as the magic in the room responded. It swirled and eddied around the council members, and then a long finger of energy slowly extended toward Lucy. It completely enveloped her, small tendrils snaking their way into her head and chest. And then I understood. The entire chamber was now a giant lie detector.

We were so screwed.

My mind raced. I was pretty sure if I went full Ollphiest, I could get us out of here. Of course, I would have to take out most of the council.

Yes.

Shut up.

I was in the same predicament I had been in when I first faced Lucy. These seven people were supposed to be the good guys. If Lucy's theory was correct, some of the council members were cabal members, but I didn't know which ones, and getting out of here would require absolute carnage. Lucy shifted her stance slightly, the back of her arm pressed against my side. It was a clear 'knock it off' gesture. She knew I was tensing for battle.

The spell complete, the council dropped their arms. Grand Poo-bah Cynthia once again addressed Lucy.

"Lucy, claims have been made that Orson possesses powers beyond that of an ordinary shape-shifter. That he is the mythical creature Ollphiest. That he is immune to magic and the power available to the Paragon Society, and therefore presents a threat to our very existence. Under penalty of death, what say you?"

Lucy didn't hesitate. "Under penalty of death, all of these claims are false."

I winced, ready for lightning and fire to rain down on the both of us.

Nothing.

A look of surprise passed over Grand Poo-bah Cynthia's face. Square-jaw stopped smiling.

Tommy, who must have regained consciousness just in time for the show, cried out, "No, she's lying." The guards surrounding him moved in closer. Tommy threw his hands up in disgust and shut his mouth.

With a wave, Grand Poo-bah Cynthia dispelled the magic

around Lucy and walked toward us with Creepy-eyes right behind her. The other council members spoke among themselves. The tension in the room burst like a bubble, and I felt my muscles relax.

We weren't going to die, at least not today.

Grand Poo-bah Cynthia patted Lucy's shoulder and held her hand out to me. I took it and we shook hands.

"Orson, I'm Cynthia. It's nice to formally meet you."

"Nice to meet you too, Gran, er, Cynthia." That was close. I had the feeling she wouldn't like being called Grand Poo-bah.

"This is Council Member Ellen," Cynthia introduced Creepy-eyes.

"Council Member Ellen." I shook her hand.

Ellen didn't let go. She wrapped both her hands around mine, those creepy eyes staring directly into my eyes. "It's a pleasure to meet you, Orson."

I wasn't sure how to ask for my hand back without offending her. It was starting to get weird. Elyse and her dad saved me from Ellen.

"Excuse me, Council Member. Can we borrow Orson for a minute?" Elyse asked softly.

"Of course." Ellen released my hand.

"Don't go too far, Orson. We need to talk about next steps," said Cynthia.

"Okay."

Elyse slipped her arm in mine and moved us away from everyone else, stopping when we were out of earshot.

"Mr. Kelly, I just wanted to say how sorry I am," I said. "Mrs. Kelly was—"

"Don't you say her name," he hissed.

"Dad please . . ." Elyse whispered.

Mr. Kelly refused to be mollified. He pulled his arm away

from his daughter. "You may have fooled them, but I know what you are—the Ollphiest."

I was blindsided. Mr. Kelly blamed me. His wife was dead, and he blamed me.

"Katie is dead because of you, because of what you are."

"Dad, please keep your voice down. You promised."

"Promised?" I looked at Elyse, but Mr. Kelly didn't let her respond.

"Yes, keep your little boyfriend safe. I know." His voice dripped with sarcasm. "Your mother's dead, but who cares, as long as Orson is safe?"

Elyse sobbed and turned away. Too far, I didn't care who he was. I didn't care that he was grieving or that the rulers of the magic world were standing just a few feet away. He had gone too far. I reached for him. He growled at me.

"What the hell is going on?" Lucy got between us, pushing me back. "Are you two crazy?" she whispered, glancing over her shoulder at the council members, some of who were looking in our direction. "Richard, I'm sorry Katie is dead, but this isn't what she wanted. She gave her life to protect Orson. You dishonor her memory." Lucy turned to me. "And you, do you want to die? Because some on the council are looking for any reason. I know you think you're invincible, but the magic in this chamber will end you." She glared at me until I backed off.

I went to Elyse. She let me wrap my arms around her, and she buried her head in my chest, crying. Even though I wanted to tear her dad's head off, I said, "You know he didn't mean that. He's hurting. He needs you."

"I know." A shudder passed through her. "He doesn't really blame you, either."

"I'm not so sure about that."

"He just needs time."

"Yeah, of course."

Elyse looked up at me, our faces inches apart. Tears rolled down her cheeks. I didn't know what else I could do, so I just held her tighter.

"He . . . he's going up north to the compound," she said softly.

My heart sank. I knew what she was going to say before she said it, but it didn't make it any easier to hear.

"I have to go with him. I promised my mom I would take care of him." Elyse was talking fast, trying to get it all out at once, trying to convince me, trying to convince herself.

I cupped her face with my hands and kissed her lips to quiet her. "I understand. He's your dad. You've got to take care of him."

She nodded and kissed me back. What was I going to do without her? We had wasted so much time over the years, keeping each other in the friend zone instead of just going for it. A week, that's all we'd had together, and now she had to leave.

"Maybe you could come with us?"

Even though we both knew it was an impossible sugges-tion, she was sincere, and I loved her more for it.

"Nah, I got to stay here and save a centuries-old secret society from itself. You know, because I'm the chosen one and all."

Elyse giggled through her tears. "Dork."

CHAPTER TWENTY-TWO

Things moved fast after that morning. The Kellys had their house packed and their belongings shipped to the Compound within a week. All the wedding plans were cancelled; it would no longer be a huge affair. Instead, Elyse's sister and her fiancé would be married at a small ceremony up north. The hole that Mrs. Kelly left behind when she died was huge, and I wasn't sure if it could ever be filled.

The older Kelly children took charge of closing up the Pasadena house and organizing the family's business holdings. Mrs. Kelly's body was released by the Coroner's office. The official cause of death was listed as extensive internal trauma brought on by the explosion that supposedly destroyed my house—the Paragon Society was everywhere. No funeral or memorial service was held, and the body was shipped north for burial.

Elyse and her dad left town immediately. Elyse sent me a frantic text that her dad had announced they would be leaving within an hour. I broke several traffic laws getting to the house before they departed.

"I'm sorry. He just sprung it on me this morning. I think

he was hoping we wouldn't see each other again," Elyse said, her voice tired and wrung out from crying.

"I get it, and I'm sorry if seeing me hurts him, but I couldn't let a text be the last thing we shared."

Elyse's brother and sisters were treating me with the same cold disdain as their father. I couldn't blame them. Their mom had died fighting while helping me. The only bright spot was Kevin, Elyse's younger brother. When he spotted me out on the driveway, he gave me a wave and a weak smile. I waved back, appreciative of the effort.

Mr. Kelly left the house and slowed when he saw me standing there. His eyes were dull and he looked like he hadn't slept. He ignored me. "Elyse, we are leaving, now."

Elyse gave him a small nod. Mr. Kelly walked to the Range Rover, got in, slammed the door, and the engine roared to life.

I gave Elyse one last kiss. It was slow and gentle. I tried to convey everything I was feeling, sadness at the death of her mom and the pain I was feeling at her having to leave. Elyse hugged me tight, climbed into the Range Rover, and just like that she was gone.

The compound was deep in the mountains and cell service was non-existent, and the internet was shaky at best. Elyse and I had promised to talk as much as we could. I knew it wasn't true, but it felt way too much like a final goodbye—it sucked.

Tommy continued to throw a hissy fit—he really is a dick —he even resigned from the Southern California shifter council. There was nothing except circumstantial evidence against Kyle and in a move that surprised everyone, the Society let Tommy pack up and leave town with his son.

I was officially inducted into the Society. It was more than simple. I signed my name to the bottom of a legal document. Of course, it was a magically binding contract where I agreed to keep the secrets of the blah, blah, blah.

Boring.

I was hoping for a ceremony with secret handshakes and cool, hooded robes. Lucy thought I was an idiot.

My Aunt Tina and I had to stay out of sight. It was decided that the fire at the house was the perfect cover. It turned out the neighbors couldn't identify me after all. The police questioned all the witnesses and even reviewed the cell phone footage, but because of my new height and Superman muscles, nobody could identify me for sure. The smoke and fire also helped obscure the front yard enough that Elyse wasn't recognizable in any of the footage.

It was decided that Tina Reid and Orson Reid were both killed in the explosion and fire that engulfed the house. I didn't even ask where the Society got the extra bodies as a stand-in for Aunt Tina's and my charred remains. Aunt Tina and I were officially dead. I couldn't believe that both the cops and the news reporters bought the story the Society spun, but they did. There was one part of the story I couldn't stomach, and I objected until Cynthia intervened personally and finally shut me down. Tony was cast in the role of the bad guy—or at least the crazy guy. The final police report would reflect that Tony and I had fought over the so-called prank at Costco, and that he had driven to my house in anger. The altercation escalated to the point of the house burning down. Tony was innocent and deserved better, but I was overruled and the fiction became fact.

The Society set up a whole new identity for Aunt Tina and the only thing left was the spell Lucy needed to cast.

"I'm sorry I blew up your life," I said to Aunt Tina, eyes cast down.

"None of this was your fault," she said. "Even if I had told you about our peculiar family history, what would that have done? You still would have met Elyse and become friends. Nothing would have changed."

"It feels like it's my fault."

Aunt Tina pulled me in for a hug. I now towered over her, so it was a little awkward, but we adjusted our positions and it was nice. I hugged her tight, lifting her off her feet.

"I'm going to miss you, kiddo," she said.

"This isn't forever," I promised.

"I know."

"It's time," said Lucy.

I watched as Aunt Tina drove away in Lucy's ridiculous car.

On paper, it looked like we had won. We had fooled the Society. I would begin training with Lucy and Wyatt, and the three of us would do everything we could to bring the cabal down from the inside.

Yay, us.

None of that, however, changed the fact that being the Ollphiest had cost me everyone I loved. Even though that loss was supposedly temporary, it hurt like hell.

So, I was determined to root out every person responsible, uncover every dirty secret the Paragon Society was hiding, and clean house.

They will all fall before us.

Yes. Yes they will.

The supernatural thrill ride continues in:

GYPSY WITCH
A Paragon Society Novel

Available in the Amazon Kindle Store

Thank you for giving *Orson* a chance, I hope you enjoyed reading his story as much as I enjoyed writing it. As you may have noticed the subtitle for the book is *A Paragon Society Novel*, even though this is Book 1 of a new series I've made the decision not to label the books by number. The reason behind my madness is that I will be changing POV from book to book. This was Orson's origin story, and so it seemed natural that he should be the narrator. When it comes time to tell Lucy's origin story, it only makes sense to me that she will be the narrator of those events.

If you're currently shouting at your eReader, calling me names and cursing my progeny, please take a deep calming breath. I promise there will be a progression of the overarching story-line of Orson, Lucy, and Wyatt fighting the good fight and cleaning house in The Society. Weaved throughout that story, however, will be the history of how our three heroes and others (The Kelly clan?) arrived at the current point in time we find ourselves.

If you enjoyed the story, you can make a big difference...

Obviously, Orson (and the follow-up books) are not classical literature, but that's okay because I did not set out to write classical literature. My only goal is to tell a fun, exciting and engaging story and hopefully, you agree that I've succeeded in that endeavor.

I'm a pulp fiction writer, and I embrace that title with pride.

Hands down, reviews are one of the most powerful tools in an author's arsenal. I would be tremendously grateful if you could spend a few minutes leaving an honest review. It can be as long or as short as you like. Reviews help me gain visibility, and they can bring my books to the attention of other readers who may enjoy them. Thank you, in advance for your help!

PARAGON SOCIETY NEWS

I love getting to know my readers because without you I'd be mumbling to myself in the dark somewhere.

I occasionally (very occasionally—no spam ever!) send out newsletter updates with details on new releases, excerpts from upcoming books, sneak-peeks at cover art and more importantly free or discounted Paragon Society swag.

I also sometimes invite readers to join my advance reader team, which gets them copies of upcoming books before they are officially released—for free.

If this sounds like something you may be interested in, please drop me an email at:

david@davidadelaney.com

Or find me on Facebook @therealparagonsociety

All my best,

David

Made in the USA
Monee, IL
03 November 2020